AF245171

A NOVEL BASED ON THE LIFE OF

MARIA AGNESI

THE WITCH OF AGNESI

Eric D. Martin

THE MENTORIS PROJECT

The Witch of Agnesi: A Novel Based on the Life of Maria Agnesi is a work of fiction. Some incidents, dialogue, and characters are products of the author's imagination and are not to be construed as real. Where real-life historical figures appear, the situations, incidents, and dialogue concerning those persons are based on or inspired by actual events. In all other respects, any resemblance to actual persons, living or dead, events, or locales is entirely coincidental.

Mentoris Project
745 South Sierra Madre Drive
San Marino, CA 91108

Cover photo: Old Books Images / Alamy Stock Photo
Cover design: Karen Richardson

More information at www.mentorisproject.org

ISBN: 978-1-947431-47-8

Library of Congress Control Number: 2022936023

All net proceeds from the sale of this book will be donated to the Mentoris Project whose mission is to support educational initiatives that foster an appreciation of history and culture to encourage and inspire young people to create a stronger future.

Publisher's Cataloging-in-Publication
(Provided by Cassidy Cataloguing Services, Inc.)

Names: Martin, Eric D., author.
Title: The witch of Agnesi : a novel based on the life of Maria Agnesi / Eric D. Martin.
Description: San Marino, CA : The Mentoris Project, [2022]
Identifiers: ISBN: 9781947431478 (paperback) | 9798215999028 (ebook) | LCCN: 2022936023
Subjects: LCSH: Agnesi, Maria Gaetana, 1718-1799--Fiction. | Women mathematicians--Italy-- History--18th century--Fiction. | Women college teachers--Italy--History--18th century-- Fiction. | Women philosophers--Italy--History--18th century--Fiction. | LCGFT: Biographical fiction. | Historical fiction. | BISAC: FICTION / Biographical. | FICTION / Historical / General.
Classification: LCC: PS3613.A77829 W58 2022 | DDC: 813/.6--dc23

The Mentoris Project is a series of novels and biographies about the lives of great men and women who have changed history through their contributions as scientists, inventors, explorers, thinkers, and creators. The Barbera Foundation sponsors this series in the hope that, like a mentor, each book will inspire the reader to discover how she or he can make a positive contribution to society.

Contents

Foreword i

Prologue: Milan, 1722 1

Part One: A Spark of Genius 7

    Chapter One 9

    Chapter Two 24

    Chapter Three 36

    Chapter Four 43

    Chapter Five 48

    Chapter Six 60

Part Two: The Child Prodigy 67

    Chapter Seven 69

    Chapter Eight 81

    Chapter Nine 92

    Chapter Ten 102

    Chapter Eleven 118

    Chapter Twelve 129

    Chapter Thirteen 136

    Chapter Fourteen 148

Part Three: Matters of the Heart 161

    Chapter Fifteen 163

    Chapter Sixteen 176

    Chapter Seventeen 185

    Chapter Eighteen 193

    Chapter Nineteen 207

    Chapter Twenty 215

Chapter Twenty-One 226

Chapter Twenty-Two 234

Part Four: Finding a Calling 243

Chapter Twenty-Three 245

Chapter Twenty-Four 253

Chapter Twenty-Five 262

Chapter Twenty-Six 272

Chapter Twenty-Seven 282

Chapter Twenty-Eight 289

Chapter Twenty-Nine 297

Epilogue 307

About the Author 311

Foreword

First and foremost, Mentor was a person. We tend to think of the word *mentor* as a noun (a mentor) or a verb (to mentor), but there is a very human dimension embedded in the term. Mentor appears in Homer's *Odyssey* as the old friend entrusted to care for Odysseus's household and his son Telemachus during the Trojan War. When years pass and Telemachus sets out to search for his missing father, the goddess Athena assumes the form of Mentor to accompany him. The human being welcomes a human form for counsel. From its very origins, becoming a mentor is a transcendent act; it carries with it something of the holy.

The Mentoris Project sets out on an Athena-like mission: We hope the books that form this series will be an inspiration to all those who are seekers, to those of the twenty-first century who are on their own odysseys, trying to find enduring principles that will guide them to a spiritual home. The stories that comprise the series are all deeply human. These books dramatize the lives of great men and women whose stories bridge the ancient and the modern, taking many forms, just as Athena did, but always holding up a light for those living today.

Whether in novel form or traditional biography, these books

plumb the individual characters of our heroes' journeys. The power of storytelling has always been to envelop the reader in a vivid and continuous dream, and to forge a link with the subject. Our goal is for that link to guide the reader home with a new inspiration.

What is a mentor? A guide, a moral compass, an inspiration. A friend who points you toward true north. We hope that the Mentoris Project will become that friend, and it will help us all transcend our daily lives with something that can only be called holy.

—Robert J. Barbera, Founder, The Mentoris Project
—Ken LaZebnik, Founding Editor, The Mentoris Project

Widely regarded as a brilliant mathematician, Maria Gaetana Agnesi's great contribution to the field was her textbook, *Instituzioni analitiche ad uso della gioventù italiana* (*Analytical Institutions for the Use of Italian Youth*), published in 1748. This volume was received with great enthusiasm across Europe, and quickly became the gold standard for the instruction of calculus in all its forms.

Today, Maria is best remembered for the cubic plane curve that bears her name: "The Witch of Agnesi." Though her talents were remarkable and rarely encouraged among women in her day, Maria was a devout Christian and never accused of witchcraft. Instead, this curious name is the result of a mistranslation. Maria used an innocent-sounding nautical term, *versoria,* but at the time, witches were sometimes called the very similar-sounding *versiera.* Whether by mistake or intentional pun, English translations rendered it as the latter form, and so the name has stuck.

Prologue

MILAN, 1722

For three hundred years, the people of Milan had been building the same church.

Christos had sailed to all the shores of Europe, and even some of Asia, and nowhere had he seen another church so large. The Duomo's towers and spires and arching windows went up and up and higher still, half vanishing in the morning mist. It felt to him almost like the topmost steeple pointed straight to God Himself. Platforms and scaffolds enclosed the building's face, where masons labored fearlessly, never worried they might fall.

Six times Christos had come and gone from the city of Milan. The cathedral had changed, the scaffolding had shifted, but somehow it never seemed any closer to being done. How many people had passed away since someone first dreamed of building it, he wondered? How many people had struggled for something only their children's children might hope to enjoy?

He admired that about the Italians. They were never content with something good enough—they chased after perfection.

"Sir," he called out from his market stall. "Sir, stop and look a moment!"

His was just one voice among many. Merchants from all over Italy and beyond pitched their stalls in the market square, offering everything Italian gold could buy. Most desirable of all were the clothes. Silk and linen, velvet and lace; the folk of Milan had wealth to spare and they dressed with cultured pride. Selling the right bolt of fabric could feed a family for a year. Some men had been known to beggar themselves for the perfect jacket. The locals quite literally wore their fortunes on their sleeves.

But Christos could not hope for such a sale. His fortunes had left him with nothing but vegetables. Life was like that sometimes. So there he was at the edge of the market square, hollering in a broken Italian that he had once thought very good, back home in Greece.

One man stopped and leaned on his hardwood cane before the stall. He had a long look at the goods on offer. As the moments passed, he furrowed his great and fearsome eyebrows.

"The finest produce, fresh from Tuscany," Christos said, which was even true.

But the man didn't seem to care. He shook his head and moved onward. Whatever he was looking for, it wasn't in Christos's stall.

That was when Christos first noticed the girl.

An odd person to notice, perhaps. A tiny child wouldn't be much of a customer, let alone a child hiding behind her mother. But somehow she stood out—perhaps because she was trying so very hard not to. She walked with her shoulders hunched and her eyes turned down, as if to make herself as small and insignificant as possible. Whenever another shopper pressed too close in the throng, the girl was quick to maneuver as far away as she could manage. Or at least as far away as she could get without leaving her mother's side. One hand clutched at the bright blue skirt of her mother's dress, her eyes staring hard at the flagstones underneath her feet.

A crack and a holler cut through the air, followed by a peal of childish laughter. The market crowd parted around a fast-rolling leather ball. Maybe half a dozen children went hurtling headlong after it, jostling and bumping each other in their determination to catch it first. It wasn't quite clear what game they were playing, or if it was even a game with rules at all.

Some girls might have joined in the fun. This one only buried her head against her mother's leg.

The mother was the image of a well-to-do Milanese woman: Hair pinned up, dressed just so in pleated layers, it was clear she was a woman of means. That she was here by herself doing her own shopping was a touch unusual, but hardly unheard of. Perhaps she wanted to personally scout material for a fine mantua dress.

No, that wasn't it, Christos suddenly realized. She was coming right to his stall. He immediately straightened himself and put on his best smile.

Before he could get out so much as a word, the Milanese woman spoke. Hers was a clear, clipped voice, and the words flowed out swiftly. "*Dieci carciofi, se vuole, buon signore. Quelli più freschi che hai, naturalmente.*"

Christos understood perhaps three of those words. Without realizing it, he lapsed into his native Greek. "Artichokes? You're looking for artichokes?" He had them, of course. More than he knew what do with.

The only problem is that the woman didn't understand so much as a word of Greek. Her thin-lipped mouth twisted off to one side, and she rapidly fired off a series of questions in Italian, so quickly that Christos could feel the limited vocabulary he possessed flying away from him. She held up her fingers, gesturing emphatically in the way Italians were uniquely fond of doing, but it didn't help illuminate the mystery of her questions.

"No, no," he insisted, holding up his hands. "Three coins each. I can't go lower."

They went back and forth a few times, but it felt like the more words they exchanged, the further away they got from understanding.

Finally, the Milanese woman let out a pointed sigh and looked down to the small girl at her side. Christos had altogether forgotten she was there.

What happened next nearly made him jump out of his skin. This young girl—she couldn't have been more than five years old—looked up at him with mildly exasperated eyes. "My mother was wondering if perhaps you might be able to give her a small bargain on artichokes, since she wants to buy rather a lot of them."

Not only was this very well-spoken for a little girl, but it was also the most perfect and fluent Greek that Christos had heard all week.

He stood there a moment, mutely opening and closing his mouth. "I . . . yes, let's call it a five *denari* discount," he eventually managed to say, reaching for the box in which he kept his coins. After quickly checking his ledger, he gave the combined cost. The girl cheerily repeated the figure back to her mother in Italian. Where on earth had she learned to speak Greek so well? The days when it was a universal language were long gone. These days, only scholars and travelers would be likely to study it.

The girl's mother started parceling out money from her purse. Christos duly began making change.

"Thank you very much, Mister Merchant, sir," said the little girl. Her eyes sparkled as she watched him scribble figures in his ledger. There was certainly no sign of her earlier shyness now. She watched the simple calculation with unusual intensity. Apparently, even though ball games did nothing to seize her interest, mathematics were an object of fascination.

Standing at the next stall over, an older woman wearing a broad-brimmed hat was watching all of this with a touch of amusement. She elbowed her gray-haired husband while tilting her chin toward the girl. "What a remarkable little woman," she called over. "How did she master a second language at such a young age?"

Christos was distracted by an insistent tugging at his wrist.

He looked down to find the little girl wearing a dreadfully serious expression. "You made a mistake," she told him, with the blunt honesty of which only children are capable.

"Nonsense," he assured her. "All your mother's change is here. I wouldn't cheat her."

Without waiting for his permission, she reached for his ledger, pulled it toward her, and started pointing. "No, not like *that,*" she said. "You're giving us too much."

"That's very honest of you," he told her, not wanting to believe her. This was his profession.

But now that he looked, he saw that she was right. He could feel the stares of the very small crowd that had gathered landing on him as he took back two diminutive silver coins.

"And you did it twice earlier today," said the girl, already flipping back a few pages in his ledger. "You ought to be more careful."

"*Grazie,*" he told the girl, after a very long pause. It was the only thing he could think to say.

The girl's mother shook her head slowly, the same exasperated look in her eyes that Christos had seen on her daughter's face just a little while ago. She reached down to ruffle her daughter's hair, and then tugged her off into the ebb and flow of shoppers through the square. Soon enough, they were lost to sight, leaving Christos alone to frown over all the day's calculations.

The girl's name was Maria Gaetana Agnesi.

In time, the name would grow famous in all the world's academies.

Part One

A SPARK OF GENIUS

Chapter One

Maria had always been very good friends with numbers. Whenever she got home, they were there waiting for her, as reliable as her mother's smile. She bounded in, knowing all the sums without counting. Two stout doors, five tall windows, a townhouse with seven spacious rooms. Nineteen steps to the second floor, though that one was admittedly a little bit like cheating, since she always had to hop over the very last step to make the total come out right. Twenty just wasn't as beautiful as nineteen, and anyone who said otherwise simply hadn't examined the world closely enough. Prime numbers were the best numbers; that should be obvious to everybody.

A close second were the numbers divisible by three. When she thought hard enough about them, certain figures inevitably got tied up with colors in Maria's head. Threes were always very particular shades of green. She couldn't say why, but something about the crisp certainty of such things was comforting.

She supposed there must have been a time before she

thought about mathematics, but it was probably a more boring time, so she didn't much care to ponder.

The maid her father had hired a few weeks ago was busy puttering about with her feather duster, polishing all the vases and painting-frames and other things Maria wasn't allowed to touch, since apparently they were *worth a fortune,* one of her father's favorite phrases. Maria wasn't sure what exactly she was supposed to do with a fortune, which was apparently something grown-ups were always chasing after instead of more intriguing things like bugs.

"Hello, Maria," said the maid, whose name she hadn't bothered to remember. "It's me, Isabella, you remember?" Isabella used that high-up voice that grown-ups used when they thought you weren't very smart. Unfortunately, most grown-ups tended to think that way about every child they met.

Truthfully, Maria wasn't entirely sure she could trust the woman yet. "Did you go in my room?" She stood poised behind the edge of the sofa, half her face hidden. Safer, really, to not have to look at someone any more directly than you had to.

"Not yet," said Isabella, wiggling her duster in Maria's general direction. "Perhaps you'd like to handle it for me?"

Not the worst idea, really. Grown-ups' idea of mess was just Maria's idea of accessible.

Before she could answer, they were interrupted by a series of low-pitched *plonks.*

Maria dipped back behind the couch and darted away from Isabella into the music room, where her father kept his most prized possessions of all. The centerpiece, of course, was the huge concert piano he was now struggling to play.

"Maria Gaetana Agnesi," said her father, his sun-tanned face crinkling with the very slightest smile. His fingers walked along the length of the piano's keys, drawing out a sound that was frankly only a poor imitation of music. He had only recently resolved to learn, but kept at it with the same dogged persistence he applied to everything else.

The look of concentration on his face might have appeared sour to someone else, but Maria knew better. It was subtle, but the smile was unmistakable. Probably he'd sold something. A good market day was the surest thing to bring up her father's mood. Sure enough, the back of the piano was covered in great big bolts of cloth, some of them the kind of silk you couldn't find anywhere in Italy. That silk formed the cornerstone of all her father's make-a-fortune obsessions. To her, he was just Papà, but to the world he was Pietro Agnesi, and she knew people went mad for the fabrics he bought and sold.

He tapped a single key, *plink plink plink,* looking over at her from across the room. "Have you seen your mother?"

She shook her head rapidly. "Not since earlier."

He shifted to another key, *plonk plonk plonk.* His eyes swept away from Maria back to the impenetrable details of the sheet music in front of him.

"Your mother was asking after you," he said. "You should go see her." Well, there was no arguing with him when he talked like that.

Nineteen steps and a hop later, Maria was upstairs. She knew exactly where her mother would be. It was the room they'd set aside for her younger brother—or younger sister. Apparently no one knew which one the baby was going to be. Nor would they, until the day it finally arrived. That seemed an awfully uncertain business to Maria, but she supposed it made things exciting, at least.

There was a cradle inside the room—empty, of course. Her mother sat beside it in a great big leather chair. Warm light filtered in through the windowpanes onto her fair, angular face. Her hands clutched a beaded crucifix with familiar ease. The closer they got to the day when her baby would be born, the more often her mother took to the rosary.

Fifty-nine beads on the rosary, which Maria imagined couldn't be an accident: God Himself surely also knew the beauty of prime numbers. After all, He'd designed them, hadn't He? That's what her mother was always saying. Ultimately, she insisted, every good thing in the world stemmed from God.

High on the wall above Maria's mother was a picture of the Virgin Mary. It wasn't as good as the French pictures her father collected downstairs. It looked simple, almost plain by comparison. At some point in its history somebody had taken a knife to it, and the scar was still there in the frame. Apparently it was something called an *icon* and had come out of the Greece she'd learned so much about in books. There was a simple honesty about it, even if it wasn't fancy all by itself.

After a quiet clack of bead against bead, Maria's mother startled and sat up straight, touching a hand to her chest. "Oh," she all but gasped, before laughing. "You snuck right up on me!"

"I didn't sneak," said Maria. "I'm still in the doorway."

"How terribly cheeky of you," said Anna Fortunato Brivio Agnesi—her mother's long, full name.

"Papà said you wanted to see me?" Maria stepped into the room, wondering how different it would feel when her younger sibling finally arrived. She turned in a circle, measuring the place with her eyes.

Abruptly, Maria realized she was soaring right up into the air, lifted by the strength of her mother's hands. Maria plopped down onto her lap with a little peal of laughter. Her mother's stomach was getting bigger all the time, but there was still room for a tiny Maria, balanced on top of one leg and against a leather armrest.

"You're very exuberant, you know, when you're at home," said her mother. "You could stand to show a little more of that side of yourself when we're out and about."

"I like it here," Maria protested. "Outside is . . ." She didn't have the word.

"*Chaotique*," her mother suggested in French.

Maria shifted into French with practiced ease. For her it was no harder than just thinking about a math problem a little differently. "*Je ne suis pas sûr que ce soit le meilleur mot.*" She wasn't entirely sure that "chaotic" was the very best word.

Somehow, her mother managed to sound both weary and proud at the same time. The noise she made was both sigh and pleased exhalation.

"Oh, Maria, what are we going to do with you? Your accent is even better than mine. How did you manage that? You learned all your French from me."

And books, Maria might have pointed out, but books didn't have accents at all.

"Anyway," said her mother, "I'm afraid you'll need to show a stiff upper lip because we're going out."

Maria made a low noise that expressed all she intended to say on *that* subject.

"It's not the market, at least," said her mother, delicately running her hands back through Maria's hair, making sure every strand was arranged just so. "We're going to the convent. Your mother has some very important work to do there, after all."

Well, it was going to be a struggle, but Maria knew better than to complain. Without being asked, she hopped off her mother's lap.

For her mother, standing proved a trial. Anna had to brace herself with both hands on the armrests, struggling with all the extra weight with which pregnancy had burdened her. But when it was done, all she did was smile. "Come along, Maria."

They got as far as the front door before being stopped. Her father looked up from the sitting room sofa, clearing his throat in that very particular way. "I thought we already had this argument," he practically sighed, looking his wife straight in the eye.

"And I believe I made my position perfectly clear," she replied.

Maria's father leaned forward, raising a single finger toward the ceiling. "You're almost six months' expecting, Anna. You should be spending your time here, with your family. Leave Church business to Church people. The faith got along all right without you for seventeen hundred years; I daresay it can last a few additional weeks."

"We're all of us 'Church people,'" she insisted. "Not just the clergy. We're all of us one great big living church, and they need me there. No one else is going to teach those children their French."

"Your duty is to *your* children," he fired right back, his tone growing short. "Not the children of beggars. And you promised you'd cut back your hours."

"I did, and I have." Anna was a kind and giving woman, but once she'd drawn a line in the sand, it would take nothing less than a miracle to get her to yield. She put her hand on the doorknob to illustrate her resolve. "It's just the class now. And they've got someone else lined up for next month."

Pietro Agnesi let out a long, low grumble, reaching for the book discarded on the table in front of him. "Just this once," he insisted, in the style of a man who knew defeat.

Maria's mother's face lightened up with bright, sparkling enthusiasm. "Come, come, Maria! I daresay you'll love the convent. It might be my very favorite place."

And then they were out in the streets, braving the pale mists of spring.

When the Santa Maria delle Grazie had first been built, Europe knew only one Church, and Milan was ruled by an Italian family. The Sforza family, they were called, and they paid for all manner of art and buildings to beautify the city they ruled. Those were the days that would eventually be called "the Renaissance," days of master painters and the most clever new inventions. Generations had gone by since. Foreigners had conquered the city back and forth between themselves in the intervening years, the French and the Spanish and the Austrians over the mountains.

Maria didn't quite know all the details—history never really interested her very much—but she knew beauty when she saw it. A great circular tower crowned the central church, but that wasn't where they were headed. Staying a safe, close distance just beside her mother, Maria walked across the stone courtyard into the shade of a tree-dotted square, where the buildings of a monastery and convent clustered close together.

"I'm going to need your help today," said Anna Brivio, smiling down at her daughter from beneath the shade of her very finest hat.

It wasn't often that grown-ups asked *her* for help. This was a novelty that Maria at once found thrilling and slightly worrying. "With your class?"

"No, no," said Anna, "The things I promised your father I wouldn't be doing. It's time you learned a bit about . . . ." Her voice abruptly trailed off, her eyes widening in alarm. Her hand reached for the nearest surface. It turned out to be the sandy wall of the convent. She leaned against that wall a moment, panting.

Maria felt her heart start thudding in her chest. She looked around rapidly for someone who might help, but the noontime sun was bright and everyone seemed to be indoors. Words spilled frightfully from her mouth. "Are you all right?"

Anna laughed wearily, leaning back against the sand-colored stone wall. "Just fine," she insisted, though a bit of the color was gone from her cheeks. "The baby's a little heavier than I cared to admit. I think I'll be teaching my class sitting down."

With a creak of aging wood, a frowning, habit-draped nun emerged from the nearest door, preoccupied with some sort of clerical business. She stopped, however, upon seeing Maria and her mother lingering nearby.

For some reason, just like always, Maria felt the familiar tremor of fear in her stomach that appeared whenever she met a stranger. Her instinct was to hide behind her mother, but what was behind her mother was currently a solid stone wall, so it simply wasn't possible.

"Greetings, *signora,*" said the nun, her voice a little creaky itself. Age had weathered shallow lines into her face. "As always, it's good to see you."

Though her mother had shown a moment of weakness a second ago, it was now nowhere to be seen. "Yes, Mother Angelica. Always a pleasure." Patting Maria reassuringly on the back, Anna marched the girl right inside.

Maria avoided eye contact with the nun, staring at the cracks on the sun-warmed ground until they were safely out of sight.

It took her eyes some time to adjust. The inside seemed dim

at first, the air noticeably more cool. A faint smell of incense lingered in the air like a dusting of spice. It was quiet there, though Maria could hear the distant clink and clatter of a working kitchen.

Somewhere, someone quietly droned the words of a lengthy prayer, muted by the walls between them.

It was a quiet and contemplative place. Maria liked the quiet. Turning a corner, she saw a great big rack of books, their spines marked in all manner of languages. She liked that even more. An ancient Dominican stood precariously atop a book-shelf ladder, reaching for something in what looked like Latin, a language Maria knew less well than she would have preferred.

She didn't realize she was about to walk into a wall until her mother stopped her.

"Maria," she laughed breathily, looking down at her. "You spend entirely too much time in your own head. You should mind what's right in front of you."

Maria might have said something clever about that, but the old Dominican squinted down at her, his eyeglasses making his pupils enormous. It was more than she could bear. Quickly looking away from his face, she nodded rapidly and clutched at her mother's skirt.

Eventually, they reached the kitchen. A great big pot of stew was simmering, filling the place with a savory aroma. A clerical novice and a pair of volunteers fussed over the stove and laid out a seemingly endless series of bowls.

Maria asked, "What's all this?"

"Food for the poor," said Anna. "Not everyone is as lucky as we are." She hoisted up the parcel she'd been carrying, which contained all the artichokes they'd bought the day before. "I want to do what I can for them with what we've been given."

"That'll go over well," said the young novice, looking a touch displeased over the prospect of needing to cook even more food.

"Anyway, you'll be helping out here," Anna told her daughter, beaming her ever-ready smile.

"Help?" Maria rapidly blinked her eyes. "I don't know how to cook."

"And you won't need to," Anna assured her. "All you have to do is ladle out soup and take it to the people who need it."

Very easy, perhaps, for anyone but Maria. A dreadful, worrying thought took hold of her heart as she looked at all those bowls. Each one of them represented a person. A person she hadn't met before. Her mother had just asked her to do the very thing she found hardest in all the world: Go up to strangers. Heaps of them.

"It'll be good for you," said her mother, clearly believing she was doing Maria a favor.

It took a minute before Maria realized her mother had already gone off to teach her French class elsewhere in the convent's halls. In fact, it took two whole minutes before Maria stopped staring at the nearest wall.

The people in the kitchen, at least, were extremely friendly. Easy for them, Maria thought sullenly. They hadn't been asked to face their impending doom.

~

"Just one time," said Mother Angelica, standing with crossed arms in front of Maria in the kitchen.

"I don't wanna," said Maria, wishing she didn't sound like such a child, even though she was, in fact, a child.

"Christ carried his own cross up the hill of Calvary knowing he would be a sacrifice for all mankind," said Angelica, which really didn't help Maria feel any more at ease. "I think you can carry a soup bowl across a single room to help feed a hungry woman."

"I don't *wanna*," Maria insisted, possessed of a new insight into Christ's question about why his father had forsaken him. She clutched the bowl of soup they'd asked her to carry so tightly she was a little worried she might break it.

In the next room, the sound of conversation and spoons scraping bowls mixed into a din louder than the sum of its individual parts.

Mother Angelica let out a long, careful sigh. Sternness might have worked with her initiates, but it was getting her nowhere with Maria. She smoothed out her habit and knelt down in front of Maria, bringing them both to eye level. "We all have to do difficult things," she told the girl. "And I can see this is very, very difficult for you. But I promised your mother you'd learn something about charity today. So I'm only asking you to go in the one time, for her. Do that, and I promise you're done. All right?"

Maria thought about her mother, huffing and puffing and

struggling to do the work no one had even asked her to do, carrying the burden of a child who had not yet even been born. "All right," she said finally, hating herself a moment for wanting to do the right thing. "But just once."

With a nudge at her back from the old nun, she trudged into the room where the convent admitted the poor.

What she noticed first was the *smell* of the dining hall. No city smelled great, but the acrid smell of so many unwashed bodies overpowered even the perpetual scent of incense. Maria felt her nostrils flaring as she went inside.

And then there was the look of the folk seated along all those wooden benches. Threadbare clothes, sun-cooked skin, some of them slender with hunger. One woman in the back stared at her a little too long, the whites visible all the way around her eyes. There was something about the force of a stare, and that was the worst one Maria had seen all day.

So Maria swerved toward the nearest table, rapidly looking for someone who hadn't yet been served.

The most frightful-looking old woman she'd ever seen peered right back at her. Her nose was quite big, her mouth quite small. The wispy mess hanging from her crown looked more like a drooping bird nest than a proper head of hair. It was the sort of beggar she'd seen kneeling for alms by the roadside.

With trembling fingers, Maria put down the bowl in front of the old beggar. "H-h-here you are," she managed to stammer out.

And then a very strange and unexpected thing happened. The beggar simply smiled at her, and everything was fine.

For a brief moment, there was nothing frightening about

her at all. Maria saw just an old, tired woman, someone who might have once raised children of her own.

"Thanks be to God," said the beggar, her gnarled hands flattened together in a brief gesture of prayer.

Yet for some reason, Maria couldn't escape the notion that she wasn't thanking God—she was thanking *her*, in particular.

It might have been better if she had said something nice back. But instead, she just tore out of there as fast as her short legs would carry her, ignoring Mother Angelica and ignoring the kitchen staff and heading straight for the classroom where her mother taught French.

The students were all older than Maria, and none quite so desperate-looking as the hungry poor. Maria ignored every last one, moving to the desk in the very farthest back corner of the room.

She and her mother met eyes for only a moment—before the lesson continued, the same as always.

There was nothing new in the lesson. Maria had learned every last declension ages ago. But there was something about the regular, reliable shape of their forms that slowly calmed her heart, and she silently mouthed them along with everyone else.

That night, Maria's parents had an argument.

They always waited until Maria was in bed. With a whole flight of stairs between them, they probably figured she couldn't hear them. But she was both more awake and more clever than her father gave her credit for.

The subject was the same as always: her mother's charitable

work. She was going to run herself ragged, her father insisted, but her mother only regretted not being able to do more. Couldn't she see that she was putting the baby at risk? Couldn't *he* see that God had a plan for her?

Eventually things grew quiet. Through the small gap of her partially opened door, Maria was just barely able to watch her mother come up the top of the stairs. She held aloft a single flickering candlestick, also clutching the great big stack of papers Maria knew she used to plan her lessons.

The light of the candle and the shadows it cast grew longer and ever more tenuous as Anna walked not to the master bedroom, but to her study at the end of hall. Inside, the chair and desk creaked to accept her weight.

She shut the door, but Maria could still see the light she carried. She watched it dimly dance, occluded by the intervening glass of both their darkened windows.

For all the timeless time before she fell asleep, Maria could still see the silent flickering of that candle.

Chapter Two

No one came to wake Maria in the morning. That was unusual.

Both of her parents were early risers. It's not as if she were the sort of child who would sleep until noon when left to her own devices, but the sharp one-two knock of knuckles against her door had long been a familiar morning ritual. The absence felt strange.

As surely as numbers had colors in her mind, the color of sunlight said something about the hour of the day. The light was too yellow, the angles of the shadows all different. She could tell at once that it was far later than she usually woke up.

But that was all right, Maria reasoned with herself. She didn't need help to get through her day. She pried herself out of bed and exchanged a night shift for day clothes. The shoes proved a bit of a trial, but even they yielded in the end.

The shoes clunked down all twenty steps. *Unlucky number,* she thought to herself after the fact.

Before she could worry about that, she was confronted with

another unusual thing: her father, pacing fretfully back and forth in the parlor. Maria watched him walk the breadth of the room fully four times, but he didn't even notice her, so wrapped up was he in whatever he was pondering.

"Papà," said Maria.

Her father jolted upright, turning a little too quickly. The smile on his face also appeared a little too quickly. "Oh, Maria, dear. You're feeling well?" It seemed too emphatic a question.

"Yes," she said, which was the truth, after all.

"That's good." He plainly felt relieved. "I'm sure your mother is tired, that's all."

Maria walked around the back of the tall sofa and peered into the sitting room beyond. There, she could see her mother laid out asleep on the divan, pillows stacked beneath her head. Her ever-present books and notes were nowhere to be seen, and her cheeks seemed uncommonly red.

"The physician's already come and gone," said Maria's father. "He's quite certain she'll be all right. Just exhaustion, he called it."

Oh, thought Maria, who had never imagined that someone as reliable as her mother could do something like *get sick.* She remembered her mother's brief dizzy spell outside the convent. Had she been suffering the whole day and hiding it?

"We're going to do things a little differently than usual," said Maria's father. "Your mother takes you just about everywhere, but she needs rest. And you've never seen where I do my work."

This, Maria realized with an inward sigh, meant the same trial as always: new people.

"I'll try my best," she said. Anything other than that would be promising too much.

The Agnesi Textile Company fully occupied two warehouses and a suite of adjoining offices. The façade was dignified stone; the foyer for admitting clients was decorated with the very latest rococo designs. Paintings of forest scenes adorned the waiting-room walls. Pietro Agnesi had chosen every detail himself. He was very particular about style. How could he not be? Fashion was his business.

"Keep your chin up," Pietro admonished his daughter.

Little Maria worked hard to make herself appear littler still, shying away from the clerks and avoiding all the staff. What was he going to do with her? She seemed positively terrified just from the simplest outing.

Where did all that worry come from? Maria didn't even seem to trust the maids. He'd seen to her every comfort, given her the finest of rooms, and never once had a stranger so much as troubled her in public.

Perhaps that was just the way young girls were, he consoled himself. His sisters had all been older, so he wasn't entirely sure what girls that age were supposed to be like. Perhaps young Maria Gaetana would come into herself as she grew up and discovered the world less full of monsters and magic than she feared.

He tugged off his gloves and went to the green felt–topped counting desk where he reviewed his accounts. The latest shipment had arrived.

That was good, very good indeed. He'd made new inroads

with the monopolists in Marseille, where the French East India Company brought in shiploads of the most spectacular fabrics. France was the center of cultured civilization; being on the leading edge of such things thrilled Pietro greatly.

"Come on, Maria," he told his daughter, who was for some unfathomable reason examining the beveled hinge of a cabinet. He could indulge her interests, but he didn't expect carpentry to be an abiding passion. "I want to show you something special."

Fabric filled the adjoining warehouse, stacked in great, thick bolts along dozens of racks and shelves. Silk, velvet, and cotton most of all. Little swaths of their edges revealed myriad colors and patterns. The setup was not just for ease of shipping, but also to tantalize whatever tailor or couchmaker might want to inspect the options they had on offer.

He immediately found what he was looking for: the *pièce de résistance,* as the French would have it. When a representative from Marseille had shown him a square, he knew at once that he could turn it into a sensation. It was cotton, but heavier and more firm than what you'd use in clothes. It was perfect for sofas and drapes. And most importantly, there was the *color.* Nowhere in Europe could such a vivid blue be found. The company used some sort of ingenious block-printing method, where the same pattern could be replicated with perfect regularity, rather than the laborious hand-painting of years past. Dozens of blue birds peered out from the fabric, exotic parrots the likes of which few folk in Milan would likely ever see in three dimensions.

Pietro looked toward his daughter. "What do you think?"

"Mmm" was all Maria had to say about it, tilting her head to one side.

Part of him deflated. He'd hoped she'd be a little more excited. But then, were France and India anything more than places on a great big map to a little girl?

He sighed and, turning to the nearest work table, scribbled out a note.

"Raphael!" he hollered.

The French knew fashion, and there was more than one Frenchman working at the Agnesi company. One of them rounded a corner, narrowly ducking an improperly leaning bolt of patterned brocade.

"*Signore,*" said Raphael, rubbing awkwardly at the back of his head.

"You'll take these orders to these addresses," Pietro stated briskly, "to be completed at the times written hereupon. We are understood?"

"Of course," said Raphael, frowning as he took the paper.

Maria craned her neck, watching him go to the back with a keen curiosity.

Pietro paid her little heed. He scowled at the parrots that had excited him so much until a minute ago. What if the women of the city looked at this the same way Maria had? With a shrug of boredom?

Pietro Agnesi was a self-made man. Not so many years ago he was a mathematics professor in Bologna, and perhaps he could have stayed cloistered in the walls of academia for all of his life and done well enough. But one day, something in him demanded a new venture. Using a mathematical approach to the economies of scale, he was able to operate at greater marginal profit than other textile sellers, even while offering a lower price.

And the prosperity he'd earned in so doing had earned him the notice of high society, which in turn had granted him the opportunity to meet the love of his life. Anna Brivio was part of a noble family. The match was an unimaginable fortune for a man like him, and to actually find they loved each other made it all the more precious. Not everyone was so lucky.

But what if he suddenly lost his knack for understanding the market? What if he was out of touch?

He brooded on that a minute before a clatter and a sudden uproar of laughter made him whirl around in worry. He'd been lost in his own head again. Where was Maria?

The owner of the place shouldn't be seen to do something so undignified as jog. But he outright ran. If he'd let something happen to her while he was on his oblivious, self-indulgent little sulk—on a day when his wife was sick, no less—he'd never forgive himself.

He arrived to find all of his warehouse hands clustered around a loading table, atop which sat a cross-legged Maria, speaking rapidly in French. Whatever she said next solicited a mighty guffaw from one of the newer workers and a sheepish smile from Raphael.

The center of attention, charming everyone around her? This was not the Maria he knew.

"What's all this, then?" He didn't mean to sound angry. Sometimes it just happened.

Maria spoke with uncharacteristic bluntness. "Raphael can't read Italian."

"What do you mean he can't read Italian?" Pietro knew he was scowling, but couldn't help himself. "He speaks it well enough, and I don't hire illiterates."

Raphael turned from sheepish to outright embarrassed. "I'm sorry, signore," he said, accent showing through. "I can speak it, yes. But you use . . . difficult words, and the writing, it is harder than the speaking, no?"

A third man grinned before chiming in. "Truth be told, signore, we all of us struggle a bit with your professor's words. But your daughter translated everything perfectly. Maybe you should put *her* to work around here!"

Proudly, with ink-spattered fingers, Maria held up a sheet of paper. Pietro took it and compared it against the original Italian, faintly mystified.

Pietro thought he knew French fairly well himself, but he didn't recognize half of these words. And when his daughter rambled off something to Raphael—causing yet another chorus of laughs among Pietro's men—he realized she spoke with native fluency.

He knew that his daughter had been studying French with her mother. But she was *five years old*. He'd expected *un-deux-trois, rouge-jaune-bleu*. Not proper conversation. And certainly not clever jokes.

Earlier, he'd cursed himself for being oblivious to what his daughter was doing in the warehouse. Evidently, he'd been oblivious of her for far longer than that.

~

Maria leaned back in her seat, hoping she could vanish into the couch cushions. "Am I in trouble?"

"You're not in trouble," said Pietro, scowling at the rack of books that decorated the back end of his office. "I just need to get a definitive answer to an important question."

Maria knew that look, and she knew her father was less than pleased. Though there was at least one thing she'd always appreciated about him: He never spoke to her like she was stupid.

It wasn't long before Pietro made his selection. He withdrew a thick, leather-bound book from the topmost shelf and plopped it on the table in front of Maria. He flipped rapidly through the pages, letting them wisp across his thumb, before suddenly snapping his palm flat and pointing with a single finger to a random block of text. "Here, read this," he demanded.

Maria craned her neck forward. She knew this was a Bible. The verse numbers made that clear. The last time her father had read to her, it had been stories of Noah and the Ark. Except he'd read from the Italian, and this was French.

But that wasn't anything special. She read the words on the page. "But Jesus beheld them, and said unto them: With men this is impossible; but with God all things are possible."

Pietro leaned back from the book like it had given him a fright. "Gospel of Matthew. Jesus Christ be praised, Maria, do you understand how impressive that is?"

"Oh, French is easy," said Maria, in fact not quite understanding the fuss. "I had a much harder time with Greek."

Pietro kept right on leaning back, so far it looked like he might topple out of his seat. "You don't mean to tell me you can *read Greek* as well?"

"French, Greek, and a little bit of Latin, but I don't like Latin very much."

Pietro removed his glasses. His eyes actually looked somehow wider without them. "The very opposite of Saint Augustine, apparently," he muttered, whatever that meant. He looked beside himself as he moved back to the shelf. "Greek . . . Greek . . . do I have anything in Greek . . . ?"

Usually, it's parents who read stories to their daughters. Before the day was over, Maria had read a whole set of Christ's parables to her increasingly mystified father.

"Why have you been hiding this from me?" Pietro demanded, both his hands planted on the back of his prized piano.

"I wasn't hiding anything," said Anna Brivio, propped up by more cushions than were normally used on all the beds in the house. The color lingered in her cheeks, but a whole afternoon asleep had done much to recover her health.

Were they arguing? Maria thought they were. She stayed in her familiar hiding spot behind the sofa, cross-legged, listening to them speak. They weren't yelling, at least, which made it better than a normal argument.

"I told you time and time again she was making progress," Anna went on. "But you were so busy obsessing about the kind of drapes they like in France that you didn't pay any attention."

"Making progress?" Pietro made the words sound like a declaration the sky had turned to green. "*Making progress?* Anna, darling, she's five years old and she speaks four languages!"

"Three," said Anna, placid as could be, her fingers woven together atop her pregnant middle. "The fourth isn't anything we could reasonably call fluent."

"This takes years. It takes tutoring. It takes *scholarship.* This simply isn't normal," Pietro went on, his hands in the air, gesticulating.

Maria could see him. She'd dared to sneak a glance. Somewhere deep inside her heart, she felt oddly conflicted. Her father wasn't upset. She'd realized that about halfway through her earlier reading. He was *proud* of her. Knowing that had put a smile on her face the whole way home. So why was he throwing such a big fuss now?

"Well, she had a very good teacher," said Anna with a smile.

"I'm an *academic,* Anna," said Pietro. "I know scholarship, and I know you're talented. This isn't just scholarship. This is beyond talent. This is the gift of the Holy Ghost. The genius of the finest professorial minds. We must get her a proper tutor. Who knows how much she might achieve with the right guidance?"

"No," said Anna, her voice suddenly stern. "Absolutely not."

Pietro was, for a moment, at a loss for words. "What do you mean, no? You must know genius when you see it."

Maria both loved and distrusted that word—*genius.*

"She's a girl," said Anna. "She should be free to be a girl. She can be a scholar, a wife, whatever she wants to be, when she's good and ready for it. If we push her too much now, she'll just be doing it because we tell her to."

Pietro lowered his voice. Maria knew he did this when he wanted his words to go unnoticed by his daughter, but the house carried sound better than he imagined. "I'm sure you've noticed our daughter has problems talking to people."

"She's a girl," Anna insisted. But there was a hesitance in her voice now.

"When she got to show off her French, it was like she was a completely different person. Warm, gregarious, open. We should encourage that in her."

"You have a point," Anna admitted, as if it pained her greatly to cede even the slightest argumentative ground. She sat up straighter, working up the energy needed to stand. Weary as she was, this was no fast and simple process. "But there's no need to fetch her some tutor. I can do it all myself."

"That's your problem. You're always trying to do *everything* yourself. You're in this state precisely because—"

Something clattered and broke. The sound of shattered pottery tore a yelp out of Maria, who hopped up to her feet.

Thus exposed, she saw her mother sprawled across a side table, the remnants of a toppled vase strewn across the floor. Damp flowers and spilled water darkened the foreign carpet.

Pietro was with her, helping her. Any anger that was in him before was gone now.

"Fine," said Anna, once she had her feet under her. She

didn't even look at the vase. She refused to, committed to acting like nothing out of the ordinary had happened. "We'll get her a tutor. But I have final say on who it is."

It wasn't long before the candidates arrived.

Chapter Three

"You have brought me here under false pretenses," said Professor Calabresi, "and I am not amused."

For a moment, the steadily ticking clock was the only sound to be heard in the Agnesi family sitting room. Maria sat in between her parents on the sofa, frowning at the gray-haired academic. What was wrong with her, exactly?

"We were quite specific in the letter," said Anna Brivio. "We need a tutor to help cultivate a brilliant young talent. She may be younger than you were expecting, but she's the equal of a much older student."

"And we can pay handsomely," added Pietro.

"Yes, I'm sure she's extraordinarily intelligent and you've clearly the pockets of Croesus," said Calabresi, a large book tucked under one of his arms. "There is, however, the small problem that she is a girl."

"The letter stated as much," said Anna, bristling on her daughter's behalf.

"Yes, and taking time from my busy schedule to tutor a

teenaged girl is one thing. But a small child? Frankly, I do not believe she can say any more than 'hello' in all those languages. I shan't waste her time, nor yours, and especially not mine. Good day."

Calabresi carried himself straight out of the house, never once looking back.

"What an insufferably arrogant person," said Anna. "*That* was the best linguistics expert in all of Milan?"

Pietro shrugged. "The most decorated man isn't always the best teacher. We've got more options."

Quite a lot of options, as it turned out. Maria grew increasingly impatient with the parade of well-dressed intellectuals slated that day to visit the Agnesi family home. They saw two more professors, a priest, a historian, and a visiting French polymath. None of them had felt it polite to refuse the summons of one of the city's most prosperous merchants, but none of them thought formally educating Maria was a good idea.

Maria was inclined to agree. She'd rather have had her nose in a book or a flower, or do anything that wasn't sitting on this sofa, listening to these men. If this was learning, she'd had enough. But her parents had insisted she needed to be there, so there she was, wondering if the clock had somehow begun to tick backward.

The next man was an angular, too-thin sort of fellow, his nose a knobby thing that looked just a little too big for his face. Maria briefly worried he would topple over from the simple act of brushing himself off.

"Professor Veronesi, greetings, welcome," said Pietro,

gesturing at the opposite seat. "I read your paper on differential calculus. Quite forward-thinking, I should say."

The professor did not take the offered chair. Instead he moved to the side table, where he promptly began doling out a series of papers. "I took the liberty of preparing a small test," said Veronesi, his voice a little nasal. It made him sound somehow slightly deflated. "You say your daughter speaks three languages and is already quite advanced in mathematics. I would normally have discounted this at once, but given your credentials as a mathematician at the university in Bologna, I have to imagine you at least have some idea what you are talking about." He spoke directly to Pietro, as if Anna and Maria were not there at all.

Maria realized that she would soon be asked to read all the man's papers. So she hopped right up and went over to have a look.

The professor kept droning on—something about other well-to-do students and the efficiency of his methods—but Maria paid him no heed. The things he'd brought were much more interesting than the man himself. Two of the papers were full of writing in various languages, which wasn't anything special. But the third sheet, much to her delight, was full of numbers.

Her mother had seen to her education in mathematics. But there was something about these open-ended equations—multiplication, division, subtraction, and sometimes multiple of these mixed together. The world was a confusing place, and nothing in it was more confusing to Maria than other people. The pleasure of mathematics was the unfolding of beautiful certainty. There was always a precisely correct answer, and the wonderful feeling of satisfaction when it arrived.

But she wasn't more than six problems in before Veronesi yanked the paper away. It was a quick little tug that sent the line of Maria's pen sliding askew in an ugly diagonal line.

"Hmmm," said the reedy professor, studying the paper.

Anna and Pietro both sat expectantly.

"Well?" Pietro asked.

Veronesi studied the paper a little while longer. At last, he looked up. "I regret to inform you that your daughter is a genius."

The clock ticked again.

"Yes, we knew that already," said Pietro. "That is why you are here."

"And it is why I will leave," said Veronesi, leaving Maria faintly mystified. It was bad that she'd done well?

"I don't understand," Maria told him.

Veronesi smiled wanly. "Yes, well. All well and good to teach a woman enough to keep up with her husband. But honing a woman's genius to a razor's edge will only ruin her for society."

"I scarcely think myself ruined," said a politely venomous Anna. "I would like you to apologize to my daughter."

Veronesi seemed mildly surprised to notice Anna in the room. "Signora, I am sorry, but I ask you: What is the benefit of honing the academic gifts of a woman? I thought you wanted her to be able to understand her father's business. But this girl's intellect in mathematics is of such a high grade that it would be of use only in the halls of academia. There is no place for a woman at the Milanese academy. Polished too keenly, your daughter will only become a shrewish, frustrated woman who must emasculate and bully a less clever husband."

"You will leave now," said Pietro, glancing worriedly at his wife, whose eyes had gone white all around her eyes.

"Allow me to suggest instead a more feminine course of study," Veronesi opined. "Music, perhaps. It is almost a kind of math."

Veronesi managed to escape with his head on his shoulders.

"I told you this was a bad idea," said Anna. "Are we about done?"

"We have one final caller!" hollered Isabella from the front door. "Should I send him in?"

"Send him in," said a grim, resigned Pietro.

The man who entered immediately caught Maria's attention. From the very first, he was visibly different from all the stuffy old thinkers and academics she'd seen thus far. Where they were impeccably dressed and rigidly coiffed, this fellow had flowing lace cuffs and tousled hair that suggested he didn't much care about appearances. And he was younger than the others. Gray hadn't yet colored his auburn hair.

"Vittorio Bellone, at your service," he introduced himself, touching a hand to his chest. "Adjunct professor at the Milanese university." He turned his attention to Maria. "And you are the clever little girl I've heard so very much about?"

"I think so," said Maria, never inclined to praise herself too openly.

"If you're here to tell us about how we're fools for trying

to teach our daughter advanced learning, and how women are better off living like beautiful vegetables, I'll thank you to spare us all a bit of suffering and leave." Anna remained a touch bitter over the last prospect.

"Oh, hardly," said Vittorio. "I'm not sure if you know this, but I am a Venetian. Well, *was* a Venetian, but that's neither here nor there."

Pietro leaned forward, intrigued. "Ah, then you think—"

"What I *know*," Vittorio interrupted him, "is that women have been doing brilliant academic work in Venice for decades. You have heard of Elena Cornaro Piscopia?"

Pietro nodded, but Anna was forced to admit that she had not.

"She is on the very vanguard of women's education. One of an elite few women to ever receive an academic degree from a university, and the first to be crowned doctor of philosophy. You see, there is a *movement* emerging, one which will give to women the keys of wisdom that were until now hoarded by men alone."

Anna folded her arms. "So you see my daughter as . . . what, fuel for this movement? Someone you're going to usher into university to prove a grand point about the quality of women?"

Vittorio smiled brightly. There was something slightly infectious about it. "No, my lady, you misunderstand me. It is only a matter of time before women are welcomed in all the disciplines of study. I see your daughter as a potential pioneer. If she is half so clever as I've been told, she needn't stop at studying at a university. She could very well earn the title of professor herself."

"What a splendid notion," said Pietro, features alight. "As

a former mathematician, you know, nothing would make me more proud than for my daughter to carry on the tradition."

"That all seems very premature," said Anna. She sized up Vittorio with a skeptical glance. "I think it's very noble that you want to help more women make it to the universities. But Maria is just a little girl, not political ammunition, and she's not even said a word since you got here."

"Well," Vittorio began, "that is why I've prepared a test."

"We've already had tests," Anna complained.

"Not like this one," said Vittorio. "I heard the others from the foyer. They were testing her as a child. What I will do is test her as a scholar. It will be a challenge, but we will truly know her mettle when we are done."

Maria saw both her parents looking at her, as if trying to divine her opinion on the matter. All she could do was shrug. "I'm happy to do a bit more math," she said, hoping that was all there was to it.

"I don't like this," said Anna. "But seeing as how no one else accepted the position, I suppose we've no choice but to let you try whatever you have planned."

Vittorio clasped his hands together. "Then let's begin right away."

Chapter Four

Maria sat staring at a piece of paper. Vittorio Bellone watched expectantly from the other side of the writing desk. Somewhere behind her, both of her parents likewise observed. Their collective stares became something like a physical force, boring into the back of her skull with the weight of highest expectation.

She thought she was good at reading things. So why was this so hard?

It was a series of selected passages, some short, some long; all of them were in Greek, and not the ancient kind. It was the modern everyday Greek she knew she could speak perfectly well.

But there was something different about seeing the words now. A feeling had bloomed somewhere deep inside of her that if she messed this up, she'd ruin more things than she even knew how to think about.

And then there was Professor Bellone. He sat right there on the other side of the desk, hands clasped, peering directly at her.

"You're too close," she finally told him. She could hear his breathing. The sound of it was immensely distracting.

The professor rolled his shoulders back and sat up straight—he'd been leaning forward.

"Too close," Maria repeated, avoiding eye contact. Even with the added distance, she could still hear the air whistling through his nose.

"Maria, show the professor some respect." Pietro's voice jolted her with the reminder that he was, in fact, also still right there staring at her.

Maria held her hands up level with either side of her head, the pen lying neglected on the paper. "It's hard," she protested.

"Nonsense," her father insisted, as unyielding as stone. "This should be incredibly easy for you. I saw you read far harder things with my own eyes. Don't go embarrassing yourself—or your parents—in front of the professor. I know what you're capable of! There's no sense acting like a child."

His voice was doing that thing it did sometimes, where it steadily got louder and louder. Pietro never noticed he was doing it and always denied that it was happening when it did. There was no sense in telling him to stop, or complaining that she was, in fact, a child. It would only fall on deaf ears.

Anna's dress rustled as she rose from the sofa, unable to maintain her silence. "Darling, please have a seat," she said to Pietro, in that sweet sort of voice that actually meant *You're being entirely unreasonable.*

She grasped Maria's shoulders, squeezing softly. "Everything's going to be all right, dear. Your father and I know you're very talented, so you don't need to worry about anything. Just do what you can."

All very reassuring in theory, but now there were *three* people right on top of her. Maria clunked her head down into her folded arms. That way, she at least wouldn't have to look at them all.

"See? Coddling her won't get results," Pietro insisted.

Anna shot right back, "But *chastising* her isn't going to—"

Vittorio Bellone cleared his throat. It was a quick, whip-sharp crack of a noise. His eyes flicked between both of Maria's parents before he quietly spoke. "If I might make a suggestion."

The suggestion was immediately heeded. Both Pietro and Anna shuffled out of the room and shut the door behind them. With the clunk of the door, Maria suddenly felt capable of breathing again.

"You're not comfortable around people," the professor observed.

Maria didn't answer. She just breathed out, long and slow, turning her eyes to the paper.

"Well, you'd hardly be the first academic to prefer the company of books." Vittorio scooted back his chair all the way to the wall. Patiently, he crossed his arms and hooked one leg over the other. "You can have a minute. Let me know when you're ready."

"This isn't the Bible," Maria finally realized, studying the words on the page. "Or anything like literature. It's . . . something to do with math."

It was a host of unfamiliar terms. It was like peering into the clouded depths of the ocean—it was certainly made of water, and maybe you could see a couple of shapes, but it was impossible to see the bottom.

How oddly exciting.

Maria wondered aloud: "What's *logismos*?"

"In Italian," said the professor, "we call it *calculus*."

Maria sensed a new frontier was beginning to reveal itself. "And it's a kind of math?"

Vittorio clapped his hands, just once. "If you'll turn to the second page . . . ."

Equations flashed like mathematical thunderbolts in Maria's mind, interweaving with one another into ever more complicated knots of logic. But, like a Möbius strip, they never came to dead ends, never tangled—the straight line of logic soared relentlessly from equation to sum. Page after page was filled with the evidence of her figuring.

That was because a certain professor said it wasn't good enough. He insisted on a complete record of every step.

"You must *show your work*," he demanded sharply, not for the first time.

"Why?" Maria fired back, by now well over the hesitance that gripped her every time she met someone new. "I got the answer right—isn't that what matters?"

"Because that is how the academy works," Vittorio told her, emphatically jabbing at a finished problem. "It's not enough to declare yourself a genius. People will think you are cheating. Or lying. And most importantly, the goal of learning is to enlighten *everyone,* not just yourself. How will other people keep up with you if they can't see the chain of logic by which you got from one place to another?"

"Because it's obvious," said Maria, really believing it. She'd never met a math problem she couldn't do in her head.

"Oh, it's obvious, is it?" Vittorio produced another paper, this one with two columns of text.

Maria realized with dread that all the passages, on both the left and the right side, were in Latin.

"Well, go on," he said. "Read them."

"It's too complicated," Maria protested. "I don't know Latin."

"But to me, it's obvious," said Vittorio. "So why should you need to be shown all the intermediate steps?"

The professor was a very different kind of teacher from her mother, Maria realized. Combative, challenging. She wondered just how much more than her he knew. And how long it would take her to catch up.

"I hate Latin," Maria complained, secretly hoping to master it.

Not long after that, Maria left the room to demand the professor be her new teacher—and the professor practically begged to let her be made his student. He was even willing to do it for free—not that Pietro would let him.

Maria learned Latin faster than she ever imagined possible.

Chapter Five

"We're going to see something very special today," Anna told her daughter. The two of them were out on what had become something of a weekly ritual: their visit to the convent.

Spring had given way to summer, and the mist that often settled over the city by morning was becoming a rarer and rarer sight. It was said in the streets of Milan that if you could look up in the early morning and see clearly the topmost spires of the Duomo, then the day was bound to be sunny. Maria felt that on that day, if it weren't for the roofs of buildings and the landscapes in between, she might be able to see clearly all the way to Rome.

The heat was absolutely oppressive. Anna had placed a delicate wide-brimmed hat atop her daughter's head when they first set out, but that was a bit like trying to put out a fire with a thimbleful of water. They weren't but a hundred yards out before Maria could feel sweat dripping down the sides of her face, and though her mother was as stoic as she always was, a quick glance was enough to confirm that she was suffering, too. Maria at least had the fortune of being able to wear a relatively simple child's dress. She knew her mother was under multiple layers, and even though maternity dresses weren't as structured or heavy as formal clothes, it still couldn't have been easy for her.

Anna had reached the beginning of her pregnancy's ninth month. It wouldn't be long before Maria's brother or sister was born. Maria felt certain it would be a girl, but she had no reason for the belief. It was just an instinctive object of faith, something she was confident in, much like her mother showed unlimited confidence in the loving kindness in all men's hearts.

"You and your father are talking more often lately," Anna spoke up, perhaps to distract from the weather as much as anything else. "I'm very glad. You always seemed a bit distant from each other before."

Until now, they'd never had a language in common. Maria had always had an instinctual understanding of mathematics, but only through the instruction of Professor Bellone had she come to possess the words needed to express it. The "intermediate details," as he'd called them. Every time she asked her father a question, he was only too pleased to answer; he never held back a scrap of nuance, and even if Maria was clever, she was learning there were layers to scholarship she'd never imagined. Sometimes she couldn't keep up, but after years of only knowing her father as a man to return home exhausted from work, Pietro's newfound warmth and enthusiasm were a draught to be desired.

But for all her gifts in language, Maria remained much better at articulating other people's feelings than her own. "We talk a little more now" was all she said to her mother out loud.

The weeks had become regimented. Weekday mornings with Vittorio, afternoons with her books, and, if she was lucky, evenings with her father. Weekends, however, were a time to be with her mother—and thanks to her mother's earnest piety, they were also often a time to be with God.

"Tell me a little more about the Latin you've learned," Anna prompted, and it felt like no sooner had Maria begun expounding on the mysteries of the subjunctive than they arrived at their destination.

The convent of Santa Maria delle Grazie had once been frightening, but after a few short months of visitation it now felt like a second home. Moreover, the dim stone halls were a blessedly cool respite from the punishing summer heat.

Maria beamed a great big smile at the tottering figure of Brother Hieronymus, the old Dominican who minded the refectory library. "Our little scholar returns," he enthused, turning a gap-toothed smirk up at Anna when Maria darted past him to examine the spines of books. "Got a knack for words, that one. I daresay she'd make an excellent nun."

"I think her father has other ideas," said Anna, nonetheless amused.

The nuns at the adjoining convent were most of them rather old—Maria had never quite put a thought to the notion she might wear a habit herself. How old did you have to be? Probably not the life for her anyway. Books and church and religion were all well and good, but there were quite a lot of rules involved, and that got exhausting awfully quickly.

But if there was one thing Maria appreciated about this

church, it was the depth of their book collections. Vittorio had explained there was a time when the Church had done everything they could to keep everyone from reading certain books they figured best kept out of normal people's hands, and that someone named Martin Luther had been very upset about that, but Maria didn't expect she'd suffer similar disapproval.

"Maria Gaetana," Anna admonished her daughter, who was already deep into the shelves. "Do pace yourself. Didn't I say we were going to do something special today?"

"Do twice as many chores, I bet she means," cackled Hieronymus from the back of the room, where he was polishing oil lamps. "I've never met someone so in love with service. When you get to my age, trust me, you learn to avoid work. Life's too short!"

Mother Angelica had chosen that moment to enter the room. She turning a wrinkly frown at the recalcitrant Dominican. "Yes, I am sure that laziness is a wonderful quality for a man of the cloth to encourage in children."

"Children are children," Hieronymus declared, already on his way out of the room. "And they are children only the one time. I say let them frolic."

Maria, meanwhile, had found the book she was looking for: *Philosophiæ Naturalis Principia Mathematica*. Vittorio said that this book, written some years ago by an Englishman named Isaac Newton, had changed the way the whole world thought about mathematics. He'd also claimed that Maria was too young to read and appreciate the book. They'd just see about that, she thought to herself, sliding it off the shelf.

Mother Angelica noticed, frowned, and let it pass. "Are you fond of art, young Maria Gaetana?"

It took Maria a moment to realize she was being spoken to, let alone formulate an answer. "Hmmm? What? Art?" Her small fingers traced the spine of the book. "Oh, I suppose. My father loves it, and always goes on and on about the 'Florentine masters.'"

This apparently pleased Mother Angelica greatly, for her typically dour expression become one of lightness and grace. "Oh, then I won't need to explain to you about Leonardo da Vinci. We don't usually show the Leonardo, you know, but your mother is ever a stalwart patron of our mission and she wanted to share it with you."

They had plenty of paintings at home. What was so special about Leonardo? Mathematics had gotten better and better with the years; Maria figured old art was probably much the same. Worse than the new art.

"We've had to practically seal off the room," said Mother Angelica, already leading them deeper into the refectory.

Maria might not have followed, save for the guiding influence of her mother's hand upon her back. She clutched the book to her chest with both arms. Their steps echoed on the gray stone floor.

The door had more than one lock. Were they trying to keep people out or trap the painting inside, Maria wondered? It all felt a bit silly.

"I've only seen it the one time," Anna told her daughter,

anticipation obvious upon her face. "It really is the most splendid painting."

Aged hinges creaked as Mother Angelica pushed open the door. They exited the dim hallway and entered an even dimmer chamber. At one point, the place must have been used for something, but now it was empty. Everything had been removed, leaving only whitewashed walls, a high curved ceiling, and the echo of their steps. Curtains muted the light from the outside.

There was the painting, of course. But Maria didn't see what the fuss was about.

The thing was falling apart.

Maria had seen enough paintings and enough churches to know Jesus and the twelve apostles when she saw them. But whole patches of the paint were gone. Everything was faded. Flakes had peeled away. It was well done, she supposed, if perhaps a little boring. Everyone seated around a table looking startled and upset, except for Jesus himself, who had that sort of sleepy, dreamy quality he always did whenever he showed up in art. Part of Maria wondered if what the Savior really needed was a proper nap. Naps always made her feel better.

Both her mother and the old nun made the sign of the cross and stared up with reverent awe.

"It's called *The Last Supper*," said Mother Angelica, full of intermingled piety and pride. "The finest work of the greatest master."

"It's really old," said Maria, which made her mother frown, for reasons she couldn't quite discern.

"More than three hundred years old," said Mother Angelica. "I fear it was much brighter when I was a child. Leonardo used an unusual method to paint it. We do our best to keep it from getting damaged, but I fear the day will come when nothing is left of it. It doesn't seem to want to last."

"Nothing lasts forever, except for God," said Anna, which was so earnest and pious that it made Maria slightly uncomfortable.

Mathematics were also eternal, Maria decided. No matter how much the world changed and no matter how old people got, the way things worked never changed.

An uncomfortably boring interval passed as the grown-ups kept staring at the painting.

Maria eventually wandered off, looking for a place to read.

Pain had bedeviled Anna Brivio ever since she was a child.

She was only six when the migraines began. They had been a constant companion throughout her life. When her sisters had danced and wheeled in the ballrooms of the rich and powerful, she had been in bed, suffering. When her brother had schemed to bring the family greater honors, she kneeled in church, praying for relief.

And there she was now, praying before *The Last Supper* of Leonardo da Vinci, hoping that the twinge in her skull was just the product of worry for her daughter, not the sign of another debilitated evening.

There had never been a lack of doctors, at least. Once upon a time her family had been silk merchants, much like her husband, Pietro. But for all his prosperity, Pietro could never have dreamed of matching the wealth the Brivios possessed. When the War of the Spanish Succession raged, the Brivios had opened their coffers to carry no small portion of the cost. The Holy Roman emperor had duly elevated their family to the nobility. Anna had been very young when it happened, but she had never truly felt like a noblewoman. Titles and honors were nothing before God.

Today, as always, she offered her suffering up to the Lord. That was how she dealt with the pain—and also how she hid it from other people. Prayer gave clarity, even if it did not always provide relief.

"I'd best go and see where my daughter has run off to," she told Mother Angelica, growing increasingly certain that a migraine was building. Last year she had begun to believe they were getting rarer, but the longer her pregnancy had gone on, the more her body seemed to spite her for it. At least it would be over soon, she consoled herself. Soon she would know the joy of meeting her second child.

Never show weakness, always be gracious. Those were the twin lessons her father and mother had instilled in her. As the youngest of the nobility, everyone would be watching for the slightest lapse in protocol.

The world had started to grow blurry at the edges by the time she finally found Maria. How was she going to be able to teach her class like this? She couldn't, she knew. Anna despised that weakness in herself. There were so many things she'd given up because of it. But she refused to give up being a mother. Pietro had so often insisted on a governess, but that was an argument Anna would not lose.

Maria sat in a shaded corner of the courtyard, pages deep in some ridiculously advanced Latin tome. Competing emotions stirred in Anna's heart. Pride, of course—her daughter was brilliant. She'd always known it. Even as an infant, there'd been a clarity to Maria's eyes that spoke to the cleverness that lived behind them.

But perhaps Anna had never really admitted to herself just *how* brilliant Maria was. Sneaking off on a Sunday to read mathematical treatises? This was simply not normal for a child.

On the other side of the courtyard, a group of small girls ran along, their voices raised up high in laughter and exclamation. They chased one another desperately, engaged in some game that only children could understand.

"Maria, you can't study every day of the week," Anna chastised her.

Maria looked up from the book, a bit sullen. "It's not studying," she insisted. "My teacher even said I shouldn't read it."

"Perhaps you should listen to your teacher," Anna suggested, doing her best not to frown and not entirely succeeding. "Why don't you go and play? You're young. Go enjoy it."

Anna looked over to where the other girls were playing. The tallest girl was holding up some kind of furry bug. The other girls around her shrieked with exaggerated, disgusted delight.

"Don't want to," Maria muttered derisively, touching a finger to the bottom of a line of Latin text.

Anna wondered silently: Just what was she going to do with this girl?

The world swam in a haze of color before her migraine-clouded eyes.

That night, Maria's parents had another argument. Lying in bed, Maria couldn't hear all the words through her bedroom door.

". . . slow down the pace of her education," her mother insisted.

". . . course not," said Pietro, his next few words too low to carry. ". . . genius. You would waste that? Weren't you the one who wanted her taught?"

". . . bad for her," Anna went on. Something thudded repeatedly. Maria imagined her mother's fist impacting a table. "You don't understand!"

"Do *you* understand?" her father's voice roared back. "Do you know how much money that professor is costing us?"

"He offered to teach *for free!* Or have you forgotten?"

Maria truly didn't understand adults. Shouldn't they be happy she was doing well? Happy she was learning?

But the argument didn't continue with shouts. They remembered that a young girl was supposed to be asleep upstairs, and returned to hissing whispers at each other.

Curiosity ultimately got the better of Maria. If they were going to argue about her, she felt it only appropriate that she overhear. So, silently as she could manage, she crept barefoot out of bed. Tiptoeing, she maneuvered over toward the doorway, taking care to avoid the one stubbornly creaky floorboard.

Her small fingers curled around the doorknob. So slowly that she could feel the movement of every individual sinew in her hand, she turned it open. Body turned sideways, she slipped through the narrow gap and crept to the stairway landing.

Only the one lantern was lit in the room below. Shadows deepened Pietro's face. The oil-flame's reflection flickered in his eyes.

"You're being ridiculous," he told his wife, arms crossed. "I don't even understand why we're having this discussion."

But there was no answer.

And as the moments lengthened, still no answer came.

So long as she lived, Maria never forgot the transformation in his father's eyes. The change from accusation to horror—instantaneous and yet seeming to last forever.

Maria heard the quiet, muffled thud of a heavy thing falling. That wasn't the part that scared her. She thought Anna had simply dropped something.

What truly worried her was the wheeze her mother made after she hit the ground. Like all the breath went out of her at once. It was not a noise she'd ever heard a person make before.

Maria's feet moved of their own accord. Before she realized it, she stood in the doorway, looking at where her mother had collapsed into a heap upon the floor. Her father kneeled beside Anna, holding her hand too tightly.

Hearing Maria's steps, his head snapped toward the doorway. They met each other's eyes.

Maria knew at once just how very, very bad this all was—because her father didn't chastise her for being out of bed.

"The doctor," he said, too quietly. "I need to fetch the doctor."

Chapter Six

"It's just exhaustion," Maria told Vittorio, seated at her familiar study desk in the parlor. No one had told her that, actually. But she remembered her father saying those words the last time this happened. And her mother had got better then, hadn't she?

She'd get better this time, too. Maria felt confident about it. Or at least she felt like she needed to be confident, for her mother's sake.

Vittorio's eyebrows scrunched downward. He had arrived at the usual midmorning time, but hadn't yet opened the bag that contained all his papers.

The commotion upstairs was hard to ignore. There were a whole bunch of people Maria had never seen before coming in and out of her mother's room, and also a woman called a "midwife," which no one had explained to her. Her father was there, though, so it was doubtlessly all fine. The sound of their shoes and voices was a kind of droning backdrop that muffled the parlor clock.

It was probably fine. But no one was talking to Maria about any of it.

"Well, if you think you can focus, and you're certain everything's all right," Vittorio said doubtfully, "then I suppose we can at least do a review of yesterday's material."

Before he could pull out his chair, yet another doctor arrived. He was the fourth one to arrive that day. Maria had no idea what his name was, but he wore pinch-nose eyeglasses and he seemed to be in an awful hurry. He marched right upstairs to Anna's room, Isabella leading the way. His arrival caused a sudden outburst of voices above.

"The subjunctive," Maria prompted Vittorio.

"Never mind the subjunctive," said Vittorio, leaving the bag on the seat of the chair, unopened. "Wait here a moment."

Vittorio's boots were awfully heavy. Maria could hear the *thunk* of every boot-fall as he marched toward the stairs. He did not climb them—instead, he waited patiently at the bottom until Isabella began her own descent.

"I'd like to speak with the master of the house," said Vittorio.

"Oh, he left word for you." A poorly disguised fatigue put a slight tremor into Isabella's voice. "He said you were to carry on your lesson as usual. Lady Anna Brivio has always had poor health, you see, but she bounces back like a spring."

"I'd like to speak with the master of the house," Vittorio insisted, voice dropping lower.

It wasn't long before Pietro appeared at the top of the stairs. He and Vittorio regarded one another with vague displeasure until Isabella abruptly excused herself.

"Given the circumstances," said Vittorio, "I'd like to cancel today's lesson."

Pietro took three steps downward, lessening the distance between them but further accentuating the distance in height. "Listen," he said quietly. "This is a difficult time. There was a bit of stress, so we're getting the baby a touch early. The doctors are just a precaution."

"One doctor would be a precaution," said Vittorio. "But this many—"

"Are a wealthy man's excess of preparedness," Pietro described it. "That's all. My daughter will be happiest if her mind is elsewhere. God knows I wish mine could be."

Vittorio couldn't muster a reply. Pietro hastened for the bedroom, where Maria now realized that her sibling was being born.

The subjunctive *did* suddenly seem rather less important. Maria could feel all the tiny hairs on her arms and neck stand on end. For an instant, she felt like she was looking down at herself from the ceiling, rather than just sitting there at the table.

Eventually she realized that Vittorio had joined her. Neither of them immediately spoke.

Maria felt as shy as the first time she'd met him. "I . . . ."

Vittorio fussed with one of his shirt cuffs, looking sideways to the stairs. "Do you think you'll have a brother or a sister?"

"I'd like a sister," she admitted quietly. "Though I think Papà wants a son."

"Men always do," said Vittorio with a sly sort of smile. "Carry on the family name, the family business, that sort of thing. But in this case, well . . . maybe he wants a son because he knows he already has the very best daughter he could hope for."

Maria had never heard her father say anything like that. She hoped it was true.

Finally, she managed a weak smile of her own. "You were right," she said. "Isaac Newton was too hard."

Vittorio burst out with startled laughter. "You actually tried to read it? Goodness, I need to be careful what I say around you. Well, don't worry. Today I've brought something a lot easier. We won't learn anything new—you can just read quietly."

It was all about ancient Rome and the time before Jesus Christ was born. Did Jesus ever have any brothers or sisters? Maria realized she'd never heard anyone say a word on the topic. She began to daydream, wondering what it would be like to have God Himself as an older brother. Probably it would be very hard to live up to the example.

"Maria." Her father's voice cut into her thoughts.

Maria suddenly realized a great deal of time had passed. Pietro stood in the doorway, flanked by doctors on either side.

"Your sister has been born," he told her.

Which ought to have been a happy thing. But the way he said it was all wrong. Too tense, too matter-of-fact. Like there was something wrong with it.

Pietro looked like he might fall over at any moment. In fact, Maria realized, one of the doctors gripped him by the elbow. Without the help, his feet might very well have failed him.

"Your mother needs to see you right away," said Pietro.

The second doctor grimly extended his hand to Maria. She leaned back into her seat, unwilling to take it.

Vittorio kept a cautious silence. But he pushed his hand to Maria's back, gently nudging her forward.

She took the doctor's fingers and went up with him to where her mother lay dying.

Anna seemed almost at peace. She held a sleepy, red-faced infant in her arms, as healthy a child as one might wish for. Cradling the baby to her chest, she lay in her maternity bed beneath a sunlit window. Were it not for the ashen, bloodless pallor of her face, it would be easy to believe she was just tired, as all women must be after such a trial.

But Maria knew better. They'd cleaned it up as best they could, but the smell of blood was overpowering.

She wanted nothing more than to run from the room, as far as her feet could carry her. She'd close her door, bury her head beneath a pillow, and stay there until everything was over. She'd wake up in the morning and her mother would be just fine, ready to take her to one of the old churches of which she was so fond.

"Maria," said Anna, trying and failing to hide her suffering. "I want you to know two things."

Maria felt like she'd lost control of her own body. Someone else, surely, was guiding it to the bedside, taking her mother's hand.

"First," said Anna, her fingers much too cold. "You're my oldest and dearest daughter. And I love you very, very much."

Maria couldn't bring herself to answer out loud. She

squeezed her mother's hand so hard she feared she might bruise her fingers.

"And second, I want you to take that," Anna continued. Baby in one hand, Maria's fingers in the other, she couldn't point. Instead she nodded at the bedside table, on which was placed an aged and time-worn Bible. "It was my mother's before it was mine. Now it's yours."

Maria took the book. She tucked it mutely beneath her arm. Holding it so tightly would surely damage a thing so old, but if she didn't squeeze hard, she might lose her grip not just on the book, but also on herself. Her cheeks were already wet.

"I'll take good care of it," she promised her mother.

A familiar scent filled Maria's nostrils—the heavy, spice-laden odor of the incense burned in churches.

In the doorway stood a priest, scalp shorn bald, the formal robes of office weighing down his broad shoulders. He intoned his words with the gravity that comes from practice.

"I am here to perform the sacrament of extreme unction."

Seeing the priest inspired Anna to speak again. Something, perhaps, she had not originally meant to say. "Remember that books and learning aren't everything," she told her daughter. "It's what we do with them that matters. Service to God, service to others, that's just more important than words on a page."

The grip of her mother's fingers was getting weaker. The priest gently reached out to part mother and daughter from one another.

Outside the room, Maria listened to the soft-spoken words of life's final sacrament.

~

They came in the evening to take her mother's body away.

She never saw them. Nor did she see her father. Both of them preferred to feel their grief alone.

Maria wondered if she ought to cry more. She had been to a funeral once where the dead man's wife wailed so loudly she needed to be dragged from church. Didn't she owe her mother that much?

But she found she had no more energy for crying. Instead she lay in bed, staring out her window to the opposite wing of the house, at the room where her mother used to stay awake and read. For all the years of her childhood, she'd been able to look across one window to the next, where the flickering candlelight stood in testament to her mother's presence.

No one would light that candle now.

Maria forced herself to rise, to shuffle to the corner of the room, where her own lantern burned. She watched the fire a moment, until the brightness of it left lingering pinpricks of light in her vision even when she closed her eyes. She lifted the lantern and set it on her own windowsill.

Her fingers ran over the books stacked haphazardly on her desk. Like her mother, she liked to stay up reading.

Part Two

THE CHILD PRODIGY

Chapter Seven

In the waning hours of twilight, a pack of Milan's erudite rich gathered to observe the city's latest curiosity.

It was not a city that lacked for curiosities. Relics of saints, a nail of the True Cross, art from across the ages—but all of those were inert things to be viewed through glass cases. What held their interest now was not a masterpiece, but a person.

"Not since Blaise Pascal has there been a greater child genius," said one man to another as they approached the palazzo. "Mark me, you will be amazed. It is greatness in the making."

"Speaks seven languages is what they claim," said his companion, shaking his head skeptically. "I will believe it when I see it."

A well-dressed servant stood at the doors of the Palazzo Agnesi. After taking the guests' names, he bowed his head and duly opened the door.

The Agnesi family, always prosperous, had only increased their fortunes with time. Of late they had bought a truly magnificent residence. A local master had been hired to paint the foyer's walls with arboreal splendor, and everywhere was the evidence of good taste expressed through enormous outlay of wealth.

These men had arrived late. There had already been food, already been conversation, and now was the show.

A circle of older folk regarded a young woman. She was perhaps twelve years of age. The golden flower brocade blooming on her mantua dress suggested the splendor of Versailles; the deep blue of its fabric recalled motifs of the Virgin Mary in art. A portrait of the Holy Family that hung on the wall behind her had no doubt been positioned quite intentionally to evoke the connotation. And yet there was a plain, approachable simplicity about her.

"I have heard it said that you will defend your scientific propositions against any challenge, in any language," said a reedy fellow with a wispy mustache.

"So long as it is, in fact, one of my own propositions," confirmed Maria Gaetana Agnesi, poised like statuary, fingers laced together in her lap. "You may challenge my theses in Greek, Italian, Hebrew, Spanish, German, or Latin. It makes no difference to me."

The reedy fellow switched immediately into Latin. No one spoke Latin like a native—it was always colored by the idioms of their homeland. But this challenger had clearly chosen his words in advance, for they had the formality of the Latin used in church. "You earlier suggested that the Empire adopt a policy of variolation for all its nobility and doctors. I proclaim this variolation simple madness. Cure smallpox by infecting a man with smallpox? That would not avert an epidemic—it would *cause* one. For what is to stop the variolated man from passing it on to others in turn?"

Maria did not need even a moment to prepare her response. "Fully one third of those who contract smallpox perish from the disease. Best estimates from England would suggest that at most one percent of those who undergo variolation succumb to the infection. It is a certainty of our age that physicians will, at some point in their lives, come face-to-face with an outbreak. Would it not then be simple prudence to ask them to face the less risky trial to prepare them for what we know must come?" She let that sit rhetorically for a moment before continuing her defense. "As far as the risk of an outbreak . . . ."

Vittorio Bellone sat amid the onlookers, keeping his silence. He'd heard Maria expound on this and other topics before. There was no field of the natural science in which she did not have at least working knowledge. And yet he felt nervous for his pupil regardless.

Or perhaps he was nervous for himself. He had given up a lot of his own personal research time to cultivate this talent on the long shot that she would find success in academia. What if people thought Maria just a parrot of his own ideas?

Hence these events—proposing and defending theses all by herself. Building her reputation. Her father's idea. A bit cynical, Vittorio could not help but notice it gave Pietro an excellent excuse to drag more rich customers into his orbit.

Now a different man spoke to Maria, this time in Spanish. The draw of this performance was as much the variation in language as any content of ideas. "More importantly, your thoughts on calculus are far more revolutionary. Explain to us how you came by such notions."

Maria wore her first smile of the whole evening. "Well," she proclaimed airily, "religion we take from the Bible. But in matters mathematical, I received a personal revelation from the Gospel of Newton."

Polite laughter. More challenges. More defenses. It seemed there was no modern topic on which Maria could not expound.

Vittorio knew full well the preparation that had gone into such seeming effortlessness. Maria was a sponge for information, but even with so fine a student, comprehensive knowledge took time. She'd stayed up late many nights, always of her own initiative, cramming as much knowledge into her head as she could. He wasn't sure how she came by such a desperate need for learning.

Eventually, the hour set aside for the novelty of testing a child's genius came to a close. A harpsichordist—yet another reflection of Pietro's prosperity—took up the instrument bench and began to play. Vittorio had heard Pietro say more than once that he preferred the piano. But the piano was new, and the well-to-do had not yet developed a taste for it.

Which is not to say that Pietro was above trying to guide the public taste. He simply picked his battles.

Pietro stood in front of the room, ready to sally forth on just such an effort. He waited for his daughter to slip mutely away before he spoke. "Gentlemen, if you'd please look to the box on the table in front of you, you will find the most intriguing export of the New World, but rarely sampled on our shores. They are called *cigars,* and I daresay they shall be a fixture of society before many years have passed . . . ."

Vittorio had seen this routine before. He couldn't stand the stink of the cigars. So he followed after Maria.

When he found her, she was slouched on the side room's divan, her shoes kicked off and a pillow over her face.

"You shouldn't do that," he criticized her reflexively. "It's not ladylike."

"I don't like being in front of people," she declared, her voice muffled by the pillow. "I have to look at them looking at me."

"You were absolutely perfect," Vittorio told her. "Even the business about the Golden Ratio, which gets a little too close to religion for my liking."

"Religion and science are closer together than you think," said Maria, lapsing into her presentation voice even with the pillow over her face. "Through such means as the curves of the Golden Ratio, we can observe—"

"All right, all right," said Vittorio, holding up his empty hands even though she couldn't see them. "I concede. You've earned your rest. Thankfully, you don't have another one of these for a couple of weeks."

Maria finally took the pillow off her face, sighing heavily. "Then I suppose that's something. I love learning, but I hate having to *prove* that I've learned. It's such a waste of time."

"We agree on that, actually. But this will lay the groundwork for your university study. Hopefully, no women will need to go through so many trials after you."

"What if . . ." started Maria, two dangerous words coming

from her. They always preceded some wild, unworkable idea. "What if I gave the talks with my back to the audience? It would be so much easier if I could just focus on the ideas instead of the people asking about them."

"I don't think that would go over well," said Vittorio.

A plume of pungent cigar odor announced the opening of the door. Pietro shut it behind himself, rubbing his forehead with a cloth. "Blasted smoke always makes me sweat."

Maria's transformation upon her father's arrival was immediate. Her smile radiated good cheer, her posture spoke of limitless energy, and somehow, she'd even manage to trick her shoes back on. The transformation was a bit startling.

She asked, "How'd I do?"

"Adequate for our purposes," said Pietro, peering down at a scribbled note. "Your challenger was too clumsy in his Latin to notice, but there was a flaw in your defense of gravity's effects on tidal motion."

Maria's eyes widened. "What do you mean, a flaw?"

"You explained the effects on the ocean well enough, but regarding why the tide is not so visible in smaller bodies of water like ponds and fountains, I think your supposition was too much sophistry and deflection. I'd have preferred an outright admission of ignorance in the absence of a firm mathematical basis."

"Oh," said Maria, clapping her hands together rapidly. "Oh, that gives me the most interesting idea."

The young woman careened off to her study desk, overcome by some obscure flash of inspiration. She began scribbling almost immediately. Vittorio imagined the day was not so very far off that he would have nothing left to teach her. She did enjoy the work, there was no doubt about that. But lately, it had become so *much* work.

"I've never met a man with a louder face than yours," said Pietro, speaking quietly so as not to disturb Maria.

"I hadn't said anything," Vittorio answered reflexively, realizing that he sounded like a bit of an idiot.

"Anyway, there's a reason I'm pushing her. But I want you to keep it between you and me, do you understand?"

Maria had better ears than half-deaf Pietro realized. Vittorio took it upon himself to move them a whole room away from her, then asked: "Right, what's all this, then?"

"I haven't told her yet, but she's received an invitation to give a public speech." Pietro once again dabbed at his brow, even though it was wholly dry. "We'll need to decide on the topic."

"Let her decide," Vittorio suggested. "She's clever enough."

"Yes, normally I'd agree. But this invitation is from the imperial governor of Lombardy."

"The emperor's new appointment?" Vittorio felt momentarily dizzy.

Austrian nobility. And they'd invited a girl from the merchant class. That *did* make things tricky.

"I'll tell her soon," Pietro promised, looking back over his shoulder. "But not tonight. She deserves some rest."

If there was one thing Maria couldn't stand, it was her body's need to rest.

Ever since her mother had died, she'd grown only too aware

of the limited time God had granted to every one of His children on earth. Every second wasted was a second you wouldn't get back. Every second frittered away on something frivolous was less time you could spend to meet your full potential. If it wasn't learning, religion, or charity, she had no time for it.

Which is why she sometimes found her stepmother incredibly tedious.

"What do you think of the blue drapes? For weeks I was thinking blue. But then, blue is so very out of fashion," said Oriana, a young woman of some twenty-five years who had already given the family several children. She stood fussing with the curtains at the end of the hall. "You know, you don't want to be seen chasing trends too directly, but you have to at least *acknowledge* them or people start to wonder if you're paying attention."

Oriana was broad through the shoulders, utterly tireless, and, if Maria was being perfectly honest with herself, not very intelligent.

She tried not to hold it against her. God did not give everyone the same gifts, and it was petty of her to hold middling wits against anyone. But for some reason, Oriana's fixation on the finer points of interior decoration made Maria more acutely appreciate the linear nature of time.

"No, I simply can't abide the blue," Oriana decided. "It's last year's trend."

Maria, who so happened to be wearing a blue dress, decided not to state her opinion on the subject. "I wanted to speak to you about the children's education."

"Oh! Yes. I got their tutors to put together a lesson plan, just like you suggested."

Maria nodded. "Yes, I've read it."

"And so did I," said Oriana pleasantly. That was how she did everything—pleasantly. "Some of it went a tad over my head, and I wonder if it's a little ambitious to teach all of them Latin, but it all seemed very reasonable to me."

"I don't like it," said Maria. "It's inefficient and assumes they're all stupid. If I were you, I'd fire them and do it myself."

But then, Oriana couldn't do it herself, could she? Anna Brivio could have. But God had taken her back to his side.

The children presented a problem Maria didn't know how to solve.

Bluntness wasn't something Maria aspired toward. But on matters of education, sometimes she got that way. She'd learned she *had* to be that way, sitting in her father's salon, to get older men to take her seriously.

Maria took her potential—and the potential of her brothers and sisters—very, very seriously. She realized she should apologize for being rude to Oriana, and to the teachers the woman had chosen. Most of them were her relatives in some tenuous way or another.

Something of Maria's old awkwardness had never quite gone away, no matter how many times she got up in front of a crowd. She avoided eye contact with Oriana, pretending to look through the window, even if the only thing outside was a gray stone street.

Oriana took her time to come up with an appropriately

pleasant response. Much like Maria studied the window, she studied the drapes.

A convenient distraction came screaming down the hall on two legs. It was Savio, and he was trying to rip off all his clothes. Again.

Maria couldn't help but smile. What a little troublemaker he was growing into. She swooped down to grab him by the arms. "No no no," she chastised him playfully, earning a snot-accented squeal for her efforts. "You look so dapper like you are. Hands off the buttons."

Lately, if he wasn't running around screaming, Savio was toppling priceless furniture. That was also a problem Maria didn't know how to solve. Savio needed a way to keep busy. This enormous, palatial house they'd moved into—it was too easy for him to get into trouble, Maria decided, picking him up as best she was able.

"I think it's time Savio began taking lessons," she told her stepmother.

Oriana remained skeptical. "Maria, dear, Savio is three years old."

Maria genuinely did not understand what point she was making. "Yes, and?"

"Well . . . we can see if he's got the knack for it," Oriana said, taking Savio from Maria's arms. "I think you should go have a rest in your room."

That was not at all what Oriana was thinking, and Maria knew it. She waited for the inevitable addendum.

Oriana enthused, "It'll give you a chance to see your *letters*! How exciting!"

Downstairs, Teresa was banging on the harpsichord again. The cacophony bounced off the walls, turned tinny by distance. At seven years old, Teresa was the oldest of Maria's five siblings, and she'd lately developed the idea she could be a musician.

"Are you expecting again?" Maria suddenly wondered, lips pursed.

Oriana was not subtle. She gasped. "How did you know?"

Because if Oriana wasn't pregnant, she soon would be. Time had borne that out. Judging by her reaction, the family would indeed grow by yet another child. Another younger brother or sister. Maria was the oldest; she had to take care of them.

But how was she supposed to do that? She barely had time to take care of herself.

"Go on, go on," Oriana encouraged. "You got the most delightful letters."

With funereal enthusiasm, Maria went into her room. At her increasingly stubborn insistence, it was largely undecorated. Simple surroundings helped her stay focused.

So the garishly bright wax seals stamped onto the letters atop her desk stood out all the more.

She took one letter in her hand. To Maria, the family crest impressed upon its yellow wax represented not excitement, but the dreadful, unwelcome attention of Society.

This happened every time she gave one of her thesis talks. She didn't have to open these letters to know what they were.

They were invitations. Her father's visitors, seeing her be the centerpiece of her father's parties, wanted her to be the centerpiece of *their* parties. Maria supposed someone else might have loved it all: being invited to such things before she'd even reached adulthood, treated like a guest of honor.

But they'd want her to *talk* to people. To *meet* people. To *perform.* Doing that in the family home was bad enough, but this was the one place she felt comfortable. Who knew what horrors and expectations might be waiting at some stranger's house?

Oriana fussily intervened. "Maria, dear, you're crumpling the letter."

So she was. She set it back down.

"If you'd like advice about which ones to accept," Oriana spoke in all earnestness, "I can help you."

"I don't have the time," Maria declared, moving to where she kept her most important books. She pulled a tome on all things geometry from the shelf and placed it on top of the letters, like its weight could banish everything they represented from her life. "There's no time for parties."

Not enough time for anything. She still had so much to learn.

Chapter Eight

"You look awfully tired," said Teresa, idly kicking her legs. She was seated at the piano bench and her feet didn't quite make it to the ground.

"I didn't sleep well," said Maria, which wasn't entirely true, if she was being honest. The issue was more that she didn't sleep. She hoped the misdirection wasn't a lie in the eyes of God. Maybe it was, but surely just a lie of omission at the very worst. "Don't you have Latin study today?"

"Mamma's got me a brand-new music teacher," Teresa enthused, her cherubic face beaming with a child's joy. "I'm going to get all warmed up."

Teresa made a great big show out of flexing her fingers, selecting sheet music, and cracking her knuckles—even if they didn't actually pop. She had seen one of the musicians their father hired do something similar. Ever since, she had adopted it as her own personal ritual.

Maria did appreciate her sister's enthusiasm. It was hard to imagine that *she'd* ever been that excited about anything, although she supposed she did still look forward to new frontiers of learning. Amazing how excited you could be for something new, only for it to fade into so much background scenery once you moved on to another frontier. Humans were always striving for the next thing.

Perhaps that was what Maria needed. A new next thing.

Teresa bounced in her seat with a child's energy, flourishing her stubby fingers down the keys. She paused a moment for dramatic effect, then began to work through the motions of a scale.

Maria stood there, listening. She knew she should be checking on the other children. She'd volunteered to look after them while Oriana went to some intolerable social function with her even less intelligent friends. But perhaps Maria could afford fifteen minutes of rest.

At the very least, she owed it to her sister to listen to her music.

Teresa was Maria's only full-blooded sister. She thought no less of the other children for having a different mother—they were all born of the same father, and she accepted them as her kin. But only Teresa seemed to have that odd quality Maria had begun to realize set her apart: the need to be excellent at something.

Who had first invented music? wondered Maria. A Greek, probably.

There was something mathematical about a scale. About certain entire forms of composition. If Maria had been a musician, she might have loved the art of the fugue. A theme and its contrapuntal answer played out like equations for the ears. She had read the basic theory of how it all worked, but it seemed immensely complicated. Perhaps someday it might be worth examining.

Maria knew she shouldn't sit down. If she sat down, it would be hard to get up again. But she'd spent so long navel-gazing that the scales were already over, and Teresa had plowed headlong into the spritely, refreshing themes of Antonio Vivaldi.

Maria didn't allow herself many pleasures, but she *did* like Vivaldi, and what her sister lacked in technique she made up for in enthusiasm. She allowed herself to imagine the green fields of spring . . . or what it might be like to lie in the sun of an early autumn day . . . .

Entirely by accident, Vittorio had become a successful man. His mother never would have believed it.

As Maria's fame grew, people inevitably began to wonder who had seen to her education. It wasn't as if Vittorio boasted—teaching her had never been about his own prestige—but someone had found out anyway. Probably they bribed one of the Agnesi family maids.

At first he'd refused new students, even from wealthy merchants and lesser nobility. He was a professor, he told them; he was busy.

But they kept coming back with more and more money. Everyone had a price, and to his amusement, Vittorio inevitably discovered his. So now he had a couple of extra students on weekends. When exactly was he supposed to *spend* the money? Just crafting lesson plans ate up his scraps of free time.

Part of him wanted to quit the university entirely and use the money to get into business. That had been Pietro's strategy.

From the streetcorner, he regarded the palazzo Agnesi. Even the townhouse of a few years ago had seemed a palace by Vittorio's standards. This one felt less like a home and more like a fortress.

"Come in, come in!" hollered the maid from the door. "The young mistress is waiting for you."

Vittorio came in, bid the staff good morning, and narrowly avoided careening into a pair of stampeding barefoot children. Bewildered, he watched the two small boys bound off into the deep recesses of the house, wholly unattended. Shouldn't someone be looking after them?

He shook his head, and in the music room, he found the reason for the neglect.

Maria Gaetana Agnesi lay sprawled over a desk, her cheek flat against her folded arms. She looked pale and haggard.

Worried, Vittorio touched the back of his hand to her brow—but she wasn't feverish. Just tired, and in desperate need of a nap. He sighed wearily and decided to let her sleep for as long as it took him to set up the day's lesson.

The "Seven-Tongued Orator." That was what people were calling her around town. He'd taught her half of those languages, but nobody called him the "Seven-Tongued Professor." Not that he minded especially. It was simply amusing that no one valued in an adult what was wondrous in children.

"I'm awake," Maria announced erratically, only accentuating her fatigue. She jolted straight upright. "Oh, bother. The children need to be marshaled for breakfast, and—"

"I believe you have slept through breakfast," said Vittorio, causing Maria to startle all over again.

Her mouth opened in horror. "What time is it?"

The clock was right next to her. She didn't even think to look at it.

"I am sure your brothers and sisters can endure," said Vittorio. "They're all perfectly fine."

Something clunked noisily in the room above them. Vittorio might have worried about whatever-it-was breaking, but Pietro probably could have afforded to commission a whole church if he wanted. Whatever the damage might be, his coffers could endure it.

Maria pinched her nose. It drew her youthful features into a severe expression that somehow reminded Vittorio of his own late mother's disapproval. "Fine," Maria decided. "Just . . . fine."

"Today," Vittorio offered gently, "we have geometry. But we could always put it off for later and instead look to—"

"No." The word came out like a gunshot. Maria slapped her hand on the table. "Today we have geometry. It's scheduled. I made the schedule; we're going to follow the schedule."

Vittorio twisted his mouth to one side. "Maria, you seem very tired."

"I'll be fine," she insisted, before yawning.

"Perhaps a couple weeks' holiday from education would do you good. You could visit your uncle, perhaps. I bet he'd like to see you."

He'd hoped the idea might lighten her mood. Instead, it looked like a chasm had just opened up beneath Maria. Her eyes widened until the whites showed all around them. "Certainly not! Are you suggesting that I'm *lazy*?"

Vittorio had never been clever on his feet. He echoed Maria's own words right back to her. "Certainly not."

"Are you suggesting that I can't do the work? That I can't keep up with a normal schedule because I'm a woman?"

Maria wasn't even a woman, he might have said. She was still a girl. She'd just somehow managed to avoid anything that might be called a childhood.

An inner voice asked Vittorio: *Whose fault was that?*

"I have to imagine your friends would be happy for an opportunity to see you," he tried again, immediately regretting that line of attack.

"I don't have *time* for any of that," she said dismissively. "Friends are a pointless distraction from learning and from God."

To Vittorio's great discomfort, he saw not even the slightest hint of a lie in Maria's words.

"I have a big family," she added. "That's already more than enough people to look after."

"Geometry, then," said Vittorio, knowing better than to argue with genius.

It was the same with the more gifted university students. Even when they were wrong, they were so accustomed to everyone else failing to understand them that they wouldn't entertain contrary ideas.

"To resume our discussion of mathematical proofs . . . ."

On his way out the door, Vittorio found Pietro considering squares of silk fabric.

The Agnesi patriarch set down the samples. "Professor Bellone," he greeted Vittorio. "How's my very brightest daughter doing?"

Vittorio considered telling a pleasant lie, but decided against it. "Not well."

Pietro's sun-lined brow scrunched with yet more furrows. "What's wrong? Is she falling behind schedule?"

Things that Vittorio had been pondering for months, hiding even from himself, began to crystallize inside his mind. "Bit of a fatigue problem," he hedged, struggling to figure out how to express what he was feeling.

"She's always like that after we have guests," Pietro said dismissively. "Give her two days; she'll bounce right back."

She'd bounce, certainly. But when you dropped a ball, every consecutive bounce was shallower than the last. Maria's enthusiasm had ebbed and flowed, and Vittorio began to worry she was circling a drain neither she nor her father had looked far enough ahead to notice.

"Tomorrow," said Pietro, "I'll tell her about the governor's invitation. This is what it's all been building toward. I think the perfect subject for her speech would be a defense of the value of women's education. Don't you?"

Vittorio had to admit it would be perfect. Wasn't that what he'd devoted himself to—educating the very brightest girl in the city? His sister might have been nearly so brilliant herself, if only she'd been given the chance. Instead she'd been forced to marry an idiot at age fourteen, and turned to drink instead of books.

He didn't want another woman consigned to the purgatory of wasted potential.

Maria could make a sensation in the push for women's education. But then, Maria was not just a symbol. She was also a person. After so many years teaching her, seeing her genius bloom, he found he cared less about abstract categories and more about a single girl.

"We are asking too much of her," Vittorio finally said. It was one thing when they wanted to help her find the path to academia. But making her a society darling on top of this business with the governor? Any one of those was a burden. All of them together would be too much.

"I'll not hear this," said Pietro. "Not now."

"It's the truth," said Vittorio. "Any more pressure and she'll break under the weight. Make her take a month off. Tell the governor she's taking a holiday on account of poor health."

"I will do nothing of the sort." Pietro was the kind of man who got loud when he got angry. But today, he was very quiet. "Count Wirich Philipp von Daun, governor of Milan and favorite of the emperor, has asked a service of my family. He was the savior of Turin, viceroy of Naples, governor of the Netherlands, and conqueror of Gaeta. He is a man such as you and I could not hope to equal. And you want me to tell him that a child is *too busy to see him*?"

"Yes," said Vittorio. "That is exactly what I believe you should do, for that child's sake."

"You are being ridiculous," said Pietro.

Vittorio couldn't help himself. He went right for the jugular, like when he went scrapping as a lad. "What would Anna Brivio have said?"

Pietro was on his feet in a second, and in two seconds he was arm-close to Vittorio. His already quiet voice dropped lower still. "You have taken this argument to a place you will soon regret."

"She would have agreed with me." Vittorio dug in his heels. Too late to back down now. "Maria is not being allowed a chance to live her own life. She's either with adults more than twice her age or chasing after children who are half of it. Your wife doesn't seem even to help her look after them. I don't think Maria has a single friend. Have you noticed that? Have you done anything to help her find one?"

Pietro calmly turned to the side table. On it were any number of letters. Delicately he grasped one, running a finger along the envelope's pointed edge. "You know, my Maria has become somewhat famous lately."

"Yes, you've been quite keen to cultivate the fact," Vittorio agreed, no longer bothering to hide his disapproval.

"As such, I have had no end of offers from a whole range of

experts seeking to become her tutor. They are every last one of them far more accomplished and far more prestigious in their fields than an idealistic mediocrity like yourself."

Abruptly, Pietro struck Vittorio across the face with the envelope. The stiff crack of impact resounded in the air, the whole house silent save for the laughter of children.

"You would *dare* insult me, in *my* house, using the name of my dead wife!" Pietro roared, all his self-composure gone. He flung the letter to the ground and shoved the others to the far end of the table. "Out! Get out, before you force me to demand a more violent satisfaction!"

Mutely, rubbing his cheek, Vittorio carried himself into the streets of Milan. He would have liked to say something clever, something cutting, but he'd never been good on his feet.

He could hear his mother laughing at him. How could he hope to start a business now, when the city's most powerful silk merchant desired to bring him ruin?

The next day, Maria trudged down the stairs into her study and found a strange man sitting in her teacher's chair.

A stranger. Unannounced. In her *home*. Her whole heart quailed.

He was perhaps sixty years old, dressed conservatively in religious garb. His bald head and jutting chin resembled a butcher's block, and the natural set of his mouth lent him the air of a perpetual frown.

"Brother Melchor, Ordinis Praedicatorum, at your service, young mistress," he told her in clipped, precise tones.

A Dominican, then. She'd known Dominicans. But why this one?

"I am here to see to your education henceforward. Your brilliance is widely remarked upon. I trust you will find my services adequate to your needs."

"But my schedule!" she protested, horrified. And then she realized it. "Where is professor Vittorio Bellone?"

The Dominican scarcely blinked. "I know no such man. I would suggest you ask your father."

It was altogether too much. Vittorio had always been there. He'd taught her before her mother died. He'd kept right on teaching her since. Who was going to critique her geometry?

"Your father has given me the honor of sharing with you a special announcement," said the Dominican, smiling as best as his dour face allowed. "It pertains to the Governor of Lombardy and his forthcoming visit to our city."

Chapter Nine

Maria quite literally burned the midnight oil.

She had a special set of lanterns she used exclusively for late-night reading, after everyone else had gone to bed. Someone who knew her less well might think that superstitious. But for her, such specific, reliable details were simply another way to try to bring order to the chaos of the world. The flicker of her three very particular lamps had been a familiar companion for quite some time.

The bigger the family grew, the more she found she had to stay up late to get anything done. Never mind looking after all the children, never mind making sure they were ready for meals and behaving themselves—there was all the *noise* they made. She loved them all, but God preserve her, their racket made studying a chore.

Not that Maria was studying now. That had been the original idea, but her nerves had disagreed.

She paced restlessly back and forth across the length of her room. Her feet narrowly avoided all the stacks of books and papers the maids had finally learned never to touch. They weren't exactly organized by subject, and she couldn't explain the system even to herself, but it made a certain intuitive sense. Almost.

More books lay open on her desk, on her bed, on her floor, all of them turned to passages that stirred her imagination. But she could not find an answer to the question that bedeviled her.

A speech! They wanted her to give a *speech*! What on earth was she going to talk about?

When she proposed scientific ideas at her father's parties, she always drew from her studies. Things she felt she had come to understand, explained in whatever language the visitors dared bid her to use. In truth, if it weren't for all the strangers, she would have found the intellectual exercise stimulating. On evenings when more faces were familiar than not, she sometimes even enjoyed herself.

But this time, she would be the invader. She would be forced to venture into the great unknown of the city palace, into a room she'd never seen, to . . . what, impress the governor and his guests? How?

She picked up the book on her bed, closed it, and flung herself onto the covers in its place. Her groan was briefly the loudest noise in the house.

Silently, she stared at the ceiling, listening.

In the quiet of night, there was almost never any noise. Eventually, she discerned the clip-clop of horse hooves on stone. A passing carriage, some few streets away. The sharp and rhythmic hoofbeats punctuated the silence of a dreaming city.

In other parts of town, she'd been told, things stayed raucous until the rising sun. It had never been so in the Agnesi family's well-manicured corner of Milan. What time was it, anyway?

She decided she didn't want to know.

She had to pick something to discuss. She had to impress the governor and his gleaming entourage. She had to bring order out of chaos. That was mathematics to her: the resolution of the infinite into the specific. But here was an equation not so easily solved. *People* were always the most troubling variable: They could be so many things at once.

Maria hated change. Yet there was no escaping it.

Every second she lay there fretting, not studying, Maria swore she could feel her brain shrinking. The dream of geometric mastery felt further away than ever.

Perhaps she was being ridiculous. Change was inevitable; only God was eternal. But then, all men were called to imitate God, and what could be more pious than pushing back against disorder?

Ultimately, Maria was forced to admit to herself that she could only do so much.

She reached for the nearest stack of books. Whatever the top book was, she'd pick that up and read it until her eyes were tired. At least it would distract her from the onerous burden of listening to her racing thoughts.

It was, she noted with mild surprise, her mother's old Bible.

By the time Moses parted the Red Sea, she finally fell into fretful, shallow sleep. Far too little time would pass before the waxing light of dawn.

～

"I've read your study schedule," said Brother Melchor later that morning.

Yesterday, an inconsolable Maria had insisted upon it. That stridency now embarrassed her. She was fairly certain they'd be stuck together whether she liked or not. Her father still refused to explain where Vittorio had gone, but she felt confident that she would never see him again.

She didn't believe he'd "sinned against the family," as her father had claimed. But who else could she ask for details? The children certainly wouldn't know, and Oriana would not have been told.

Melchor cleared his throat. Unlike Vittorio, he had no tolerance for her lapses into contemplative silence. "Are you listening? I said, I think it's very ambitious, but it will need to be put on indefinite hold."

Maria had to accept the truth: This was her teacher now. She'd just have to make the most of it.

"I'm to give a speech," she said, since Melchor was going to bring that up next anyway. "We need to pick a subject." Maria would have preferred weeks of preparation, but since they only had days, days would have to do.

"You're supposed to be good at mathematics," Melchor proposed. "Why not speak on recent advancements in the field?"

"Because I'm not actually good at it," Maria said, believing it. She was *enthusiastic* about mathematics. But she hadn't even managed to fully catch up to the likes of Newton, let alone make any innovations of her own. "If someone smarter than me is in the audience and asks a question I don't know the answer to, I'd wind up making myself look foolish."

Melchor had no time for Maria's insecurities. His perpetually dour face sank deeper into impatience. "Do you really believe the governor and his hangers-on smarter than your father's guests?"

It seemed a ridiculous question to Maria. "Of course. Vienna is the center of all the world's civilization."

Melchor snorted. "They'd like us to believe that. This may not be entirely clear to you, young mistress, but men are much the same everywhere: sinful and stupid. And you are the very most intelligent youth in this city."

"Blaise Pascal discovered geometry, on his own, at the age of twelve," Maria pointed out dully, sinking back in her char. Her own words surprised her. The priest had brought up sin. Where had her own sudden jealousy come from? "I have never invented anything."

Melchor eyed Maria impatiently. "A fine story. The French are in love with fine stories. Frankly, Pascal probably did exactly what you did, and read ahead in his Euclid."

She would have to read even further ahead, then. She refused to be left behind. If only she didn't have to sleep.

"You have your whole life to come up with something new." Melchor was perhaps trying to be reassuring, but he came off impatient and stern to Maria's ears.

She wasn't going to invent a new discipline in a week. What did she know *right now*? What did she know better than anyone who'd be in that room?

She began to develop the beginnings of an idea.

That evening, Maria's composition was interrupted by a sharp knock at her door. She knew the sound. It was her father.

"Come in," she said, her wrist aching dully from a too-tight grip on her pen. Her handwriting was compact and tidy, but she had never learned to hold a pen entirely the right way.

Pietro opened the door, but he did not enter. His body cast a shadow across the room. "How is it coming?"

"It's not done yet," said Maria.

Pietro wondered gently: "Can I read it?"

"It's not done yet," she repeated.

Pietro took that in stride. "Well, someone's here to visit you."

Here? Now? To visit *her*? Maria didn't exactly have a long line of friends beating down the door. She lived a very regimented life, and she liked it that way. Oriana could do all the social adventuring on her behalf.

"That doesn't make any sense."

"It makes perfect sense," Pietro grumbled, already moving off down the hall. "It's one of your relatives. It would be rude to ignore him, seeing as he's come all this way."

One of *her* relatives, he'd said.

Someone from her mother's side of the family? She'd never been close to any of them. There were quite a few, and most of them were off being nobles and doing whatever nobles did, in Hungary. So who?

Hating that her train of rhetoric had been interrupted, Maria set down her pen.

Etiquette suggested that she summon the maids and have them insert her into one of the wide-hipped monstrosities that were the very height of fashion. Maria did not have the time for such things. She'd say hello and come to goodbye as quickly as possible.

Gripping the banister, she marched right down the stairs.

Near the door was a thirtysomething man with the most perfectly calibrated mustache Maria had ever seen. You could probably plot its lines along mathematical axes. His clothes were stylish in yellow and gold and white, yet hopelessly rumpled, like he didn't much care about how they looked.

He held Savio up above his head, grinning wickedly as he whirled the boy around. "I've got you now, you little rascal! How are you getting out of this one?"

Maria felt suddenly dizzy watching them spin. Her hand reflexively reached for the banister, even though she was already holding it. Thanks to that, she lost her balance and was forced to grip it that much tighter in order to stay on her own two feet. She wasn't spinning, nor was the house, she reminded herself. Sometimes it just felt that way.

This was why she hadn't wanted to stop working. Once she got off track, it got harder to ignore the frailties of her body.

"Oho! She emerges!" The mustached fellow set Savio down and let him dash off to make mischief elsewhere. He threw out his hands to either side. "Come and hug your uncle Giuseppe!"

Maria just stood looking at him for a moment. She had an uncle? Was he really her uncle or just some older cousin thrice removed?

Giuseppe eventually realized that a hug was not in the offing. Undeterred, he beamed a yellowed, toothy smile. "The last time I saw you, you were *this* tall," he gushed, as all adult relatives must.

"I've tried my best to do otherwise, but I do seem to keep getting older," said Maria, a line she'd used at a couple of her recitals.

Giuseppe had not been to those recitals. He croaked out his amusement. "Hah! And as sharp as I've been told. I heard about your big day, you know. The business with the governor. Are you excited?"

Maria still had yet to descend the final step. Her knuckles whitened around the banister. "I am not sure I would say excited, exactly."

"God's blood, if I were you, I'd be knocking my knees together. I hear he's an absolutely intolerable man, but oh well. He's got good taste and he pays my wages, so I can forgive most else."

Giuseppe was not helping, Maria decided.

But even if she was not widely socialized, she at least knew how to be polite. "To what do I owe the pleasure of your visit?"

He spent a moment adjusting his haphazard cuffs and collar. "You got my letter, presumably?"

"Presumably," said Maria, thinking of the pile of discarded, ignored missives hidden under stacks of her thickest leather-bound books in the corner of the room. She imagined his letter had made Oriana's cut, but that didn't mean she'd read it.

"If you hadn't put it together, I'm the director at the Royal Palace these days. The music director, that is. So when I saw the program for the upcoming visit, I saw your name. And I thought: Goodness! My dear cousin Anna's child has certainly come up in the world, and at such a young age, too."

A musician. That somehow made sense. But she hadn't any idea he existed until just now. How young had she been the last time they'd met?

"And I'm told you're not . . . mmm . . . how to put this."

"I hate going outside," Maria helped him.

"You're not keen on unfamiliar places. So I thought I'd come and give you a chance to see the Royal Palace in advance. You see, I've got a concert tonight."

Well, Maria did like music. "You're playing?"

Giuseppe barked a laugh. "No, no. I composed! At least part of it. The other part, I'm told, is someone near and dear to your heart. How would you like the very best seat in the house for a performance of Antonio Vivaldi?"

It was like someone had sent Mephistopheles himself to come and tempt Maria away from her mission. Her words came out almost as a gasp. "Who told you I like Vivaldi?"

"Apparently you told your stepmother she should fire all her tutors. You know, I took that a little personally, seeing as I'd just volunteered to teach your sister Teresa the harpsichord."

Teresa had told him. Well, Maria had told Teresa that Vivaldi was her favorite. Repeatedly.

"I can't go," she told her uncle. She hoped God would give her the strength to resist.

"Nonsense," said Giuseppe. "You will see the place, you will hear the music; you will still have days to prepare after the fact."

"My father wouldn't like it," said Maria, actually thinking he would probably even enjoy going himself.

"I'll give you time to get dressed," said Giuseppe. "We could also invite your stepmother, perhaps, if that would put you better at ease. Your father says you have a fine rapport and Oriana's been a guest more than once."

Maria's mind was immediately made up. "I'm sorry, but I have to finish my composition," she told Giuseppe.

"I'll wait for you to finish," Giuseppe promised. "It will give me time to meet your other brothers and sisters!"

In the end, Maria did not find out how long he stayed, waiting for her. It was very late at night before she had a speech she could be confident in giving.

Chapter Ten

A carriage awaited outside the Agnesi family home. Maria was not in a hurry to board.

She'd recited her speech so many times she could do it all from memory. She suspected she could translate it extemporaneously into any of the seven languages she spoke. In fact, if she'd had another few days to practice, she probably could have done the whole thing backwards, but she suspected that trick was probably more impressive in fugues than spoken oratory.

She was as ready as she was going to be. But it had, in fact, been half a year since the last time she'd left the house.

"Young mistress, everyone's waiting," came the voice of one of the younger maids from the other side of her door. "You certainly can't be late for your big day."

She sounded so exhaustingly cheerful about it all.

Maria had, for once, actually managed a proper night's sleep. She knew she would need it. But that didn't mean she was going to pop out with a buzz of childish glee. Instead, she donned what she thought to be her most resolute expression and thrust open the door.

The maid giggled upon seeing her. Wonderful for her confidence, that.

Feeling at least forty pounds heavier thanks to her formal dress and its heavy pinned-up train, Maria braved the stairs. To her immediate embarrassment, she saw that her entire family was there waiting.

There stood her father, Pietro, impeccable as always. Her stepmother, with more jewels than Maria was previously aware they owned. Young Savio, younger Francesco, Giulia, even Sofia, still in the arms of her wet nurse. And, of course, Teresa. They were all lined up to see Maria off, even though her brothers and sisters wouldn't be coming.

A symbol of women's education. That was what Vittorio told her she could be. And so that was ultimately what she had decided to speak about: the right of women to be educated. The *need* for it.

But did she really have the strength to be that symbol? Forget all the other women of the city—would even her sisters look up to her if they knew how nervous she was? She wasn't a symbol; she was a fraud. All she'd done was study more than everyone else.

"Good luck, Maria," said Teresa, echoed by a chorus of her siblings, all save the very youngest. "I'm always so proud of you!"

Well, if they were going to be like *that,* Maria couldn't even dream of showing she was scared.

"I'll tell you all about it when I get back," she promised them. Hopefully it wouldn't be a tale of disaster.

After a firm word from her father to the driver, they were soon in the carriage. She sat next to him, Oriana opposite. For the two adults, such rides were an everyday occurrence. For Maria, it all represented a tremendous novelty. The bounce and rattle of the carriage, the whinny and whicker of the horses, the traffic on the streets—all of it was new.

Somehow, inside the confines of the carriage's four sturdy walls, the city was easier to take. The people were at a safe remove, allowing Maria to appreciate the streets and buildings. She tugged up the small drapery covering the carriage window. The Gothic, antiquated spires of the city's massive church were already visible above the nearest rooftops.

"It's been so long since the last time I saw the Duomo," Maria realized.

"What you'll never see is the blasted thing finished," said Pietro, unimpressed. "They've been working on it for hundreds of years. I think I heard they're on something like the sixtieth architect. Leonardo da Vinci was even up for the job at one point and they sacked him before he could even start."

"It's still very impressive," Maria said distantly, trying to think of anything that wasn't public speaking.

Pietro worked his jaw for a moment before softening his words. "Yes, I suppose it is. I'm thinking like a businessman again. Sometimes I should just appreciate things as they are."

Oriana chimed in: "Do you think you could get them to make *you* the architect?"

Pietro exhaled patiently. "Oriana, I don't know anything about architecture."

"Well, *she* does," Oriana said, pointing at Maria. "You should have heard her going on about . . . buttresses, or whatever they're called."

It wasn't long before the streets inevitably led the carriage to the austere Palazzo Reale di Milano. A blocky, imposing structure, it had at one time been a fortress. Modern touches around the windows and doors softened the façade with a certain elegance of function, but there was no escaping its rectangular, unyielding shape. Maria found it slightly intimidating.

As the seat of city government, the palace contained no shortage of activity. People came and went across the wide central plaza. They passed through oversized doors under the watchful eyes of soldiers, sharp bayonets affixed to their muskets.

"It would be nice if the governor could come to our house instead," said Maria, knowing it was a little late for that.

"Count von Daun is a very busy man," said Pietro, visibly suppressing his amusement at Maria's suggestion. One corner of his mouth twitched.

Knotted, fluttering tension seized hold of Maria's stomach when the carriage door swung open. The coachman stood with hand outstretched, ready to help her down. Maria, unmoving, found she could only stare at his fingers.

Seeing her dismay, Oriana intervened. She reached over to capture the offered hand herself, as if it had been meant for her all along. No sooner was Oriana out and on her feet than she turned and reached for Maria exactly as the coachman had.

A familiar grip was the best compromise she was going to get. Maria seized Oriana's hand. The long step down from the carriage felt like falling into open air. All the tension in her stomach felt momentarily like the bubbles in a glass of champagne—rushing upward to burst and fizzle. She hoped her face didn't look green.

Two hands clapped at the nearest palace door, drawing all their eyes.

Much to Maria's surprise, the person waiting for them was a woman. She had expected an austere old valet, but instead she saw a smiling, portly German. At least, some instinct told Maria that she had to be German. Or an Austrian, which was nearly the same thing, wasn't it? It was something about the set of her nose and style of her hair, to say nothing of its bright blonde color.

"Oh *my*, you are the little genius?" the woman asked.

"I suppose people do call me that," said Maria, reflexively averse to praise.

"Yes, yes they do. Come along then, all of you." She was fat enough that her gait seemed a touch unbalanced, but it didn't slow her down at all. Her clothes likewise fit her perfectly, done up with print and brocade that even Pietro must have admired. Perhaps some relative of the count, Maria wondered.

The answer came immediately.

"My husband, the count, has declared we will use the *salone di audienzia* for the evening's entertainment," the woman said. "It's our very newest room. There was a fire some years back, you see, and the renovations were completed during our recent visit to Vienna. He's absolutely in love with the place. He's talking about setting the architect on the Duomo next. Wouldn't it be grand if someone could finally finish it?"

Pietro looked skeptical.

Maria, meanwhile, concerned herself with the building they were already in. The whitewashed walls had a brightness that reflected the natural light pouring in through the windows. What captured her attention most were the ceilings. She knew that her father had an unusually large amount of money, but this was an entirely different scale of wealth. The building reflected the combined grandeur of both the Holy Roman Empire and the centuries-long history of Milan. What would have been excessive in a family home was here not only acceptable, but expected. The tall ceilings boasted in some places interlocking geometric panels, and in others grand paintings of things celestial by masters both living and dead.

Neck craned back, Maria tried to make sense of saints and angels and parse out what Bible stories the paintings corresponded to, but they were moving so fast she didn't get enough time to really guess.

"Maria, you're walking into a wall again," Oriana whispered, lightly gripping her stepdaughter's shoulder.

So she was. But looking at the art kept her from having to look at the people in the rooms.

"We're expecting some of the city's best and brightest," said the count's wife, who had neglected to give her own name. Probably used to people knowing it, Maria supposed, and she didn't feel adventurous enough to ask. It was hard enough to keep from feeling like the walls were spinning.

"Your uncle Giuseppe mentioned you're a touch shy, so we've set a room aside for you to wait in," the woman went on, after leading Maria into a baroque sitting room. "Our guests should begin arriving in an hour."

Blessedly, the room was totally free of people. But only when the count's wife excused herself did Maria notice she'd scarcely been breathing. She immediately sucked in a great big breath of air and collapsed into an overstuffed armchair.

Oriana had left along with their hostess, nattering about something or other, which left Maria alone with her father. She had known Giuseppe for all of five seconds, but she would have to thank him for his insight in getting her a private room in which to meet the governor.

"Well, at least it looks like there aren't going to be that many people," said Maria, looking around the room. This wouldn't be so bad. No bigger than one of her father's events at home.

Pietro cleared his throat. "I don't believe you'll be giving the speech in here," he said, in that particular tone of voice adults used when they hadn't figured out quite how to phrase bad news.

There were the bubbles in her stomach again. "What do you mean?"

Pietro indicated a panel in the back wall. So cleverly did the trellised motif continue across the joinery that Maria hadn't even realized it was a door.

"I believe the audience hall proper is through here," he said.

Before Maria could warn him against opening it, he found and turned the knob. Maria's fingers involuntarily clutched the armrests of her chair. He only opened it the slightest crack—but that was enough for Maria to peek at the salon beyond.

It was at least twenty times the size of their assigned sitting room. Rows and rows of chairs and tables had been set up for the pleasure of guests only just beginning to arrive. There had to be dozens. No—hundreds. Could there even be a *thousand* seats in there? It felt like the count must have expected the entirety of the city's well-to-do intelligentsia at this event. An event in which every single one of their eyes and expectations would be turned wholly and solely on Maria, judging and weighing her every word.

Desperately, Maria sputtered out: "Please close the door."

Pietro did so with casual ease, oblivious to his daughter's distress. "I wonder who he got to do the remodel. We could stand to maybe have someone look at our . . . ."

He chattered on, congenially clueless. Maria's ears had started ringing. She didn't get headaches, but sometimes everything went vertiginous on her. She sank down into the cushions of the chair, clinging to the solidity of it. The lights were too bright, her father's voice too loud. Even the chafing texture of the seat suddenly had an uncomfortably immediacy, to say nothing of the pressure of the stomach panel on the front of her dress.

"But above all else," Pietro went on, "I need you to know that I am extremely proud of you."

Those words momentarily cut through all of Maria's anxiety. "You are?"

Pietro beamed a smile. "How could I not be? Powerful

men spend their entire lives trying to earn the attention of the Empire's luminaries. You have done it as a young woman."

Yet Maria's stomach refused to settle. Her father was proud of her, yes. That meant something to her. But pride would only make him that much more disappointed when she went out there and wilted under the pressure. When she refused to even walk through the door.

If she so much as stood up, she was certain her stomach would flip upside down.

"This will be wonderful for the future of our family," Pietro went on, fully confident in his daughter's success. "With you as an example, all your brothers and sisters will find no shortage of doors opening for them. To say nothing of what it will do for our business."

"Papà," Maria said quietly, "I believe I am going to throw up."

Pietro's mouth stayed open a few moments. "What?"

Maria felt the twisting, churning certainty that preceded the inevitable end of nausea. "I'm going to ruin the governor's carpet," she realized, clutching her hands to her dress and wishing it weren't so heavy.

Pietro rapidly surveyed the room. "Hold on, hold on. There must be a . . . chamber pot, or a . . . ."

Maria disgusted herself with the horrible, choking noise that escaped her throat. Her stomach voided itself of all the food she'd eaten. When it was gone, she retched again, and again, her gut heaving nothing but dry air.

Pietro kneeled in front of Maria. She realized she had thrown up into her father's incredibly expensive hat.

"Oh no," Maria croaked. "Your hat."

"Never mind the hat." Pietro scrunched the brim shut, then used a corner of the fabric to dab at Maria's chin. "Hats can be replaced. I've only got one daughter."

She slumped to one side and let her forehead hit the armrest, muttering the first lines of her speech.

Outside the room, Pietro flagged the nearest servant. "Dispose of this," he told the man, more terse than he meant to be.

The servant took the hat, at first confused and soon disgusted by the damp mess slowly soaking the whole thing through.

"And fetch water," he told the man, flicking his wrist irritably. "A whole pitcher. Swiftly."

What a perfect fool he'd been. How long had his daughter been suffering? How long had he willfully ignored the way she was working herself to exhaustion? He'd made the same mistake as everyone else—thinking her a tireless paragon of wisdom propelled by the wind of the Holy Ghost. She might talk like an adult, she might think like an adult, but she was still a child. *His* child—a girl he should have been looking after. And he'd taken both her health and excellence for granted.

He had done the same with his first wife. He would not make that mistake again.

Suppressing the urge to lapse into profanity, he slipped back into the waiting room. His daughter sat vacantly in the chair with her chin on her knees.

"We're going home," he told her.

"What?" Her eyes widened. "No, we can't do that."

"You're ill," he told her. "We should have you lie down. Get the physician. I'm sure the governor will invite us again if he truly wants to see you."

"I'm not sick," Maria insisted stubbornly. "I'm just . . . I'm just . . . ." Her hands moved a little erratically, like she could pluck the right word directly out of the air. "I'm a little nervous," she finally decided.

That idiot Vittorio had been right, Pietro thought. As much as Pietro hated to admit it, he'd been blind to the problem, even though he talked to his daughter every day. Maria worked herself like a dog.

Pietro took his daughter's hand. "I know it's mathematics that's your passion, not speeches. Or . . . people. Trust me. We can go home. I won't be angry." Even if his wife would be aghast. She'd just have to find a way to deal with it.

Maria did not answer immediately. As was often the case in matters of nausea, throwing up seemed to have settled her nerves and ended her pain. She walked over to the audience chamber door, turning her head to listen to the sound of what was going on beyond it.

By now, people were arriving. Circulating. Even without proximity to the door, Pietro could hear the building hubbub and occasional laughter of the guests.

A realization suddenly dawned on Maria. "You know, I'll bet I've met most of these people already."

Pietro furrowed his brow. "What do you mean?"

"They only came ten or twenty at a time, but you've invited just about everyone who's anyone to come to visit our house," said Maria.

"That . . . may be true," Pietro admitted.

"So it may be a little more frightening. But I've already won most of these people over." Maria sounded distant, like she was observing her own life from a distance, rather than living it in the flesh. "Half, or perhaps even most of them, will simply be waiting to hear what I have to say."

"And they'll be happy to wait to hear it another time."

"No," said Maria. "I promised my brothers and sisters that I'd tell them how it went. And I don't think my mother would have been happy if I told them a story about how I ran away."

Pietro knew he'd been defeated. He'd been both wrong and right. His daughter *was* just a girl—but she was a tremendously special one.

With her own small hand, Maria opened the audience chamber door.

Maria stood before Milan's assembled noteworthies in a room lit by the sparkling fantasia of crystal chandeliers.

It was not difficult to pick the governor out of the crowd. The imperial dignity of Austria was something he wore like a mannered garment, his posture the sort of thing you'd usually see in a painting. Perhaps he had sat for so many paintings for so very long that stiffness had become his more natural state of being. The powdered wig atop his head reflected the very latest vogue sweeping across the world, a huge white-tufted artifact that looked like a bunch of rolling pins wrapped in yarn.

Maria thought he looked absolutely ridiculous.

She'd been scared of him? He was a peacock.

Somewhere out there, Pietro and Oriana were watching. Somewhere, Giuseppe was no doubt marshaling the musical entertainment. And perhaps her debate partners from her father's salon were once again itching to be impressed.

But she would ignore every single one of them and make her appeal to a single pair of eyes. That was the trick she thought she could play on herself: She would speak solely to the governor, like no one else was there.

She knew she did not have the loudest voice. But she did not shout. She relied on the audience's attention and their silence.

"I have been asked to speak to you today because I am a young woman with certain talents," she began, speaking in Italian.

She would give them the trick they always desired—the whole span of her linguistic roster.

In German, she continued: "Some of you have come from as far away as Vienna to this city I call home." In Latin: "Some of you are sworn to the Church, brothers and sisters in Christ."

She greeted the rest of them, all in their own tongues. The Habsburg dominion held people from every corner of the world.

No matter what language she used, there would be someone there that night who knew it. But such a grand flourish wasn't her aim. It was only a means to establish her credibility, especially among those who had never seen her before. She segued into the substance of her thesis.

"Today," she said slowly, "I am here to speak in defense of all women's right to—and a single woman's *desire* for—an education."

Silence threaded tangibly through the room.

"I have long been in love with mathematics," she told the governor. "I have loved numbers like we love our dearest friends, used them like the fingers on my hand. They are the brush that God used to paint the world to life. The laws of motion govern every step our feet take, every movement of the bodies in the heavens. It is my belief that someday an equation will be written to describe the blooming of a rose. That is what I most love to study: that beautiful, sublime logic."

With every word she spoke, it became easier. The words she'd polished and honed and fretted and lost sleep over unfolded from her lips, propelled by mounting enthusiasm.

"But I have always heard voices that bid me *stop*. Since I was a child, people have ever smiled and shaken their heads, as if my learning were a fancy and a game, a quaint distraction from more feminine ends. What purpose has a woman's education, they said, beyond what she needs to raise her children safe at home?

"But is it not woman who first inspired Pythagoras? Was

it not a mother who cradled Newton and taught him the first words he spoke? Was Athena not a being born of mind? Is inspiration not a muse, and is a muse not woman?

"Before, my theses have always been those of science. Today I postulate a more social question: Why should a woman *not* be welcomed into our academies to pursue her wisdom's highest dream?"

She paused, and let silence fill the room.

Maria was used to arguing her points. Today, point by point, they let her logic reign.

The carriage rattled on the road back to the Agnesi family home.

"You should be very proud of yourself," Pietro told his daughter, not for the first time that night. But he felt every word with a deeper conviction than ever. He felt certain God could not be more proud when He beheld the stars He'd put in the sky.

The speech had proven a sensation. For every person who found it a tedious transgression, there were five stirred by Maria's rhetoric. Pietro took even the fact that a few people were upset as a good sign: Even if they disagreed, Maria had been too well-spoken for them to write off and ignore. The earnest appeal of a child touched people in a way that purely cerebral arguments from adults could not.

Pietro knew it was his own failing that he still wished she'd agreed to more of his corrective suggestions. So he didn't mind that she wasn't answering him. He didn't mind that the governor hadn't so much as spoken a word to them after the fact. Right now, everything was just fine. Fine enough that he didn't notice the fact that his daughter was asleep until her head slumped over and clunked against his shoulder. She'd passed out the moment they'd sat down in the carriage.

This was the last time, he promised himself. She didn't have anything left to prove.

Chapter Eleven

The inevitable avalanche of letters followed. Days later, Maria lay on the divan, knuckles pressed into her forehead, wondering why the reward for success should take the form of yet another trial.

Oriana bounced on her feet, toe-heel, toe-heel. "And *this* one is from the Simonetta family, one of the very finest and most well-heeled in all of Milan. The Pallavicini, Borromeo, *and* the Simonetta, all in one day! You should be very impressed with yourself."

"Tell them I'm too sick," Maria croaked. If anything would make her feel more ill, it was the notion of entering yet more mysterious salons.

"Oh, you mustn't pass up the chance," said Oriana, holding the invitation like it was a holy relic as she swept around the sitting room. "I'll make all the arrangements. You won't even need to think about a thing. You can just show up and have a good time."

The front door clunked with the force that only her father applied to it. Maria stoically endured Oriana's nattering until he appeared in the room.

"Did I not leave instructions for Maria to be allowed to sleep as long as she desired?" he asked his wife.

"Pietro, darling, it's been almost a week. She can't keep sleeping until noon."

Maria was inclined to agree with Oriana. It was past time she got back to work. Without the structure of work, she didn't know what to do with herself. She felt like if she sat on the divan long enough, she might become a piece of furniture herself.

The question was what work to do. Everything had been designed for her talks at her father's grand events. Now she was at loose ends. Without her schedule, she didn't know how to conduct herself.

"She'll rest until she's well," Pietro insisted. "I don't care if it takes two days or two months."

Oriana might not have been very smart, but she was canny about social matters. Maria recognized the gleam of that artifice in her eyes now as she fanned out the various letters of invitation across the table.

"Maria is your very favorite daughter," she began, dusting the paper with her fingertips.

"I don't have a favorite child," insisted Pietro, that familiar parental lie. "I love all my children equally."

"Maria is your oldest and most intelligent child," Oriana corrected herself, in the style of a woman unconvinced. "And while a girl might more normally be introduced into society at the age of her majority, I think it is safe to say that our Maria has, at this point, been very much introduced."

Maria narrowed her eyes. What was her stepmother scheming?

"Come to your point," said Pietro wearily.

"There comes a time in her young life when every young woman must eventually marry," Oriana declared, hands clasped tightly together. "And these events provide an excellent opportunity to start hunting for an advantageous match."

A sudden tightness constricted Maria's stomach. Her pulse briefly elevated; she sat bolt upright on the divan.

"See, she's already excited," Oriana proclaimed.

Pietro eventually managed to voice his daughter's objection. "It seems a touch . . . early."

"I'm not entirely certain how to be pleasant about this, so I'll just be rude," said Oriana. "Your daughter is extraordinarily intelligent. Finding her a husband who can keep up with her, let alone equal her, is going to be something of a challenge."

It occurred to Maria that while she had a lot of experience talking to men, she had absolutely zero experience dealing with boys. They were like a mysterious and foreign species, often discussed but almost never encountered. "I don't like this," she groused.

"Oriana has a point," Pietro conceded. The letters drew his eye. "The Borromeos have a boy who is more or less her age, don't they?"

It was a family with that most sparkling quality: prestige. As she grew older, Maria increasingly realized that the world more often respected a family's pedigree than its wealth. That was half of why she'd endured public appearances. If she increased her fame, it would only increase the standing of the Agnesi family. In the end, it was the very best thing she could do for her siblings.

"Fine. I'll go," Maria said.

"Oh, this is going to be so much *fun,*" said Oriana, bouncing all over again.

"I am ever so charmed to make your acquaintance," said a young teenage boy in whom Maria held no interest whatsoever.

"Mmm" was her reply as she looked out over the Borromeo family lawn. The beauty of its well-manicured hedges provided her an excellent excuse to avoid making eye contact.

It had been a long ride to the outskirts of Milan to reach this place, a picturesque country retreat built precisely for this kind of intolerable party. Stars twinkled above. Lights flickered below. People circulated freely from the house to the external loggia, whose balustrade she now leaned against.

Notably, not a single other person had approached her for the past five minutes to tell her how brilliant she was, which was her first clue that this moment had been carefully engineered. The second was that her father was suddenly nowhere to be seen. The third was that there was not another person present who was even remotely their age.

"Everyone says you're the most brilliant young woman in all of Lombardy," the boy went on. He'd mentioned his name, but in her haste not to look at him too directly, Maria had already forgotten it. Every moment that went by, it became more and more rude to ask him to remind her, but with every additional moment, rectifying the problem became a more frightening prospect.

Maria realized she was supposed to say something, even though he hadn't even done her the courtesy of asking a proper question. "Mmm," she intoned, risking a sidelong glance.

She supposed he was not unattractive. Neither fat nor slim; an approachably rounded cheek structure, but with a sharp jaw to balance it. But Maria's understanding of "attractive" was largely built on remembering other people's comments and trying to slot them into a mathematical appreciation of facial geometry. What strange alchemy transmuted the self into a thing suddenly being bewitched by human flesh? Would she eventually suffer the same fate when she was a grown woman?

Evidently silence was not something the boy knew how to handle. "My father's gone to see you speak," he said. "He was very impressed with the quality of your Latin."

And what was Maria supposed to say about that? "Your father being . . . ?"

The poor boy opened and closed his mouth. Maria realized then that he must be somebody terribly important. Never in his life had anyone failed to recognize the greatness of his house. "Signore Borromeo, the man whose invitation you accepted to come here."

Oh. She really ought to have something to say about that. "I am pleased to meet you as well," she managed.

That, at least, put things back into an arena that whoever-he-was understood.

"Would you have an interest in seeing the gardens up close? We're quite proud of them."

Maria was clever enough to recognize this as a courtly gesture. The gardens even seemed worth seeing up close, though she doubted that in the darkness of night they would see much more than the outlines of each other's faces.

Oh. That was the whole point, wasn't it? To escape the watchful eye of their chaperones.

Maria was wholly at a loss. She couldn't come up with a way to politely decline. Her eyes swept the yard, searching for inspiration. Details she'd previously ignored now withstood her most intense scrutiny.

Then, as if it had been deposited by the hand of God, she spied the finest scientific device she'd ever seen.

All at once she left the boy behind and crossed to the far end of the patio. There, two gentlemen and one woman clustered around a standing telescope. Its metallic surface gleamed with a reflective sheen that caught the dance of the patio lights. Someone must have assembled it here for the event as a kind of showpiece.

The older of the two men leaned over the device, making minute adjustments as he narrated to his fellows.

"It will change your entire conception of the world to see the planets directly. Not as lights, but as discrete objects." He spoke mainly in Latin, perhaps for the greater specificity it offered in scholarly terms. Maria sensed from his accent that he must have been a visiting Austrian. "It is like seeing the mighty red eye of God," he added.

"Oh," Maria enthused in the same language. "You must be watching the passage of Jupiter."

The old fellow let out a pleased yet raspy laugh. "Why, yes, my dear. Would you like to have a look?"

"I've only ever read about it in books," said Maria. "The mathematics are absolutely fascinating. Did you know we're so skillful these days as to be able to estimate the difference in gravity present on Jupiter and Saturn?"

The second man looked to the first, unfamiliar with the Latin word. "Gravity?"

"The force described by Newton," supplied the sole woman present, possessed of an even, deadpan voice. "That which draws all things back toward the ground."

"Yes, yes, I know what gravity is," the man said defensively, even though he'd just asked.

"In fact," Maria couldn't help the words spinning out of her mouth, "Christiaan Huygens wrote in his *Cosmotheoros* that we can determine the speed of the rotation of Mars simply by observing the features upon its face, or posit the existence of rivers on Jupiter, due to presence of clouds and rain, observable to the naked eye."

"I have heard of no such book," said the man who did not know what gravity was.

"That is because you don't know anything about physics," said the woman.

Maria began to realize that she might, in fact, be the intellectual heavyweight in this little circle of amateurs.

But why shouldn't she be? Maria suddenly appreciated an uncomfortable fact—even she wasn't immune to the tendency to think of women as less intellectually serious. That troubled her. All of her struggle to earn the notice of a university would feel wasted if it was just for her own sake.

"I'm Maria Gaetana Agnesi," Maria introduced herself. Thanks to Oriana's instruction, she curtseyed with the best of them.

"How could you be anyone else?" The woman's eyes sparkled and she inclined her head respectfully toward Maria. "I read the text of your speech on the necessity of women's education and found it entirely salutary."

Someone had *written down* her speech? They had been circulating it? Why hadn't she heard anything about that?

The younger man spoke up. "Allow me to introduce—"

"Laura Maria Caterina Bassi Veratti, at your service," she cut in to introduce herself. "I am a physicist by inclination and, God willing, soon enough by profession."

Something about the ease with which she proclaimed it shocked Maria. To sum up one's own existence so completely in a single phrase: *I am a physicist.* Never once had she been able to look at herself and declare confidently: *I am a mathematician.* What would it take for her to forge that river?

"You're staring at me like I just turned into a goat," Laura Bassi teased Maria good-naturedly. "I know as well as you do that a woman has never been a professor, but I am not without sponsors." She elbowed the older of the two men beside her. "Nor are you, I'd wager. But we needn't wait for the permission of the world to appreciate physics. Here, come have a look."

Maria allowed herself to be tugged toward the telescope. Delicately, she held back her hair and leaned into the eyepiece.

Within, Maria beheld the miracle of science.

In the sky, Jupiter was only a point of light. In the lens, it became a world. Bands of striated color wrapped across an alien globe like the layers of freshly excavated stone. This was a planet with neither continents nor oceans, instead seeming like an accident of the painter's palette. Stripes of red and white and orange encompassed the whole of its face, save for a single blood-red spot.

A gasp of surprise escaped her. She'd read all sorts of books— but none of them had truly prepared her for the beauty of the real thing.

"It truly is wonderful, isn't it?" said Laura Bassi.

Maria could hear the smile in her voice.

For a time beyond measure, Maria etched the shape of Jupiter into her memory.

Out of nowhere, an explosion of blinding red light sent Maria falling onto her backside, squawking in alarm. A powerful *crack* tore through the air with the force of a thunderbolt. Briefly, against all rational thought, Maria wondered if someone had fired a cannon.

That wasn't entirely too far from the truth.

Dozens of party attendees all clapped appreciatively, their gazes turned up toward the sky. There, the slow-fizzling remnants of fireworks were already fading from sight. The brightness of their explosion, magnified by a telescopic lens, had left one of Maria's eyes temporarily blinded. Only slowly did her sight return, bleeding back in around a fading splotch of electric color.

There are moments in life that stay with you forever. There, on the grass of the Borromeo estate, Maria had one such epiphany.

She had seen fireworks before, through the window of her family home. Then, they were distant blooms. Here they roared. Far out beyond the gardens, she saw the tiny shapes of the men who lit the wicks. She saw the fires catch and the trails glare. Pure, glorious force propelled the rockets upward, higher and higher, as if they might reach all the way to distant Jupiter, a light looking down upon a sky now studded with blooming fire.

It was mathematical, all of it. This was geometry realized.

"That's it," Maria said, still sprawled on the ground, supporting herself on her elbows.

Both Laura Bassi and the old Austrian knelt down to coax Maria up to her feet. Distractedly, she let them help her, but she was too busy thinking to do much with her own limbs.

"That's it," she said again, a whirlwind of inspiration coursing through her mind. "Thank you so much," she told Laura Bassi. Without thinking, Maria hugged the woman.

Bemused, the physicist wrinkled her nose, leaned back, and touched a hand to the top of Maria's head. Clearly she was not a hugging person. If truth be told, normally, neither was Maria.

"You are . . . welcome," Laura Bassi said. "Though I confess I know not the reason why you seem so pleased."

Maria had yearned for a goal. Something she could do that no one else had done. Now a single desire was written on her heart—a need to understand that glorious, free-flying upward motion.

Chapter Twelve

Once again, Pietro was forced to confront the fact that he did not understand his daughter.

"Ballistics," Maria was repeating now, puttering about the family library. "Ballistics, ballistics, ballistics."

The word didn't make sense coming out of her mouth. He highly doubted she'd suddenly developed an interest in artillery pieces. "You appear to have made something of an impression on the Borromeos' middle son. 'Remote and mysterious' it seems he called you."

Maria wasn't listening. She kept right on muttering, perhaps for her own benefit as much as for her father's. "Equations of motion can be described roughly with two sets of logic. Dynamics, concerned with force and energy as described by differential equations, and kinematics, concerned with positions of objects in time. Galileo, Newton, Descartes, Leibniz, all indispensable . . . but we don't have the correct Leibniz in the original. I need to see his equations, not his monads."

She'd been obsessed with equations ever since they got back from that night at the Borromeos' home. Reams of paper scattered across the library desk hosted all sorts of figures, many of which didn't even make sense to Pietro, and mathematics was supposed to be a field in which he held expertise. His daughter's wisdom was rapidly leaving him behind, and evidently outstripping what they had available in his library collection.

This was the same obsessive monomania for study she had shown before. Pietro had promised he wouldn't let her do this again. "You want me to send for a book?"

"There are seven or eight that I require," said Maria.

"There are also seven or eight of the finest patrician households who wish to meet you," Pietro pushed back. "To toast your excellence. Your every appearance is a sensation. Trust me, Maria, you do not want to waste that opportunity."

"Every second I spend at a party is a second I could better spend studying," Maria replied dully.

Pietro stood there for a few moments. "I'll get you as many books as you want," he told her. "Just humor me and go see a few people first."

Maria fixed her father with the most baleful, dead-eyed stare of which she was capable. "If I must."

"It's a very interesting idea," Maria told the visiting professor, seated in the salon of one of Milan's wealthiest families. "It is, however, completely wrong."

Pietro, seated some distance away, felt his stomach clench. Maria being seen about town was wonderful for her and wonderful for the family. He'd told her as much. Insulting an established professional, however, was not without certain risks.

Professor Colombo sputtered incoherently for a moment. A dozen eyes awaited his response. "This is a new field," he attempted, trying to save face, clearing his throat awkwardly. "Your brilliance is widely remarked upon, but my papers on probability earned the notice of the pope himself. Perhaps if you would let me explain in more detail—"

Maria's voice cut right through him. "It is not a new field. It is a problem that was already solved years ago by the Bernoullis. You have reinvented the wheel, replaced it with a triangle, and called that progress." Unamused, Maria looked to her left, where a family valet was doing his best to look invisible. "Fetch pen and paper. We will see whose method is more efficient."

Pietro could not help but notice that the perspiration on Professor Colombo's brow seemed to outstrip that which was merited by the evening's heat.

It was a risk, Pietro knew that. But on the other hand, if she could outdo a professor in his own field—who could deny her genius then?

And who could deny how proud he was, seeing her confidently sketch out the shape of the Bernoullis' curve? Perhaps he'd been worried for nothing.

Another day, another show. It was the third that week. Maria's head pulsed from the burden of it all. "A few parties" seemed to steadily be transforming into "meet every wealthy person in existence."

"You must be very driven," said a young daughter of some rich family whose name Maria had already forgotten.

They sat in another salon, as finely decorated as all the others. Days of appearances had become months before Maria realized any time had elapsed at all. Oriana always told her she must do a better job remembering all the details of Society, but the more of it Maria saw, the more interchangeable it all felt. She was constantly trying to pour the sum total of human knowledge into her brain. There simply wasn't room for social niceties on top of that.

The girl was still talking. "Seven languages, at your age? It seems almost impossible. I felt myself very clever for learning three."

"Your mother told me you were something of a scholar yourself," said Maria. It would be nice to find someone her own age with whom she could discuss things that mattered. This girl was certainly older than her, but not by much.

"Oh, heavens, no," she said, laughing. "I can't stand it. If it wasn't for her insistence on studying, I'd be out riding."

Maria was disappointed once again. Horses, like vapid society functions, did not interest her at all. As the stranger began chattering about the finer points of different breeds, Maria felt her consciousness growing more and more remote from the present time. It felt like she was a spirit outside her body, looking down at herself. She swore she could feel the revolution of the earth and the ever-faster passage of time. Deep down, she wished only to return to her books at home. All around her was the life so many young women coveted. To see and be seen. To wear the finest clothes. To have the ear of the wealthy and powerful. It all made her feel so very, very tired.

The talk of horses had ended. The woman whose name she had forgotten frowned. "Are you all right?"

Maria realized she was supposed to be talking. "I need to go home and work."

"I'm concerned about Maria," Oriana told Pietro, eyeing the ever-deeper pile of formal invitations.

"If you had seen her the other night, you wouldn't have worried," said Pietro, seated in front of the piano. He'd never really managed to get the proper sense of the instrument, but it didn't stop him from trying.

He grinned to remember that old hack mathematician's humiliation. If that hadn't made an impression, what would?

Ever-pleasant Oriana wore a very unusual frown. "I'm concerned nonetheless."

"Let me remind you that getting her out in front of society more was your idea. I think it's been wonderful for her. She's finally shown proper *confidence* lately. I think she's beginning to realize just how special she really is."

Oriana settled her fingers on Pietro's shoulders. Her fingers were small, but her grip was surprisingly firm. "You may not have noticed this, but she's wearing the same dress as yesterday."

Pietro didn't see what that had to do with anything. "Yes, and?"

"It is also the same dress as the day before that."

"Then clearly she likes it. Perhaps we should get her a few more in the same style."

"No, uh . . . ." Oriana dug her thumbs into Pietro's skin. "You don't understand. I don't think she's been sleeping. At all."

Pietro decided not to dignify that with a response. His fingers played across the piano keys.

Eventually, Maria tromped through the room to the library beyond. If she'd heard them discussing her, she gave no sign.

They watched her in silence for a moment. She sat right back down where she'd been before that evening's outing, picked up her pen, and resumed her calculations. Of late, all her days had played out in that very spot. Each of her movements had the rote, heavy quality of clockwork.

Oriana's features scrunched up tightly. "You know as well as I do that she hates being paraded in front of the world. I thought she might learn to enjoy herself, but instead she's just staying up to make up for all the time she spends being social."

Tempted to again distract himself with music, Pietro let his fingers lay still upon the keys. He remembered the way Maria had thrown up at the governor's mansion—and the way she'd passed out afterward, sleeping in for days. Perhaps there was something to be said for easing back on her schedule of appearances.

He had almost made up his mind before the world intervened.

One of the servants practically stumbled into the room. "Master Agnesi, sir," he all but stammered. "There's a . . . you need to see this. It's another invitation for the young mistress."

"Put it in the pile," Pietro said dismissively, waving the matter aside.

"Master Agnesi, sir," the servant spoke again. "You really should see this right now."

The young man all but thrust the missive into Pietro's hand. As Pietro looked at it, his spine locked as straight and firm as steel.

It was the seal of Charles VI, the Holy Roman emperor and ruler of the unequaled House of Habsburg.

The imperial family was coming to Milan—and they demanded that Pietro's daughter reprise her speech on women's education. Princess Maria Theresa, heir to the Habsburg throne, had signed the letter in her own hand.

It was the kind of offer one simply did not refuse.

Chapter Thirteen

When she'd first been summoned to speak before the imperial governor, Maria had gone by carriage. Today, the imperial governor had sent a carriage of his own to pick her up. That would have been surprise enough. What *really* surprised her, however, was that the governor and his wife were both seated inside.

"Well, come on," grated Count von Daun from the carriage window, his enormous powdered wig doing a lot to make his head look small. "It's not wise to keep royalty waiting."

Together with her father and stepmother, Maria shuffled into the vehicle's cabin. It was a spacious and tremendous carriage, but the presence of five people inevitably created a slightly claustrophobic atmosphere.

What was worse was how *awkward* it felt inside. The horses began moving, but no one said a single word. Maria didn't know how to talk to a man this important, and evidently, the adults in her life didn't know either.

And this man was nothing at all compared to the people they'd be meeting. Her father hadn't even told her until this morning.

Oh, you've an audience with the emperor this afternoon, he'd said, trying so very hard to be casual.

A horrible scheme of his to make sure she'd sleep. Little did he know she'd largely gone without, regardless.

There was a low, basso rumble to the count's voice, an effect only amplified by his courtly Germanic accent. Combined with the jowly, droopy nature of his neck and chin, Maria couldn't help but imagine what the powdered wig would look like on top of a bullfrog's head.

"You're to be a royal guest of honor," he pointed out to Maria.

She truly didn't know how to behave in front of this man. She resolved to say as little as possible. "So I have been told."

Evidently the governor found this the height of wit. He gave a great big croaking laugh, looking aside to his wife. "So I have been told," he echoed in a tinny imitation of Maria's voice before looking back at her. "You've got poise, at least."

Poise? She felt like she was going to throw up, and she wasn't sure the governor would let her use his wig like her father had let her use his hat. Although Pietro was feigning disinterest, Maria could tell both he and Oriana were watching her carefully.

"I've grown used to speaking in front of people," Maria said.

"Yes, all of it to do with science, a thing you were quite keen to make very Catholic with all of your speech's references to God, but I daresay your visit today has more to do with the devil's art of politics." He looked at Pietro. "This is all about the emperor's long-standing obsession."

"Politics is not a thing we often discuss in our household," Pietro said carefully, not at all comfortable in this arena. "We prefer to focus our children's education on more timeless things."

"Pah," the governor croaked. "Entirely reasonable of you and not at all helpful. I came here to make sure this girl knows what she's getting into. She may be the imperial guest of honor, but without my invitation, that old codger of an emperor never would have known she existed, so her behavior reflects on me as well."

It suddenly made sense to Maria. The governor's presence, the perspiration on his brow, the dryly amused exasperation of his wife. He was *worried*.

"I won't embarrass you," she promised him.

The governor inquired: "Does the phrase 'Pragmatic Sanction' mean anything to you?"

Some sort of law, wasn't it? Something the emperor wanted to be passed. Politics, like history, was a thing in which Maria held very little interest.

Before Maria could embarrass herself, the governor's rotund wife put her hand on her husband's knee. She spoke to him with delicate force in German. "Perhaps it would be best not to try to give her an education in geopolitical realities over the course of a single carriage ride. She's a genius; let's just trust in that."

The countess was trying to speak in a language Maria didn't understand. Maria decided it would be impolite to point out that her efforts had failed. And also impolite to admit she'd forgotten both their names. Again.

"My wife and I have the fullest faith in your abilities," the governor declared, easily persuaded by the woman at his side. "Just . . . be careful, hmm?"

Oriana clasped Maria's shoulder. "She's a very clever girl."

Intellect wasn't everything. Try as she might to ignore it, the seed of doubt took root inside Maria's mind.

There was something different about the way the Viennese court conducted itself. All the customs of Austria had descended upon the Milanese palace, rearranging everything to their own particular pleasure.

A painting, Maria thought, looking across the grand audience chamber. Everywhere she saw the kind of artificial, mannered poses that people assumed in paintings. The governor had done something very similar when she first met him. But here, there were a dozen people like that, all of them no doubt very important retainers to the imperial throne.

Among them, Charles VI sat large and magnificent upon the room's very grandest chair. Layers of voluminous cloth evoked the imperial eagle with their black-and-gold motifs. He was not a young man, the emperor, but neither did his spine yet droop with age. Beside him in equal splendor sat his daughter, the princess, reddish hair swept back and clipped with jewels.

Maria tried to convince herself that this was just another evening at a salon. The clinking of glasses and plucking of musical instruments spoke to an informal atmosphere.

"Ah," said a lugubrious-looking fellow standing by the emperor's elbow. "It is the young genius, Maria Gaetana Agnesi."

Maria had hoped she might go unnoticed, at least at first. Subconsciously edging closer to her father's side, she joined her family in a formal show of deference to the grandeur of the Holy Roman Empire.

"Your Imperial Majesty," they greeted him.

She couldn't hear her own words. The pounding of her heart threatened to drown out even the string quartet hidden behind a nearby screen.

"Oh, good," said the princess, clasping her hands noisily together. "After all the politics, I'd been hoping for something lighter."

Lighter for her, maybe.

Pleasantries buzzed back and forth for minutes. Before Maria quite understood what was happening, she found herself at a lectern. She didn't need notes for her speech, though. She'd seared it into her memory the better part of a year ago.

"I am here today to speak in defense of all women's right to an education."

She'd spoken in German. That surprised some of them right from the start.

The speech took perhaps ten minutes to recite from start to finish. Maria, as she often did these days, found herself feeling suddenly remote from her own body. The longer the speech went on, the more detached she felt. Like she was standing next to herself, watching a woman named Maria Gaetana deliver impassioned oratory, while the more calculating part of her mind mutely observed. An odd product of fatigue, perhaps—but not without its uses.

It allowed her to focus not on her omnipresent fluttering anxiety, but on Holy Roman Emperor Charles VI. Where the governor had been content to passively observe her speech, the emperor was dissecting it even as it came out of her mouth. The longer she spoke, the farther forward he leaned, a forearm braced upon the table. His face was an inscrutable mask that betrayed nothing, but there was a calculating gleam in his eyes that spoke of a secret purpose.

A political reason for the invitation, the governor had said. What political purpose could Maria possibly serve?

Ultimately, she decided not to worry about it. She would simply speak the truth as best as she understood it. Maria had lived her whole life in the pursuit of truth. There was no point dissembling now. She didn't really know how to lie.

"I hope someday to see you all at the university," Maria concluded, realizing she'd just finished her speech.

While the reaction had been strong the first time she'd delivered it, the applause here was polite and understated. Maria wondered if that was another part of the imperial style—not appearing too enthused about anything.

"Splendid, splendid," a reedy fellow calmly declared in French, his eyes made large by spectacles.

"You're entirely too kind," Maria answered him, reflexively humble.

Another man cut in, speaking in Spanish. "I've heard it said you speak all of Europe's languages. Is it then linguistics that you hope to study and someday teach?"

"Not all of Europe's languages," Maria answered him in the same tongue. This was another line that had served her well at her father's parties. "Just the ones worth speaking."

One of the few women in the room laughed at her response. "Come now, Francesco, were you not paying attention? It is mathematics that speaks to her. She hopes to follow in the footsteps of Newton."

"Lately," Maria admitted, "I have found myself becoming more of a Leibnizian."

It was not Francesco who spoke next, but a fat man beside him, in Latin. "Perhaps we might have a bit of sport and see how she does with some of the field's more perplexing equations. Mayhap a woman's perspective will turn some of our old idols on their head."

Things rapidly took on the tenor with which she was familiar. An increasingly impressed body of courtiers consulted her on everything from gravity to aqueduct engineering. By her father's reckoning, she could defend no less than 190 philosophical or scientific questions on demand.

Tonight was no different. Expounding, not for the first time, on Leibniz and the nature of monads, she was in her element. Confidence might have carried her all the way through the talk, if not for a sudden surprise.

Her old tutor, Vittorio Bellone, stood casually by the side entrance.

For a moment she swore she must have been hallucinating. But the door guards noticed him as well, both of them frowning in his direction.

Maria had long ago made peace with the fact that her father had fired him. But to see him now was like the sudden apparition of a person long dead. How had he gotten in here? Surely he hadn't suddenly found new employment with the imperial family.

"We're all of us very impressed with your erudition," Vittorio declared sharply, in Maria's native Italian. "I daresay there's no question about science on which you would not have an informed opinion. So I'll ask you a different kind of question."

Maria could feel the discomfort emanating from her father. This was nothing Pietro had planned.

Vittorio spoke plainly: "When you aren't studying, what is it you like to do in your own time?"

Maria opened her mouth to answer . . . and then closed it. Because she knew as well as he did that she didn't *have* an answer.

What was he doing, barging in here and asking a thing like that?

"Your genius is plain, but what *motivates* it—that's what interests me. Perhaps horseback riding? Dancing? Or simply seeing your friends?"

Awkwardly, Maria maintained her silence, mind racing in pursuit of a witty answer that would not come. Without thinking, she eventually declared: "I do not have any time for friends."

Pietro had already made his way to the door guards, where

he was hissing out a stream of invective, a finger leveled at Vittorio in vague accusation.

Mere moments later, the guards had seized Vittorio by the shoulders. Forcefully, they marched him from the room.

Maria could just barely hear his voice as he vanished into the hallway, a smug, satisfied sort of look on his face, like he'd proved some point to his personal satisfaction. "No need to be so rough, gentlemen . . . ." Most of the nobles of the court made a point of pretending he did not exist. Only one pair of eyes studied his retreating form quite keenly.

They belonged to the princess of the Holy Roman Empire, who wore a deep, contemplative frown.

"Let us not tire out the poor girl," boomed the voice of Charles VI, the first words he had spoken since Maria arrived. "I think it a fine time to break for refreshments. Everyone be at ease and drink freely; I have sent for the very best in the cellar."

As was ever the case after one of her appearances, Maria could feel herself deflating.

"The absolute nerve of him," Pietro hissed at their table while the reception continued. "I'll see his whole family ruined."

"The professor is a bachelor, darling." Oriana did her pleasant best to guide the conversation elsewhere. "He doesn't have a family to ruin. Meanwhile, you did very well, Maria. As always. Truly, there's nothing you can't do. I daresay you're destined to claim that professorship. Perhaps even in Vienna!"

Maria could barely stand leaving the house. She didn't think she'd survive leaving the entire region of Italy. What she wanted most of all was to fall into bed, but after she fumbled her answer to Vittorio's questions, fleeing would only make her look weak. Weakness was a thing she very much refused.

Pietro carefully dissected a roast pheasant with fork and knife, eventually looking up at his daughter. "You're tired," he pointed out.

"I can't just go home," Maria said.

"Of course you can. We can go right now."

"I'm a guest of royalty."

"You're also my daughter," said Pietro, "and that's more important to me."

There was a strange, buzzing quality about Maria's head. She wasn't entirely certain what to make of it. It felt vaguely like magnetism, when you pushed two lodestones of opposite polarities toward one another. The halves of her brain seemed to be having a slight disagreement.

"I'll be fine," she insisted. "I can sleep in tomorrow."

"You know yourself better than anyone," said Oriana. "If you truly, honestly feel like you're up to it, your father and I support you."

For a brief moment, Maria considered going home. But she still hadn't divined the emperor's purpose in asking her here. What had he been looking for in her speech? Even if her whole body felt vaguely prickly, and the world felt vaguely wrapped in molasses, she could persist for the sake of satisfying her curiosity.

Free time, indeed. The thirst for knowledge satisfied was far more valuable.

A well-coiffed servant soon appeared at their table. "Young mistress Agnesi. The emperor and the princess would like to speak with you in a private, candid audience."

And so the time had finally come. Maria scooted her chair back, ready to rise to the challenge. "It would be my pleasure," she said.

Only her body wouldn't move.

The valet cleared his throat. "Young mistress, if you would please follow me."

Her fingers worked. Her jaw clenched. Nothing else in her body seemed to answer.

The buzzing grew insistently louder. All of Maria's extremities began to prickle. "Just a moment," she requested.

Something was wrong with her.

The realization hit her: She'd known for weeks that her condition was deteriorating. Months, even. But she'd always found a way to ignore it.

Perhaps there was still something she could do—some tonic or something she could request—if only she could remember from her studies of medicine just what she was experiencing.

Maria's mind worked fast at the best of times, and now it achieved the kind of rapidity that would carry a body to flight. It felt not unlike flying, in fact. It took her a moment to realize that what was really happening was that she was falling.

Her chair clattered noisily to the ground. Her head struck the heavy side of the table with a powerful *thunk*. Plates and silverware clattered and sprayed away from the point of impact. Crumpling, she momentarily remembered the third of Newton's laws, as her body inevitably experienced impact's equal and opposite reaction. Legs gone limp, she careened toward the floor's unyielding marble tile.

Her panicked, slowed-down experience of time allowed her sufficient moments to reflect on what was happening before her head struck the ground.

Oh, she finally realized, just before the world went black. *I'm having a seizure.*

Chapter Fourteen

S he heard their voices before she saw them. Strangers, all.
". . . mere seizure wouldn't have had her out this long. It
seems more consistent with extreme exhaustion."

"The whole room saw her convulsions. A *mere seizure,* as
you put it, is incontrovertible fact and central to her condition."

"Yes, yes. The question is why a seizure, and why then?
Diagnosis of root cause is the cornerstone of any proper
treatment."

Maria realized she was lying on her back. That was no
surprise. What was far more startling was that she could feel her
bed underneath her, and see her plain, familiar ceiling.

She'd been unconscious long enough not only for them to
summon a raft of doctors, but also to cart her all the way home.
How horribly embarrassing. She'd let her family down in the way
she always feared she would, in front of the very most important
people in perhaps the entire world.

The doctors hadn't noticed she was awake. Three physicians
of varying ages squabbled about how best to treat her while an

assistant sat at her desk grinding medicine. No wonder she'd woken up.

Carefully, she cleared her throat. "I'm feeling much better, thank you."

Exactly the wrong words. All three of them were on her in an instant, urging her to lie back down, adjusting the bed, checking the heat of her brow.

In between their shoulders, she could see her father in the back of the room, looking horribly guilty.

"No fever that I can detect," said the eldest doctor.

"Please go away," Maria told the doctors. And then again, louder, holding eye contact with her father. "Please make them go away."

Pietro spoke up at once. "That'll be quite enough. She needs rest now. You can prod her all you like later."

With some significant protest, the physicians were eventually exorcised from the room. Maria breathed a deep sigh of relief. *More people* was not her idea of wellness.

"I'm so very, terribly sorry," Pietro murmured.

"Not your fault." Maria was already sitting up. She wiggled her toes and wondered what the doctors had hoped to discover by removing her shoes. "These things happen."

"Stay in bed. I insist."

Maria reached for one of her room's many piles of books. She ignored her mother's Bible and the challenge of Leibniz and reached for some light reading: Ovid's *Metamorphoses*. Studying poetry was almost like a vacation, and the regularity of Latin would help steady her mind.

"Maria, the last thing you need right now is more books. You've had entirely too much of books."

"And you've have me do what instead, horseback riding?" She wasn't certain why she was being short with him. The problem had been none of his fault. "I'm the one who should be apologizing."

A sharp knock sounded at Maria's bedroom door.

"Later!" Pietro hollered loud enough to be heard past its frame. More quietly, he told his daughter: "You need to rest."

Maria, still sitting in bed, flipped through the pages to try to work out where she'd left off. "I am resting," she muttered sullenly.

The knock again, more firmly this time.

"Later!" Pietro shouted louder still.

Oriana's voice filtered in, tinny through the wood. "This is extremely important."

Pietro hissed out a breath and opened the door, too forcefully. "What?"

A wide-eyed Oriana looked like she'd seen a ghost. "We have a visitor," she proclaimed. "Here for a whole hour already, but your doctors wouldn't let me up the stairs of my own house. When I complained, they called me 'hysterical' and started threatening to prescribe me opium tinctures."

Pietro ticked his head to one side. With the door open, they could hear music. A steady, thrumming flow of musical notes filtered up from the floor below, bouncing off stair and wall. The distance muted it, but it was unmistakably a harpsichord.

"What is that horrible racket?" he asked.

Maria knew that style of playing anywhere. "It's just Teresa playing."

"No," said Pietro. "Not the instrument."

Oriana set her jaw tightly. "The princess of Austria is downstairs, waiting to see our dear Maria."

A trilling, echoing warble reached Maria's ears. "And . . . she's . . . singing?"

Oriana nodded grimly. "She is singing *very badly*. I don't know how to ask her to stop."

Silently, Maria closed her book, set it aside, and walked downstairs.

Every single servant in the family's employ was hiding in the hallway leading up to the music room, trading confused and fretful glances. Even Savio knew better than to go barging in, staying back with his governess at the furthest end of the hall. Maria's appearance so soon after her collapse only added to the general atmosphere of confusion.

Maria didn't wait for anyone's permission before she went inside.

Young Teresa sat at the harpsichord, merrily going through the program of some kind of operatic tune. Bless her, she was too young and too personable to realize how strange an honor she'd been given. Singing to her tempo, the Habsburg princess stood with her arms outstretched, forcefully belting out the lyrics of an aria. What she lacked in skill she made up for in volume. Hearing the quavering force of her voice was not unlike being struck in the face.

The music abruptly stopped. Teresa had caught sight of her

sister, features lighting up into an almost incandescent smile. "Oh! You're all right!"

"So it would seem," said Maria, privately wondering if she was hallucinating.

The lack of musical backing had brought an awkward end to the princess's indulgence in opera. She cleared her throat pointedly, glancing around at her ever-present entourage of guards, as if challenging them to find issue with her behavior.

Not a man dared.

"All right, all of you out, chop-chop," said the princess, clapping her hands together.

One man was fool enough to object. "But your father—"

"Never mind my father. I will be alone with a thirteen-year-old girl. If she proves herself a fearsome rogue, I promise to yell for help immediately."

Maria could feel her mouth twisting into an uncomfortable compromise of an expression that did not quite reach a frown. "I would never make trouble."

The princess beamed down at Teresa. "You're a very talented little girl and I hope you can play for me again sometime. Run along now. You can see your big sister when I'm done with her."

"It was nice to meet you," said a hopelessly oblivious Teresa, before she made herself scarce.

Once they were alone, the princess suddenly broke into a peal of laughter. "Won't be hard for me to remember the two of you. You're Maria, she's Teresa—and I'm Maria Theresa. Isn't that just delightfully confusing?"

"With respect, my lady, I don't believe anyone would ever dare get us mixed up."

A hoot of amusement echoed from the princess's diaphragm as she appropriated the nearest couch. "No, I suppose not. I suppose not. Goodness, but you're a dry, retiring sort, aren't you?"

Maria realized she was being rude, but the words came out anyway. "I have just had a seizure, my lady."

"Yes, a fair point. Should I return on the morrow? We're to be stuck hereabouts for days while my father begs and pleads an entourage of pig-headed French to put his sanction before their king."

Maria had already kept the princess waiting for who-knew-how-many hours. She wasn't even certain it was the same day that she collapsed. "I'll be all right. I've just had a very long nap."

Another hoot. "I can't tell if you've the driest sense of humor or if you're simply that blunt. No, don't tell me; I prefer the ambiguity." She laced her fingers together and leaned forward.

Maria was comfortable with waiting for the princess to break the silence.

"So you think a woman could be a university professor, do you?"

Maria did not have to think about *that* answer. "I do."

The princess began picking at something beneath her seemingly immaculate nails. Her posture aspired to indifference, but her words came out too pointedly for that. "Do you think a woman could rule an empire?"

Now this was a slightly thornier question.

"If she was capable, I do not see why not," said Maria. "It would not even be the first time."

"But it would be a first for *us*," the princess declared with bitter exasperation. "A first for the House of Habsburg. My father has no sons; I'm sure you've heard."

"And you're his eldest daughter, Maria Theresa," Maria said slowly, beginning to realize why the emperor had been so interested in hearing her speak.

"My father has spent his entire life doing two things—trying very desperately to have a son, and now that it's fairly clear that is not going to happen, trying very desperately to get the rest of Europe to let me inherit. He's trying to force them all to commit to it in writing. He calls it the Pragmatic Sanction. Equally pragmatic was his decision to put me through an absolute perdition of Jesuit education. All to prepare me for the role that would otherwise attend the brother I've never had. The Habsburg dominions are as numerous as they are dissimilar, and simply to speak all their languages has been a trial."

Maria began to realize, against all common sense, that she had something in common with the woman destined to be her ruler. "How many languages have you had to learn?"

"Seven!" The princess had a way of getting very loud. She belted out that single word. "Much like yourself, if admittedly not quite so well. And where you chose Hebrew, I chose Hungarian; they're part of our realm, after all."

Their conversation was in German. Maria had so often done her trick of switching languages that it had long ago become second nature. Only now did she realize that she'd done it as soon as her sister left the room.

Maria began, "Your father . . . was maybe . . . hoping I had some ideas about why women deserve to teach, which he could use in his arguments for why women deserve to rule?"

"I suppose," said the princess, pushing herself to her feet with effort. "Or perhaps he simply has faith in women's capabilities and wanted to look upon one of his empire's greatest talents." She then shifted conversational tacks. "Do you have a family chapel?"

The palazzo was big, but it wasn't *that* big. "There's a room in back suitable for prayer, but I don't know if I'd call it a chapel."

"Well, come along," said Princess Maria Theresa. "I say the rosary every day, and I've decided to spend the day with you."

The old Byzantine icon of the Virgin Mary that Anna Brivio had so long favored still remained in the Agnesi family household. The comfortable, intimate little side room that hosted it lay in the back reaches of the house. It had something of a church's atmosphere, thanks to high windows and religious art. In the years since her early childhood, Maria had learned that the damage to the icon had been at the hands of people called the *iconoclasts,* who believed that all religious art was a sin against God and a form of idolatry. This one had been narrowly rescued from total destruction in circumstances no longer well remembered.

While the princess dutifully moved through the beads of the

rosary, Maria tried to say some prayers of her own. Many intellectuals distrusted religion, and very quietly some of them even doubted God, but Maria had never been that way. The more she learned about the way the world worked, the more she saw the evidence of the architect behind it. Yet today the prayers would not come. She felt too hollowed-out to think. The racing thoughts that so often troubled her in times of quiet had now turned to an empty fatigue.

Eventually, the princess crossed herself and looked over at Maria. "Do you have a favorite church?"

Maria momentarily startled. The answer came out unbidden. "La Chiesa di Santa Maria delle Grazie."

"That's the one with *The Last Supper*, is it not?"

"Yes," said Maria. "I saw it myself as a little girl. My mother made a great point of showing it to me—but I had no idea why it was special. I walked right out of the room, bored with it."

"Perhaps because it was not a textbook," suggested the princess.

Maria resisted the urge to protest. "I liked it there. We spent a lot of time there together. The old monks were always very happy to see me. There's . . . something about a place like that. It's very quiet, in a good way."

"Your mother was of the Brivio family, if I am not mistaken?"

Maria felt herself smile at the memory of her mother, and the days she'd spent with her at the convent. The expression felt somehow odd upon her face. "Yes. And you know, she also said the rosary. Every day, I mean. Like you. She had . . . a great deal of faith, my mother. I think that was the thing she wanted to pass on to me the most."

There had been something reassuring about her mother's religiosity—a fixed, unwavering belief in the goodness of God that propelled her to give so freely of both her time and money. Maria didn't doubt for a second that if her mother had still been alive, she would have found yet more ways to be of service to others.

"Faith is the bedrock of this empire," said Princess Maria Theresa, with perhaps too firm a conviction.

"Perhaps I should go visit that old place again," Maria eventually murmured.

Suddenly, the princess asked, "Have you ever considered a religious vocation?"

Maria practically fell out of her chair. "You mean, become a nun?"

"I've spoken with you for a fair bit now, and your mother's faith and charity is the first thing to put even a hint of a smile on your face." The princess collected herself from her seat, brushing herself off. "I spoke to the servants before you awoke. They say all you ever do is study or show off your knowledge. That, my dear, is not living." She didn't wait for Maria to offer a rejoinder before bustling right out of the room.

"It is *too* living," Maria protested, following along, then adding defensively: "It's what I'm best at."

The princess channeled all the power of her voice's considerable volume, cupping a hand to the side of her mouth. Loud enough for the whole house to overhear, she proclaimed: "Perhaps young Maria Gaetana should spend less time studying and more time enjoying the rewards that ought rightfully attend to excellence."

Maria realized she was blushing. "Don't do that," she whined, knowing it was childish.

The princess clasped her on the shoulder. Her grip was unexpectedly firm. "Thank you ever so much for what you have done to further the cause of women's education. As duchess, I shall endeavor to do my own part for that goal."

Pietro had taken the hollering as an invitation to make himself known. He emerged hesitantly from behind a doorway. Oriana lingered at a yet-further distance, looking liable to faint.

"Thank you so very much for gracing us with your presence this evening, Your Highness," said Pietro.

"Tomorrow, I'm going to take your daughter to have a look at Leonardo da Vinci's masterpiece," said the princess, drawing very near to Pietro. She gripped his shoulder just as she'd gripped Maria's. Yet despite her sunny demeanor, the weight of her palm was heavy enough to turn Pietro's stance lopsided. "I intend to keep a very close eye on her growth and career. I hope to ensure she lives a life she finds fulfilling."

"Perhaps . . . we can see to a lightening of her workload," Pietro all but stammered.

Princess Maria Theresa smiled like a saint. When she relaxed her hand, Pietro nearly staggered to one side.

"Thank you again," he managed.

The princess put her fingers in her mouth and whistled. As if they'd never left, her guards reappeared. She turned to Maria. "Maria, God doesn't put us on this earth for science alone. As your princess, I command you to sleep—and to learn how to enjoy yourself."

Maria slept better that night than she had for years.

Part Three

MATTERS OF THE HEART

Chapter Fifteen

A few years' time had done much to change Maria's life, but little to cure her distrust of horses.

The great beast whickered discontentedly, not at all interested in the picturesque Milanese countryside that spilled out around them. The thing was just so *big*. Maria had grown quite a bit herself over the last while—she was well into her teenage years now—but she still felt small in the company of this particular animal.

"There's nothing to worry about," she declared to her younger sister Teresa. The person she was really trying to convince, of course, was herself. "Mounting a horse is the easiest thing in the world." Ever since her doctor assigned her to this cruel activity, she'd even managed to mount a horse once or twice without falling.

Up ahead, Uncle Giuseppe sat atop his own gray steed, a magnificent animal that Maria felt was somewhat safer to appreciate—since it was a healthy distance away.

The chestnut monstrosity beside her, affectionately named

Cagliostro by its stablehand, was to be Maria's conveyance for the day. "Nothing to worry about," she said again.

"Well, go on then," said Teresa, a wry, knowing quality in her voice.

"I've got a very delicate constitution," Maria protested. She tentatively touched the horse's flank, which drew another whicker out of it. Startled, she snatched her hand right back. "You can't rush these things."

Giuseppe looked like he was right where he most wanted to be in all the world. He sucked in a great big breath of air, waving an arm at the vineyards that wound their way up the more distant hills. "What a lovely day for a ride. Come on, girls, time's a-wasting."

"Your physician told you this was the best kind of exercise for someone with your problems," said Teresa, who at age thirteen was now clever enough with words to hold Maria's feet to the fire.

"May the saints preserve our souls," Maria murmured, steeling herself to the task of mounting the horse. This *was* exercise, after all. And part of a scientifically designed program, at that.

A risky and wobbly ascent later, Maria cantered after Uncle Giuseppe, clutching onto the reins so hard she felt certain they'd leave marks on her palms.

"Easy, girl, easy," said Giuseppe, speaking not to his horse but to Maria. "Your horse can feel what you're feeling. Show it calm and confidence, and he'll reflect it back at you."

Maria felt familiar butterflies in her stomach, a perennial

problem. "Can we please talk about something other than what I'm feeling?"

"I heard you've been writing letters to the princess," Giuseppe proclaimed as the trees slowly passed by alongside them. The canter of horses' hooves held a sharp, rhythmic precision.

"Oh, maybe once a year," Maria said dismissively. "I'm no one that important in her eyes."

"There are folk who move to Vienna and spend *multiple* years trying to secure an audience," said Giuseppe. "Why, if I were a more dastardly man, I'd try to get you to mention the brilliance of my compositions in your next letter. But if I'm being honest with myself, I could never dream of competing with the musical stars over there, so I'm quite content to dwell as a large frog in our more modest pond."

"Actually, I was thinking of mentioning Teresa," said Maria. "She's gotten really very good these years—"

"No thanks to her teacher, I'm sure," bragged Giuseppe with exaggerated pride.

"And I think she's got an idea to try to become a professional musician."

"Not that she'd ever have mentioned this to me," Giuseppe went on, good-naturedly.

"And also . . . . ." Maria trailed off, suddenly realizing they'd let her sister lag behind. She glanced back over her shoulder. "Teresa?"

Maria nearly went lurching from the saddle. Her sister suddenly flew between them, holding on tightly to the reins of a galloping pony. Its hooves hardly seemed to touch the ground, such was its speed. Wild, boisterous laughter burst from Teresa's throat as she rode full tilt for the wineries ahead.

"So I see why *she's* here today," said Giuseppe. "You, though, look a little bit like you might perish. Is this another one of your doctor's schemes?"

In that moment, Maria envied her sister. How could she be so very unconcerned with all the variables of horse and rider? "Something like that, yes."

"The last one was . . . sprinting, as I recall."

"Which we suspended, as it seemed to be making my symptoms worse, not better," muttered Maria. "I think I liked strolls around the park best, but you get heatstroke one time and suddenly no one trusts you to measure yourself."

"Today is a day without measure," Giuseppe assured her. "Let's simply enjoy ourselves, hmm?"

A few years ago, Maria had struck a bargain with Oriana and her father. Four days a week, she would be allowed to study as much as she pleased—but in return, she would devote a day to herself or to family. So far the bargain had held, and of late she hadn't even had a seizure for two whole seasons. Things seemed to be in balance.

Applause dragged Maria back to the present moment. A trio of young men, one of them glisteningly shirtless, stood at the edge of the nearest winery. The shirtless fellow, some kind of farmhand, was vigorously about the business of chopping firewood. The other two fellows, less industrious and more fully clothed, admired Teresa's ongoing sprint for the hills.

The way the one man's muscles moved in his forearms

captured Maria's attention more than she would have best preferred. Silently, she resolved to say a whole extra decade of the rosary on Sunday.

"Oh, wonderful," Giuseppe muttered. "It's him. I thought he was off in Salerno."

It was the youngest fellow who drew Giuseppe's ire. Still out of the young man's earshot, but drawing closer as their horses moved along the trail, Maria asked: "Who is he?"

"Marcello Ricci. Their family owns most of this land. His father has become a major wine dealer of late."

Maria understood at once. "They're what father always calls 'new money.'"

"Even though he's the same thing," Giuseppe said.

Marcello Ricci was a man of about twenty, with large black eyebrows and a ready smile. His white teeth appeared as he noticed Giuseppe and Maria on the approach. "Aha! If it isn't Giuseppe Brivio. My father sends his regards."

There was not so much as a whisper of Giuseppe's previous disapproval. He was all gentility now. "Young master Ricci. Your father always speaks well of you."

No doubt this was true. Maria was clever enough to notice this statement simultaneously absolved Giuseppe of the need to lie or to express his own opinion.

Marcello ignored the formality and fixed the whole of his attention on Maria. "Aha! And you must be the Agnesi girl. The one everyone's always raving about. The great genius."

"Some people say that," Maria offered in her own brand of deflection.

"They say that you'll defend any philosophical position, in any language."

There was something about the way he looked at her that Maria disliked. "I don't really do that so often anymore. For some reason people grew less and less impressed with it the more I grew up."

"Well, for old times' sake, answer me this: Which philosophy do you think is better for a man to live by—Epicureanism or Stoicism?"

Maria realized, to her great and abiding exasperation, that this young man was doing something like *flirting* with her.

These days, she didn't much like the way people used to exoticize her intellect or marvel over her learning. But at least that wisdom was something she'd chosen to obtain, not a thing visited upon her by God without her permission.

The word came to Maria's lips far more cuttingly than she meant to. "Stoicism."

Marcello scratched at his chin—a chin somewhat in need of shaving. "Well, go on. All ears attend the lady professor."

"The pleasures of sin and vice are fleeting, and wither on the vine like the grapes of a bygone harvest." Maria channeled a firebrand preacher she'd once heard. "Men are drawn to the pleasures of the bottle to escape their woes, and find neither strength nor oblivion therein. Stoicism, meanwhile, arms us with the tools necessary to endure life's hardships, even as it tells us that they will pass. The stoic lives in the world, but is not ruled by it. The epicurean is a creature who has chosen that which is fleeting over the eternal joy of service to God."

Marcello grinned in simple amusement. "How earnest. But that's not scientific; that's just a warmed-over sermon."

Maria felt her spine stiffen. "I did not come prepared for debate."

"Then perhaps you should. My father is hosting an intellectual symposium for honored guests on the twenty-fifth. It would be my honor if you would attend."

Maria glanced at her uncle out of instinct.

"The young mistress's health is sometimes an issue," said Giuseppe. "We will seek her doctor's approval and send along our reply. Meanwhile, we should catch up with the other young woman before she rides into a bramble somewhere."

"Good day," Maria closed out the conversation, spurring her horse to movement. She'd rather be anywhere else.

With that thought in mind, Maria felt the horse was no longer quite so burdensome a thing to command.

As reliably as the finest clockwork, every year the Agnesi family welcomed another sibling. Maria now had ten of them, with an eleventh on the way.

"This is all wrong, Savio, and you know it's wrong," Maria fussed over her little brother's Latin studies. His handwriting was terrible, the syntax inelegant, and frankly, she didn't think he took the matter seriously at all. "This word isn't even part of the third declension."

"It's stupid," said young Savio, this being his favorite word of late. "Why can't they just have one declension for all the words?"

"I must inform you, Savio, that of all the many languages I

have studied, Latin is, in fact, the *most* regular. Don't even get me started on the irregularities of English."

"They're all stupid." He stared sullenly at his papers. "It would be a lot simpler if everybody just spoke the same one."

"Yes, well, the Tower of Babel had its consequences," said Maria, trying to joke, but Savio didn't seem to get the reference.

In another room, young Lorenzo was crying, as he had been doing with oppressive frequency ever since his teeth had started coming in. By now, Maria was used to this phase in her siblings' development.

Her father, however, always seemed to forget that when children are born, they must spend a while as infants. The noise of the house caught him perpetually off-guard. Bleary-eyed, nap ruined, he lumbered into the study. "Good to see you're both hard at work," he croaked out.

Savio looked none too happy about the prospect of work, but Maria found herself smiling. Even in these middling years of youth, when so many young women grew to resent their parents, she felt it was important to do her father proud. "Not my work. That comes later."

Pietro rubbed at his eyes. "Mmm. Your uncle spoke with me the other day."

Maria had noticed that her father never referred to Giuseppe by name—he was always "your uncle," like connecting himself to the man directly was somehow distasteful. Maria supposed their personalities were just entirely too different.

Pietro, still a touch groggy, spent a while collecting his words.

"He says you've been invited to attend some kind of symposium hosted by the Ricci family."

"I'm not going," Maria declared. She had made up her mind immediately on the day of the invitation.

Pietro looked at his son. "Savio, run along and entertain your crying brother, won't you?"

A grateful Savio bolted before Maria could so much as utter the word "study." Long-suffering, she organized his papers into tidier composure. "You're going to tell me that it would be good for the family business if I went."

"I'm not ordering you to go, you understand. The boorishness of the family's eldest son is widely remarked upon. If you would prefer not to . . . ."

"I have a condition," said Maria, holding up a finger.

"If we can make a connection with them, it really will help."

She counted off. "For the next three weeks until that day—no more exercise, no more days off, and no more visiting relatives. I need to devote myself completely to study."

Pietro opened and closed his mouth. "What, are you worried you'll come off poorly?"

Maria had made social appearances in the last few years, certainly, but she and her father had put an end to her constant performances. What a performer needed was *practice.* By their mutual reckoning, at one time she had been learned enough on nearly two hundred topics to debate the very best and brightest minds. Lately, although she'd continued to make great advances in mathematics, no one had tested her general knowledge.

It took her a moment to realize what she'd been feeling. She'd been *embarrassed.* That obnoxious young fellow Marcello, whom she fully intended never to speak with again, had ambushed her with a question and she hadn't been prepared to deal with it.

Questions, knowledge, answers—these were the tools that gave her the minimum necessary confidence to even go out of the house. How could she face a whole room of scholars again if she was less clever now than she'd been at the age of twelve? It would embarrass the family and make both her and her father look like fools.

But what she said out loud was: "I'm out of practice. I'd just like to brush up on some things."

"Well, all right," said Pietro, looking like he thought it a bad idea, but somehow was unable to quite express why.

Oriana felt exhausted. Being a mother was as challenging an ordeal as any labor of Hercules, and she wouldn't hear it suggested otherwise. She'd spent all day trying to hammer sense into rambunctious Francesco, who simply would not give up on his ridiculous dream of being a battlefield hero. Lately that dream seemed to be translating into surprise assaults on the household staff. Even with a fleet of governesses, tutors, and servants, she barely felt able to keep up. How did the poor folk of the city manage to raise their families alone?

Reclining in a leather seat and enjoying the luxury of a rare moment of evening repose, she rubbed at her temples, wondering what was bothering her. She'd gotten time all to herself with some of her old acquaintances yesterday, which usually did a great deal to rejuvenate her spirits, but over the last week she'd grown increasingly certain something was wrong, something she couldn't quite place her finger on.

Suddenly, she realized exactly what the problem was: She hadn't spoken with Maria in weeks.

She'd seen her, of course. But only briefly over a meal, before Maria vanished back to whatever it was she kept busy with. Oriana had never understood that girl. If she was a more callous and awful woman, she might suggest it was because Maria was not her own daughter, but that simply wasn't true, because she'd always gotten along splendidly with Teresa, who happily called her "mother" without a second thought.

Maria, though.

Some people were visited by fey moods. Obsessive periods. Oriana's brother was like that—he'd vanish into art for days at a time. But Maria didn't just vanish for a day or two. It was more like she perpetually dwelled beyond a sky of mist and vapor from which she only occasionally came back down to visit the rest of them on earth.

Without realizing it, Oriana had already marched close to Maria's spartan room on the second floor. Sure enough, she could see from the light spilling beneath the door that Maria had neglected to go to bed. It was entirely past the time her physicians had prescribed.

Oriana stood with her knuckles poised, about to knock. But for whatever reason, she hesitated. Some glimmer of intuition told her it would be better to wait.

She was rewarded with the sound of horrid retching from

within the room. Maria had surely just thrown up. The unpleasant wet noise that followed spoke of a chamber pot freshly filled.

Oriana knocked. "I'm coming in," she declared.

"Just a moment," said Maria, calm as you please.

Oriana waited exactly one moment and not a second longer. She flung open the door and stepped inside. "You're sick again," she observed, more accusatory than she intended.

Maria had already gotten back to her desk. She looked completely composed. Stacks of books and papers filled every spare surface in the room. "Just a little indigestion," she insisted. "Too much dinner."

Oriana pointed right at her. "Bed. Now."

"In just a minute," Maria said patiently.

Oriana knew she was far older than the girl, so why was it Maria always acted like Oriana was the younger of the two? "If I come back here in ten minutes and you're not in bed, I'm telling your father."

A dead-eyed look came upon Maria. She immediately shut her book. "Fine. But I'll be right back at it in the morning. I've got a very important day this week and I must be ready. I already have his permission."

Oriana battled the urge to say something rude. Instead, she just took a step back. "You don't have his permission to study yourself to death. We already learned what that looks like. Bed."

"Yes, mother," said Maria, something she only called Oriana when she was upset.

Oriana felt the pit of her stomach sink. Someday, she

resolved, as she shut the door—someday Maria would call her that in fondness.

Chapter Sixteen

"Father won't be coming?" Maria asked Oriana suspiciously, seated upon a carriage bench. It rattled beneath them on the way to the Ricci estate.

Oriana frowned. "We went over this several times."

"I've been studying," Maria explained, not for the first time in her life.

"He had some very important business for the day that could not be rearranged. Uncle Giuseppe will be there as chaperone."

Well, at least there would be *some* family there, Maria immediately thought. A moment later, however, she found herself feeling guilty. Oriana was most certainly part of her family. She was the mother of nearly all her brothers and sisters. Yet Maria couldn't deny she had always felt somehow remote from the woman.

"I need to admit something to you about why I'm doing this," Maria found herself saying.

Oriana wore a subdued little smirk. "Oh?"

Maria considered how to frame her next statement. She

thought of something vicious and then tried for nice instead. "There's a particular young man whom I wish to impress."

Oriana completely misinterpreted her. "Oh ho ho! Our little girl is all grown up!" She clapped her hands delightedly.

"Not like *that*," Maria grumbled, wilting back into her chair. "I want to show him I'm smarter than he thinks I am."

Oriana practically bounced in her seat, clapping merrily. "Yes, and I'm quite sure you will! I've always said you're very, very smart. Oh, who is it? Who is he? Can I help?"

Cheeks flushed a stubborn crimson, Maria conked her head against the side of the carriage. This morning, she felt enormously confident. Her old sharpness was coming back to her. Now, she felt horribly, horribly exhausted and they hadn't even got there yet. "I don't want to talk about this," she decided.

Thankfully, Oriana was happy to do all the talking for her. All her friends had been married, and she had all sorts of recommendations about how to approach both engagement and matrimony.

Oriana did love a party. And with her husband gone, there was no one to tell her not to indulge in as much food and drink as she liked. Lucky her, since the Riccis spared no expense in creating a gigantic monument to the prosperity of their new winery. Royal courts had dined on fare less rich.

They'd set up the outdoors of the winery with banquet tables, a rather rustic touch that Oriana found charming. She didn't really know anybody there, which she also found charming—she had always found joy in making new acquaintances.

A smile, a laugh, a shared toast . . . it was all part of the thrill of simply being alive. Oriana dared to hope that today, her daughter—and Maria *was* her daughter, she insisted on it— would learn to ease up and have a little bit of *fun*. Maybe if she could just get enough wine in her, the girl would stop thinking about logarithmic what-have-yous for five minutes.

Giuseppe, rakish as ever, made a point of sitting next to Oriana and warding off any too-earnest male attention. "I can't imagine Pietro would approve of all this liquor," he proclaimed, pouring himself a fourth glass.

Oriana refused to let him ruin the moment. "And when are *you* getting married, hmm?"

"You will recall I did that already," Giuseppe said, inhaling the scent of wine.

"It was annulled the same month."

"Yes, and what a month it was. So fulfilling, truly, that I feel I need never know another woman."

Suddenly, Oriana snapped her fingers. "Oh, look, look there." She pointed out to where Maria stood near the rows of vines. "Is he the one?"

Giuseppe narrowed his eyes, eyeing the dapper and well-coiffed young man who stood beside Maria. "Marcello Ricci," he mumbled, as if it were the name of his hated foe.

"He must be the one." Oriana drank liberally. "Look at the fire in her eyes. Oh, this is so exciting!"

"I think you may have slightly the wrong idea. She hated him at first glance."

Entirely too enthused, Oriana steepled her fingers, filled

with matchmaking zeal. "That's why he's perfect. She's cold and distant, our Maria. Always agreeable, always calculating and studying. A frustrating man she can't understand, who inflames her anger and passions both! It's just what she needs."

Giuseppe remained visibly skeptical. "I don't think you and Maria share the same taste in men."

Maria, her back stiff as steel, traded words with Marcello, too far out for Oriana and Giuseppe to hear. A visibly frustrated Marcello snapped his fingers irritably, hollering toward the party. It wasn't long before more folk attended to them, including the visiting scholar and guest of honor who was meant to give a talk later.

"Drat," Oriana muttered. "This is exactly like the past. We need them *alone,* Giuseppe, alone!"

Giuseppe, with mouth full of cutlet, found himself unable to verbally reply. Raw skepticism nonetheless came through in his low grunt.

Maria seemed to be in her element. She had that economy of movement, forbidding body language, and poised demeanor Oriana had suffered through watching so many times before. Oriana had told herself over and over again that things were different now, that today would be the beginning of a new Maria, but the young woman had reverted once again to the old familiar mode. They'd never really taught her to do otherwise.

"I don't think she's feeling well," Giuseppe noted.

"How do you figure?"

Fanning herself, Maria took a few steps away from the circle of men around her. Marcello, however, would not respect her personal space. Sensing an opportunity for gallantry, he stepped toward Maria, offering her a supportive arm.

Very gallant of him, Oriana thought, but the young man had made a horrible mistake. He didn't understand what a lack of personal space did to Maria's already delicate stomach.

She held out stiff, unwelcoming arms—and then suddenly threw up all over him. All over his immaculate, expensive coat. And then again. And then on his boots. In the full view of the entire party.

Aghast, Oriana stumbled to her feet and ran to her daughter's side.

Giuseppe took a long, slow pull from his wineglass. "I suppose that's one way to help Pietro sell them new fabric."

"Before I say anything else, I need you to realize that it was your fault," Oriana told her husband, jabbing a finger at his chest. Anything less subtle simply wasn't going to get through to the man.

The old parlor clock ticked audibly. Pietro did not hurry to speak. Oriana knew he was examining his memory for any and all possible misdeeds. Given that he'd been out of town on business, he probably thought himself innocent of wrongdoing, but he eventually settled on the safest possible question.

"What's the matter?"

"It's Maria." Oriana stepped back and folded her arms. "You've started pushing her too hard again."

"I'm not pushing her. I just gave her some room to pursue her interests."

Oriana had prepared evidence in advance. She thrust a hand toward a great book on the table labeled *Propositiones philosophicae.* Maria's name was on it. "And I am sure it was wholly *her* idea that she should perform as the parrot Minerva in front of all your well-moneyed acquaintances? That all one hundred and ninety theses in this book, transcribed from her talks, are things she studied wholly of her own initiative?"

Pietro loosed a low, ragged breath that did not quite become a sigh. "We published that book years ago. We've eased well up on her since."

Interesting, thought Oriana, how it became "we" when they reflected on a bad decision, and "I" whenever he had made an excellent profit.

"She's not sleeping again," said Oriana. "Throwing up again. Does this begin to sound familiar?"

Pietro had to admit that it did. He avoided eye contact.

"She's well into marrying age and doesn't know how to talk to strangers about anything that doesn't involve academics."

"She doesn't want to. Isn't that the problem? She's just doing what she wants to do."

Oriana didn't mean to shout, but shout she did. "She's doing what *you* want to do!"

The clock filled the air again.

Pietro said, "I think that's unfair."

"Whether you realize it or not, she does these things as much to impress you as anything else. She's a devout soul, our Maria, you realize that much at least. She wants to serve God and serve her family, and you've consistently taught her to do it by learning. Now she's like a dish made with only one ingredient. She's not balanced, Pietro. She won't be well until she is."

"We tried to put her in front of people before. All it did was wind her up tighter. And given that you're like this, I have to imagine things with the Riccis did not go well."

"There's more to life than books and money and stupid parties where people show off their wealth and erudition." Oriana was proud of that line; she'd prepared that in advance, too. "At the very least, she needs to get out of the house."

"She doesn't want to do that."

"Have you ever just *asked* her? Asked her what she wants to do?"

Pietro did not have a good answer to that. "I suppose we can go speak to her."

Maria was absolutely mortified. What a disaster the day had been. Not even the Latin poetry in front of her could distract from what happened with Marcello Ricci. She'd gone prepared to have a proper intellectual debate—but had discovered that all he wanted to do was rain salacious compliments on her.

And it had ended in disaster. Never again, she resolved. She'd never bother with "being social" ever again. If these were the wages of romance, she wanted nothing to do with them. Pygmalion truly had the best idea, making his ideal partner out of a statue. Unlucky him that it had come alive.

"Young mistress," said one of the maids.

Maria nearly fell out of her chair. Her nerves were the part of her that God had made out of the weakest material. When had the woman snuck up on her?

"I'm listening."

"Your parents wish to see you in the parlor."

There it was. There would be a reckoning for her behavior this time. She'd absolutely poisoned her family's relationship with the Riccis and ruined her father's prospects. She was a horrible failure of a daughter and a perfect fool.

Thanking the maid, she marched to her impending doom. There, Oriana and her father both sat near the clock, looking at her with the most grave and intense expressions.

Maria channeled something of the old soldiers she'd seen at her father's events. "I take full and complete responsibility for my actions."

But they didn't even bring up what had happened. Instead, a smiling Oriana asked her: "Maria, we're drafting up some new plans. We were wondering—what would you best like to do with your free time, going forward?"

Maria thought about her theoretical work in geometry and calculus, as well as the correspondence she'd lately exchanged with the foremost expert in the field, an Olivetan monk. If there was any way she could bring credit to her house, it would lie there.

"I was hoping we might continue letting me have more time to study. I've made several excellent strides. I think I might even be onto something original."

Pietro, for whatever reason, covered his face with his hands. "That is perhaps not what we had in mind."

Oriana wore her fake-pleasant smile. Maria imagined it would have fooled anyone else. "I am told you did quite a bit of charitable work with your mother at a convent as a child."

"She taught there," Maria said, the memories feeling distant, like a thing that had happened to someone else entirely. "I am not sure I did any work of substance."

"True, but was it not a pleasant place for you?"

Maria remembered it as such. But she also remembered being intelligent, and recent events indicated she was less clever than she believed. "It might be all right. But I'm worried about how much time it'll take away from my work."

Pietro seized on this opening. "The foremost library in the city is but a brief walk from there. Actually, that's an excellent idea. I'll arrange for you to have a library membership, and you can go there from the convent in the afternoons. The walk will satisfy your body's need for exercise."

It was Oriana's turn to sigh and massage her face. "This kind of regimented life is exactly the opposite of . . . ."

Maria thought of the Ambrosian Library. It was quite the storied institution. She realized she'd never seen the inside. What unnoticed treasures might lie within?

"I think that sounds like an excellent idea."

She had no idea why her agreement made her stepmother look all the more grim.

Oriana laid down her ultimatum: "Fine, the library, too, but you'll visit the convent first, so help me God."

Chapter Seventeen

Nostalgia was rightly the domain of the old, or so Maria had always believed. It seemed that the older you got, the more you wanted to talk about the way things used to be. Perhaps the urge to look backward crept up on you over the years, until reminiscing about the past grew more appealing than experiencing an unfamiliar present.

Yet, despite her youth, as she stood in the annex of the Santa Maria delle Grazie, visions of childhood came upon Maria with vivid immediacy.

It was the incense. The right smell, the right taste—these could conjure up memories that the rational mind had forgotten. The patina of incense bestowed the convent with a kind of dreamlike timelessness. She wasn't sure what scent it was precisely. Looking upon the old bookshelf where she'd first taken up Newton's book, she knew only that it was familiar, albeit different from the frankincense more often used in church.

She'd arrived in a carriage, entered unchallenged, and found not a soul within. Just when she'd begun to wonder if she'd gotten the day wrong, she heard the voices of the nuns singing the Divine Office, muted by the intervening walls. In the Catholic faith, every hour of the day had its own prescribed prayers and hymns, and every church or monastery would have its own rules on who would observe them and how often. It seemed this morning hour dictated that all the sisters would be joined in prayer. Maria could tell it was Latin, but she wasn't familiar with the melody.

She had nowhere else to be and nothing else to do. She allowed herself to sit without reading. It felt strange. If it wasn't for the sound of prayer, it would even have felt indulgent.

Maria did not intend to fall asleep. But she supposed she must have, for the next thing she was aware of was a young nun gently nudging her shoulder.

The nun had great big brown eyes of the kind that looked perpetually surprised. "Pardon me, but you cannot rest here," she nearly whispered.

Maria felt her cheeks grow warm with embarrassment. "I'm here as a volunteer," she managed to say. "Maria Gaetana Agnesi. My father would have sent word."

"Oh!" The nun nodded a little too eagerly. "You're Anna Brivio's daughter. Yes, she was a fixture around here. I hadn't taken vows back then, so I didn't meet her myself, but Mother Angelica told us all about her when she received word of your intent to carry on her work."

Mother Angelica. There was a name she'd almost forgotten.

In fact, there was another old face she wanted to see. "There was a monk I often saw in here. An old fellow, a bit sly. Is he still . . . ?"

The young nun smiled wanly. "You mean Brother Hieronymus. I am afraid he passed into the Lord's embrace last year."

Maria released a breath she didn't know she'd been holding. "Oh."

The nun crossed herself, looking at the books. Evidently Hieronymus's library was something of a memorial to the man himself.

Contemplative silence was a thing Maria felt compelled to fill with words. "I'm here to help as best I can. I know my mother taught a class in languages. If the teaching ministry is ongoing, perhaps I could help in the same way?"

The nun had that placid quality seen in clergy who must make bad news palatable. "Mother Angelica, after exchanging correspondence with your stepmother, has expressly forbade you from engaging in any and all academic work here on our premises."

Maria all but sputtered. "It's what I'm best at. The Epistle of Peter states—"

The nun had come prepared. She ducked behind a nearby table and emerged with the old reliable tools: bucket, rag, and mop. "Many of our sisters are quite elderly and can no longer fulfill their duties. You will be helping us today with cleaning."

Maria had lived her entire life in the presence of maids and did not know how to clean. She swallowed very slowly upon observing the tools. "I may require some instruction on the particulars."

~

Maria walked the city streets, staring at her aching fingers. She hadn't done anything hard, so how was it that her palms could ache so? Evidently there were small muscles for fine tasks with which she had never been properly acquainted.

Looking at her hands absolved her of the need to look at her surroundings. She realized that carriages did a fine job of sheltering her from the anxieties that dwelled within her heart. Four solid walls closed off the outside world—with curtains, no less. She had not appreciated until just now the devilish detail her parents had inserted into this new schedule: the need for an unsupervised walk.

Keeping active was important to health—all of her doctors agreed on this notion—but being in public remained perilous. Not that it was physical peril that worried her. These were the high streets, wide and open and well patrolled. No, what bothered her was how disorderly it all was. At her old talks and lectures, she understood her role. In the convent, there was structure. Even cleaning had wound up being surprisingly satisfying. While academics seemed to be a path without end, a dusty room could be inarguably and beautifully improved through only a few hours of labor.

To be in public was to be within chaos.

She struggled with the noise of it. The cantering of horses' hooves, the buzzing conversation, the distant clanging of iron used for who-knows-what. Music from a public house, hollering from an unhappy couple. All the people, glancing at her as she went by, or ignoring her outright, their motives unclear. Each person was an individual universe of unknowable possibility.

Such was the whirl of worry in her mind that she passed right by the Ambrosian Library and was forced to double back a whole city block.

The façade was less grand than the library's reputation might have led her to expect. In gray stone with columns, it reminded her of a miniature Greek temple. Her father had fussed about the need for a membership, but no one asked for her name or proof that she could enter. Instead, she opened the door and stepped right in.

The noise of the city blessedly vanished as soon as she closed the door. Her feet made little padding noises against the carpet and uncomfortably loud clacks upon the wood. Past the vestibule, the building opened up into the largest collection of books she'd ever seen.

The room was a long rectangle enclosed by books. The ceiling went up and up, bookshelves atop bookshelves until they were well out of reach; the uppermost collections had to be approached from somewhere on the second floor, where a narrow mezzanine adjoined the shelves.

Maria stood in the center of it all, ignoring people silently reading or transcribing at the low tables in the room. She turned in a slow circle, unable to keep from taking in the sweep of the place and imagining the possibilities.

It was on her second revolution that she came face-to-face with one of the library staff, a woman scarcely older than herself, hair pulled back into a bun that left her hairline tight and severe.

Maria smiled, for once wholly at ease. This was her sort of place. "Oh, pardon me. Where can I sit?"

This was apparently exactly the wrong question. The librarian held a finger to her lips, hissing out the librarian's universal shush.

Maria tried again in a whisper, furtively glancing to see if she'd bothered anyone. "Where can I sit?"

The librarian released a silent sigh and gestured with both her hands. *Anywhere you like,* Maria supposed it meant.

Resolving not to be bothered, she busied herself with finding the mathematics collection. Luckily it did not entail climbing ladders or exploring distant floors. Less luckily, they had nothing of the new and innovative works of Euler, a man whom the monk she'd been writing to had gushed about ceaselessly, but her father had already sent to Vienna for a copy of the man's writings. Several rare editions nonetheless caught her eye, and these she took to what looked like an empty table.

As was often the case for Maria when confronted with an especially interesting book, time began to blur. Reality eventually reasserted itself with the arrival of a young man at her table.

He was perhaps eighteen, or maybe twenty at most. His was no athlete's build, but the slender look more common among young scholars and clergy. His skin's golden hue nonetheless indicated a man who spent time outdoors. Something about the shape of his mouth distracted Maria and made her consider what it might look like—in speech, or . . . .

Recent experience with a certain Ricci left Maria less than

enthused about conversations with unfamiliar young men. She ignored the man completely, and to her grateful surprise, he ignored her, too.

The Ambrosian Library proved equal parts peaceful and familiar. Maria went home refreshed.

The next day at the library, after Maria had finished work at the convent, the boy was there again.

This time, he'd arrived before her. Maria briefly entertained the notion of going over to join him at his table, but decided it was a distraction she didn't need. She sat alone.

Not half an hour later, after retrieving a new book, he chose to sit back down at *her* table.

Maria laid her palms flat, glancing up at the slender young man. She might have challenged him . . . but he didn't speak a single word. He didn't even glance up to acknowledge her staring. Instead, he was hard at work on some kind of Latin study.

None of her business, Maria decided, happy to ignore him.

But over the course of the next few days, there he was, as sure and regular as clockwork. And every day, he chose a seat one chair closer to Maria's. By some mutual unspoken compact, neither of them acknowledged or spoke to one another.

Each day, the mystery of it gnawed at Maria a little bit more. Perhaps it was just the fact that they were, generally, the youngest people in the library. Who was he, anyway? Did he want to speak to her? If so, why didn't he just do it?

The notion of why *she* did not just speak to *him* did not even occur to Maria.

At least not until the day when he sat directly across from her.

There was a limit even to how much evasion Maria could stomach. She lifted her chin, laid eyes upon the man, and cleared her throat.

His eyebrows twitched, so she knew he could hear her. But still he did not look up.

Maria lowered her gaze, considering his Latin. Judging by the repetition of phrases, he was still an early learner and struggling with the language's preponderance of tenses. "You wanted the pluperfect there," she told him softly, to no answer whatsoever.

Undeterred, Maria continued in louder and more direct terms. Let him try and ignore that. "You should try writing the same sentence in every tense. Pick perhaps a few at random, starting with different forms. It's a useful drill. *Repetitio mater studiorum est.*"

Maria realized someone was standing next to her. She looked up to behold the tight face of the humorless librarian she'd met before.

"Shhh," the woman all but hissed at her.

With a long, pointed sigh, Maria looked back down at her own work. If she was going to be here, she wasn't going to let this taciturn boy distract her. She needed a strategy either to draw him out or get rid of him.

The latter would be easier. And yet for some reason, she was intrigued by the harder approach.

Chapter Eighteen

The next day, Maria chose the most obscure corner of the library she could find. An auxiliary room apart from the main floor, set aside for the study and transcription of rare manuscripts. An unpleasant dust-mote patina lingered in the air that spoke to the room's infrequent use. No one could claim to wander in there by chance.

Nonetheless, it wasn't long before the same slender young man entered and sat down near Maria. If he thought she was going to let him get away with being her shadow this time, he was in for a rude awakening.

"You could at least tell me your name," Maria said to him, flatly.

The poor fellow looked like he'd just been thrashed upside the head. "I . . . ." He opened and closed his mouth several times.

"Well, you can talk, at least." Maria knew what he was feeling. If her father hadn't plunked her in front of symposiums on a regular basis, she'd probably still have been just as tongue-tied in the face of strangers. "Have you been wanting to talk to me all this time?"

This simpler question proved well within his power to answer. "Yes," he said, as though relieved. "There aren't . . . I don't usually see young people here. Or women. And you're—"

"Both of those things," Maria finished for him.

"Carlo," the young man said, as though it took the strength of Sisyphus. "I'm Carlo."

"Maria Gaetana Agnesi."

If he recognized the name or had heard of her, there was no indication whatsoever. Maria discovered she much preferred it that way.

"Pleased to make your acquaintance," he said.

The silence that followed lasted long enough that Maria could have declaimed poetry. The moment Carlo looked back down at his book, she decided she had to break it.

"You're a member of the library society?"

"Well, my brother is, technically. But . . . my . . . I . . . I'm interested in academics."

"I think that's admirable," said Maria, privately wondering about his field of study. He must have come to academics later than she did if he was still struggling with Latin. It was a foundational skill.

"Well, you must," he said. "I can't help but notice you're reading some very, very challenging mathematics books."

"I don't know if they're challenging, but they do require some reflection. What are you specialized in yourself?"

"Not Latin, clearly." Abashed, Carlo rubbed at the back of

his head. "I'm much better at French, but actually, it's history that excites me most. I'd love to be a historian."

Now there was a subject about which Maria knew very little. A rare thing for her. "Is there some particular time period that excites you most?"

Carlo did not even need a moment to ponder his answer. "Charlemagne."

Maria knew a little about him, at least. It was a very masculine sort of answer. "The French king with all the paladins and legends."

"The legends are what make him so interesting. King Arthur probably never existed, but Charlemagne certainly did. How could he not capture my imagination? A man so amazing that his story transformed into myth."

Carlo's voice and hands both grew steadily more animate here on a topic he understood. It offered him the opportunity to forget about himself and his own awkwardness. Once again, Maria reflected that this was a phenomenon she knew quite well.

He continued: "I've read near all the matter of France, and seeing the way the truth becomes fiction is just utterly fascinating. For instance, did you know that King Pepin . . . ."

Maria listened attentively. Carlo had a surprisingly rich voice once he managed to get the tremor out of it. Given the prize of a captive audience, he used that voice to sketch out images of chivalry and kings. Part of his mind lived in the bygone ages of crusaders and of Saracens, when violent and passionate people wrote their destinies by the sword. From Tours to Stamford Bridge, it had always felt to Maria that history was a pageant of the brutish and the foolish, only occasionally interrupted by the wise. The ancient preoccupation with conquest had always kept Maria disinterested. Yet Carlo spoke of these things with such vibrant immediacy that she felt it important to listen.

And so listen she did, content for now to let her book stay closed. It was not until the bells tolled that she realized she'd listened for an hour and did not feel the passage of time at all.

While Maria's mother had always walked to the convent, Pietro insisted they use the carriage. An important marker of status, he called it.

As the weeks went on, it became a familiar ritual: casual chatter with her father, the bouncing carriage, the plodding horses. They would reach the convent, Maria would bid farewell, and off her father would go to his business, only for them to reunite later at the library doors.

That week at the convent, Maria found her chores interrupted by the age-stooped figure of Mother Angelica. "You are truly taking to this work," she declared in a voice gone creaky with age.

"Hmm?" Maria, who had been reflecting on Carlo's latest tale—this about Cicero, the greatest senator of Rome—paused in her work. She'd been polishing candlesticks, of which the convent and nearby monastery had an incredibly large number.

"Every day it seems you get your work done a little bit faster and go to the library a little bit sooner."

Maria could only shrug. "Well, I suppose I look forward to it."

A knowing look sparkled in the depths of Mother Angelica's eyes. "We'll still be here when you get bored of whatever it is."

"I like it here, too," Maria said, breezier than usual. "Don't worry. I won't be disappearing."

"Our Maria seems much improved," Oriana told her husband, inspecting the new season's flowers. She'd insisted they have a planter installed, and she was always fretting about whether it got enough sun.

Pietro had only stepped out for air. He hadn't expected serious conversation and felt vaguely ambushed. "I'm not sure about that."

Leaning down to inhale the scent of roses, Oriana hummed. "The last month or so, she's been much less tense. There's not as much of that little frown she always wears. She's laughing more. She's even talking to the servants."

Pietro hadn't noticed any of that. An entirely different phenomenon concerned him. "Yes, about that."

Oriana straightened her back, up and away from the flowers. The ghost of a frown appeared on her face. "Must you ruin my belief that all is well?"

"I've spoken with Maria's latest tutor."

"The Jesuit?"

"He says that in the last two weeks, she's made no progress whatsoever. It's like she hasn't been studying at all. And when pressed, she has nothing but excuses."

Oriana gently grasped the stem of an especially thorny rose. "All in all, I consider that a positive development."

~

"You know," Carlo told Maria, seated near the mighty shelves of the Ambrosian Library, "I've talked a whole lot about history, but we haven't talked very much about you. Why are you studying so hard?"

Maria felt that she'd never studied less hard in her life. But perhaps that said something about normal people's standards. "I suppose it's just what I've always done. I have to fill the time somehow and—"

"Shhh," hissed the librarian whom Maria had come to actively despise.

Carlo modulated his voice down to a whisper. "That's not how most people spend their time. Most people prefer . . . you know, liquor, dice . . . ."

Maria knew such people existed, but she had never really spent much time around them. "I like structure," she said.

"Yes, you're always here at the same time, I've noticed."

Now it was Carlo's turn to earn the wrath of the librarian. "This is an important research library. I'm tired of the two of you jabbering back and forth like it's some kind of lover's retreat."

Maria practically squawked. "Lover's retreat?!"

The librarian raised a finger. "If the two of you insist on nattering on every day, I'll have your memberships revoked."

Carlo had turned a shade near to crimson. He may have grown comfortable talking to Maria, but other people remained a problem. "M-maybe . . . maybe we should go outside and talk there," he stammered.

Maria felt absolutely mortified. "Yes, I think that's probably the best idea going."

Standing in front of the library proved likewise too horrifying. After significant awkward silence, Carlo made a suggestion. "Would you, uh . . . maybe . . . walk with me, a little? I know this area pretty well."

Maria realized that despite coming here for some time now, she had only become familiar with the straightest, most direct line between the convent and the library. More time outside meant more time in the company of strangers. But Carlo was no longer a stranger, and his company no longer a thing to be feared.

"I'd like that," she decided.

And just like that, they were off. Dimly, part of Maria imagined her father wouldn't have approved of this outing, at least not without a chaperone to follow at a discreet distance. Oriana probably would have given it her full-throated and enthusiastic support.

"You're thinking about your parents," Carlo observed with a bit of a smile.

Maria, rounding a street corner beside him, found that startling. "How did you know that?"

"Because you do everything to schedule. You've pointed that out before. When was the last time you didn't do something they planned in advance?"

Maria realized she had no frame of reference for where they were walking, other than the great spires of the Duomo on her right. She'd spent her whole life in the city and explored so little of it.

"That's not true. I choose what books I want to read on the spur of the moment all the time."

"Ah, but you scheduled 'reading time,' didn't you!"

Maria scrunched her mouth. "I suppose you're right about that."

"So why all the studying, eh? You know I want to be a historian—what about you? Is there some scholarly man you're trying to woo?"

Maria shook her head far harder than she needed to. "No, much the opposite. I'm the one who wants to be the scholar. A professor, even. In mathematics, if I have my way about it. You can't imagine how deep a field it is. And how . . . ." She put apart her hands, gesturing at the small neighborhood church that was drawing closer ahead of them. "Even a building like that couldn't have been made without the mathematics that inform its architecture."

"And why do you want to do that?"

"What do you mean, why would I want to do that?"

Carlo gave her a bit of an odd look. "You don't know why you're doing the thing you've devoted your whole life to?"

Maria found her steps slowing. Momentarily, she lagged behind Carlo. "It's just . . . what I've always been working toward."

Carlo eyed her a moment before shrugging and closing the rest of the distance to the old neighborhood church. "Come over here."

Maria couldn't help but notice that the place was in disrepair. It looked like some of the doors were boarded over, and an incomplete scaffolding in back spoke to repairs started yet stalled. "You want to visit a church? I don't think they'll let us speak in there. It seems closed. Are we even allowed inside?"

"I don't see any signs telling us we can't go," said Carlo. "And I guarantee there will be no one who complains. I used to come here all the time as a child. They don't say services here anymore, but there's an old fellow who comes by to keep it tidy. And so do I, sometimes. You'll see why in a minute."

Carlo actually had a key to the place. Perhaps he too was a kind of volunteer. He slipped the key into the small access door positioned next to the full-size ones that would've been opened during services. It creaked unpleasantly as it opened. Maria went unworriedly along inside. In a town as devoutly Catholic as Milan, even empty churches were safe and protected spaces.

The inside had a strangely tranquil atmosphere. The afternoon sun hit the old stained-glass windows just right, beaming illuminated shafts of color into the empty nave. With all the candles doused, these shafts of light were the sole source of illumination, and they lent a fantastical air to the old half-cracked paintings depicting the Stations of the Cross.

"Not that," said Carlo, already headed elsewhere. "Up here!"

Maria followed him up a whitewashed stairwell, up and up and up, past narrow slots of windows. Only after a moment did she realize they were ascending a bell tower. Bemused, she held her questions, only hesitating to emerge out onto its platform.

On two sides, openings in the tower's stone revealed the

entire sweep of the city in all its intermingled poverty and prosperity. The palazzos of the wealthy and the insulae of the poor
were like a tapestry of lives, sprawling out as far as the eye could
see.

Incongruously, there was a writing desk taking up some of
the tower's limited standing space. Maria had to ask: "You work
here?"

"Well, used to," said Carlo. "My brother doesn't think it's
safe, since the façade's gone all crumbly, which is why he got me
a recommendation to use the library."

Maria found her gaze drawn inevitably back toward the city.
"Wouldn't it be your parents' opinion that matters most?"

Carlo rubbed at the back of his head, looking out the opposite window, as if averse to getting too close in the confined space.
"I'm afraid they both passed away when I was very young."

"Oh," said Maria, immediately feeling guilty for having
asked. "My mother . . . something similar happened to me, I
suppose."

Carlo didn't say anything. Sore subject, perhaps. Maybe his
brother had been looking out for him all this time.

"I think it's because of her," Maria suddenly blurted out.

That finally got Carlo to look away from the window.
"Hmm?"

"That's why I've always tried so hard to become a professor,
and to learn as much as I can. It's because my mother was a teacher.
That was her passion. Learning and teaching. So I suppose that's
why I've tried so hard to learn . . . well . . . everything."

"Well, I know for a fact my brother's pushed me toward either the academy or the clergy," said Carlo.

"I could see you as a priest," said Maria.

That made Carlo frown, which confused Maria, but she listened to him speak regardless. "He's in business, my brother. Shipping. He's always had to worry about money, since we didn't have our parents to rely on, and I think he wanted to spare me that."

"What sort of man is he? Your brother."

"Ah, everything I'm not. Tall, confident, outgoing . . . I always let him do the talking whenever I can. I think this is the most I've talked in ages."

"You're perfectly pleasant to listen to," said Maria. She suddenly felt embarrassed. The words had just sprung out on their own.

"You see, uh . . . ." Carlo trailed off.

Maria waited patiently.

"I spent a lot of time with him last Sunday. He knows all about where to buy things, and there was this particular thing I was wanting to buy." Carlo looked a bit green around the gills. He looked like he might need to lean over the side of the bell tower like a seasick man might lean over the rail of a ship. "There's this woman I'm in love with."

Maria felt her stomach sink. She'd never have imagined hearing such a thing would make her so unhappy. "Oh," she said distantly.

"A-and they say that the best way to show your love for a

woman is with a rose. Ask anyone, they'll agree. But I didn't want just *any* rose, I wanted the best one, and they say the rarest ones are blue, and you can't find those just anywhere, you need a specialty supplier. But it turned out they're not even *real,* so I had to settle for the next rarest, which is white. If it was me, I would have stammered my way through it all, but he grabbed me by the shoulder and got it all done."

"Well, I hope your someone is very happy," Maria told Carlo. "You're thoughtful, kind, and would certainly make a better scholar than you would a priest."

That compliment seemed to ease Carlo's nerves, even as it felt bitter in Maria's mouth.

"Come on," she said. "Let's get back to the library. It's almost time for me to leave. And I do need to respect my schedule."

For whatever reason, the walk back transpired in dreary silence. When they reached the door to the library, Maria found that neither of them could abide to touch the door handle.

"I'll see you tomorrow?" Maria asked tentatively.

Carlo did not answer with words. Stiffly, he thrust a flower toward Maria.

It was, to her intense surprise, a white rose, partially flattened by the time it had spent inside his satchel.

"I-I hope you will accept it," he managed to get out.

"Of course," Maria said quietly. And louder: "Of course I accept it."

The whole world was spinning around her. She didn't know how to describe what she was feeling. It was like the butterflies that always bedeviled her stomach, yet different. An anxiety not born of fear, sublimated into something else.

So preoccupied was she with the shape of the rose that she did not notice Carlo leaning in to kiss her until it was already happening.

Neither of them knew what they were doing, but Maria did not care. The firm, awkward, earnest kiss lasted for two whole seconds, but they were the longest two seconds Maria could remember. The tension in her stomach bloomed into a buzzing intensity of feeling that narrowed her world and quieted her ever-noisy mind.

She didn't know what to say to him when it was done. "I—"

But Carlo was already leaving. Unable to face the consequences of his own bravery, he retreated as fast as his legs could carry him, tearing off into the city.

No doubt this was a thing he had planned in advance. Days in advance. In fact, he'd probably meant to do it in the bell tower, but hadn't been able to work up the courage until the very last moment.

Maria leaned back against the wall of the library, hiding her smile by raising the flower to her nose. What a hopeless and ridiculous couple of people they were. And what a very lovely thing, the scent of a rose.

She did not have long to enjoy it before she became aware of a man-shaped figure in between her and the sun.

"I'm here to pick you up," said Pietro. His voice came out dead and flat, arms folded as he stared down at his daughter.

After he plucked the rose out of her hand, Maria had no doubts. He had seen the entire exchange.

206

Chapter Nineteen

It was now the fourth week since Maria had last left the house.

"This is excessive," Oriana told her husband, once again assaulting him with a jabbing, pointing finger. "You should be reaching out to the boy's family, not sequestering her away in here. For all you know he's a perfect gentleman."

Pietro ignored the pressure, both the physical and the verbal. He made a show of examining the book of sheet music he'd had shipped in from Vienna. "She can leave when she's caught back up with her studies. We'll find a place for her to spend her time other than that library."

Oriana could have torn out her hair. It was like dealing with one of their children, except he had bigger words to conceal his mistakes behind.

Pietro stubbornly insisted, "I'll not have my daughter get a taste for . . . carousing."

"If you think Maria's the one to worry about, then let me tell you some things about your second daughter . . . ."

Upstairs, Maria sat in her room, considering the desiccated remnants of the flower Carlo had given her. Already flattened from Carlo's bag, it had again been damaged by her father, who had left it thoughtlessly crumpled on the carriage seat. Maria had rescued it and fixed it as best she could, but a rose clipped from the vine could not last long without water. One by one the petals had dried out and fallen off, until only a stubborn, wilted few remained.

There were ways to preserve flowers, but Maria had never learned them. Such girlish arts had always felt beneath her.

Now it was mathematics and scholarship that felt pointless. She had spent days in a morass of emotion, drowning her sorrows in poetry. Her father had denied to let her see Carlo again, denied even to leave word at the library about where she had gone. Oriana took her side, but Oriana would never go behind Pietro's back to send word.

Day by day, Maria grew ever more worried that Carlo would think she had spurned him.

Pacing there in her room, she considered her options. Her brothers and sisters were too young yet really to go out unsupervised, so she could not trust them with the task. The servants and her tutors were all on her parents' payroll, and years ago Vittorio Bellone had demonstrated what happened to those who disobeyed her father's program. She would not have asked them to risk their livelihoods for her, even if she had believed any of them sympathetic enough to do so.

In the end, she could only rely on herself. She would go and see Carlo and explain everything, and return before anyone was the wiser. Among her various talents, time had borne out that she was very good at staying awake all night when she set her mind to it.

She donned her most practical and durable garments—the riding clothes for her doctor-prescribed outings. The tough, comfortable footwear gave her a certain confidence she'd never have had in her nightgown.

And then she waited. Hour by hour, children went to bed, servants went home or found their own rooms, and lights went out in all the house's windows. A shuffle of steps near her room indicated that someone was checking on her, but she'd doused her lantern well in advance.

It was a bit odd how easy it was. If this were a more dangerous part of the city, Maria might have to contend with household guards, but they'd never had any trouble at their house and her father had never hired anything of the sort. All she did was slip down to the bottom floor, slide open a window, and drop a few feet down. A little uncivilized, but the door was big and creaky and far more likely to give her away.

A single-minded clarity of purpose, combined with the relatively empty nighttime streets, kept her usual anxieties at bay. She knew the carriage route by heart, and without stopping at the church first she was able to cut down considerably on time.

It was only when she'd gotten close to the old neighborhood church that Carlo had shown her that she realized there were two fatal flaws in her plan.

First, she didn't know Carlo's surname, or his brother's name, which would make looking for his family residence slightly difficult. Second, she had absolutely no idea where he lived.

So much for calling up to his window.

She really could have been more rational about this, Maria chastised herself, rubbing her elbows. Matters of rationality were supposed to be her specialty.

Eventually, after a touch of blind wandering in the hope that she might somehow run into him, the latent danger in what she was doing caught up to her.

She had always felt safe from violence on the streets of Milan. But she had only ever spent time on its broadest and brightest streets, in the bustle of day. Even she had heard the odd story about what might happen to lone wanderers after dark. Straining her ears, she could distantly hear the raucous, drunken laughter of people stumbling out of some kind of liquor-house, and decided she had a choice to make.

Rationality did not enter into it. She *had* to see Carlo. What was it Caesar had said in Carlo's tales of history? *Alea iacta est.* The die is cast.

Soon enough she found herself again in front of the Ambrosian Library. She would wait for first light, when the librarians came in to clean the place, and leave a message for Carlo. There would be hell to pay at home, but it was a hell she was willing to suffer.

Near the library, a hay cart sat unattended, out of the view of the open street. There she sat, resolved to wait.

~

"I told you," Oriana all but howled early the next morning. "I told you that you were being excessive, and now you've only yourself to blame!"

"Be quiet, woman!" Pietro had no patience for the shrewish bullying of his wife, not right now. His daughter was in danger. "We need a plan. We should send for Zanobi. He's done security for our shipments before. His men can be everywhere in the city looking and we have the money to hire the lot."

"Listen to yourself!" Oriana never got up this early, but Pietro had to admit he'd made quite a fuss. "Sending out crime fighters to hunt down your own daughter?"

"Do you have a better idea?"

Pietro paced the room. How long had Maria been gone? She got up earlier than any of them—her schedule demanded it—and none of the servants had seen her leave.

"I knew that boy was a problem the moment I laid eyes on him," Pietro continued. "She said he was some kind of orphan. For all we know his family *are* criminals. He's a bad influence."

"No, Pietro, darling." Oriana had suddenly become very calm. "What I need you to understand is that *you* are the bad influence."

This accusation was so sudden, so uncalled for, so ridiculous, that all Pietro could say was "What?"

"As someone with significantly more experience in being a young woman than you, let me tell you something. The interest of young men is normal. Not the political, fiscal, scheming sort of match you were trying to sort out for her years ago, but the honest feelings of the heart. She had just felt that for the first time, and you took that away from her."

"She'd lost all discipline," Pietro said, though the words weren't coming out as persuasively as he desired. "For weeks she'd been on a downward slope. It was only right to intervene."

"No. You were the one who'd lost, and what you'd lost was control," Oriana said, placing her hands on Pietro's shoulders.

Pietro promptly removed them. "Maria is in love with learning. You'd let her lose sight of that?"

"Perhaps," said Oriana, "she had taken a moment to be in love with *love*."

Pietro found himself scowling. His anger had run out, and with it, his clarity about what to do. Perhaps he had judged the boy too quickly, but that wasn't the issue now.

"We still need to find her."

Natural light struck Maria's closed eyes from above. The sun's needling warmth proved enough to rouse her from her sleep.

With a half-muted yelp, she rolled off the hay cart. The hay cart! She'd fallen asleep in a hay cart. Could there have been a more trite and ridiculous failing? She wished she had more experience with foul language so she could curse herself with greater fluency.

Checking herself over, she found straw clinging to her clothes, her hair a mess, and about her body there lingered an overall odor of horse. Wonderful. She was sure to impress Carlo now.

Undeterred, she emerged from the mouth of the alley. It was still early in the day—likely too early for him to be there.

An aging attendant near the door stepped aside for Maria. It took a moment for him to recognize her. "Sleepless night, signora?"

"Not exactly," murmured a self-conscious Maria, once again patting herself down as she stepped inside.

It had been a month since Carlo had last seen her. He must be worried about her.

Or what if he was mad at her? Would he be mad at her? The thought was enough to summon back up the roiling sea of worry that so often lived in her stomach.

She glanced quickly at the desk where the stern young librarian so often lingered. Blessedly, she was gone. There was no sign of Carlo, either.

That could be a blessing. It would give her time to come up with something clever to say to explain what had happened. But before she could sit down and compose her thoughts, she needed to check the whole building and make sure he wasn't there.

Crossing from the main collection into the annex, she found the accursed librarian. She was not alone. Maria would have believed her to hold all the passion of old granite, but she was in the process of messily kissing a young man.

The young man was Carlo. He had not let a month apart go to waste.

Maria could only stand there. Her mind had gone blank as white canvas. As white as the rose the librarian was holding—a far fuller and more beautiful specimen than the one he had given Maria.

It did not take long before the librarian noticed Maria staring. Pulling back abruptly from Carlo, she flushed with embarrassment.

Carlo did the same. But when he saw who had caught them, his embarrassment turned to dread. "Maria?"

No doubt he had an excellent explanation. Maria did not stay to listen to it. She turned and left, all her thoughts muffled by a disquiet sea of feeling.

Pietro had finally resolved to go and hire every problem solver in the city when his daughter quite suddenly and unceremoniously came home.

"Maria!" he called out to her as she shut the front door behind her. The feeling of relief that flooded through him was nearly enough to knock him off his feet.

But Maria didn't say so much as a word. She marched right on upstairs to her room, with all the grace and vivacity of lead.

Chapter Twenty

"I am afraid I have reached the peak of what is possible with strictly Milanese learning," Maria told her parents, as businesslike as you please. The Carlo incident had done very little to improve her relations with her father, but as the months went by, even though no one spoke a word of apology out loud, peace had returned to the Agnesi household.

Family dinner was always an involved affair. So many children necessitated a very long table, even with some of them still too young to join in the proceedings. Pietro had hired a full-time chef years ago.

"Francesco, not so much, you'll make yourself fat," said Oriana, pointing down the table. Her own stomach was currently enormous, but not for reasons of diet. Another child would soon grace the family. Maria privately wondered if eventually she would have so many brothers and sisters that they'd no longer all fit in one dining room.

"Are you saying you're ready to apply for university

admission?" Pietro wasn't skeptical; far from it. He'd long anticipated the day.

"No," said Maria. "I'm still perhaps too young. It would be too much to ask them to make multiple exceptions on my behalf. Rather, what I need is the help of a particular tutor."

"Name him."

"Ramiro Rampinelli. He is a monk of the Olivetan order and one of the very foremost scholars in the field of infinitesimal calculus. We've been exchanging letters for years."

Pietro considered this. "I have heard of him. If he is interested, find out what he needs and I will make the necessary arrangements."

Savio, the oldest of Maria's brothers, scooted his chair back. It made an uncomfortably loud noise scraping along the floor. "Food was good. I've got things to do. I'll see you all later."

He was still young. This was an exaggerated imitation of an older man's confidence.

Oriana frowned. "Savio, you are not excused. Sit down and wait for your family to be finished."

But he was already gone. Oriana looked to Pietro for support and found none present.

"Boys will be boys," Pietro said, permissive with his male children in a way he never would have been with Maria or Teresa. "Do you think our next child will be a boy? You've guessed right almost every time."

Oriana did not answer him. She looked down the table. "Lucrezia, darling, would you please pass the salt? There's a good girl."

∼

That evening, Oriana took Maria aside to her ever-expanding rose garden. "I need you to do something for me," she said earnestly.

Maria felt stiff and cold and would rather be in bed with a book. The winter air did not agree with her. "How can I help?"

"Your next brother or sister is going to be born very soon," Oriana told Maria, gravely serious. "As such, I expect I'll be preoccupied with both that and the newborn for a time. I need you to start taking a more leading role with your siblings."

Maria grasped her own elbows to better warm them up. "Don't we have a whole bunch of servants whose only job is to keep track of them?" She had never felt comfortable having the ever-growing fleet of them around.

"Yes, but they need someone to direct them, and frankly, you're smarter than all of them. Plus, you need something to do that isn't work."

A certain statuelike impassivity came over Maria. "I am perfectly content with my work."

"Maria." Oriana's features softened. "I want you to understand something. Your father feels awful about what happened with that boy. You shouldn't let it hang over you."

If he felt so very awful, thought Maria, then why hadn't he made any effort to apologize?

"He's not good with his emotions," Oriana went on. "I think you understand a little bit of what that's like."

"I have decided I would prefer not to have emotions," Maria

muttered, which sounded as ridiculous as she felt. Her father wasn't the only one against whom she nursed resentments. Carlo had not even waited a month before throwing himself at someone else. He had seemed so awkward, so earnest. Had all of that been an elaborate pose?

"Maria."

"I'll look after my brothers and sisters. It's the reasonable, responsible thing to do." Maria exhaled, thinking of the nuns at the convent. "And the Christian thing to do. You can count on me."

"Good, good," said Oriana, beaming a smile. "Just, ah, keep an eye on Savio. He's reaching that particular insufferable age."

"This is stupid," Savio told Maria, feet on the table, fingers laced together behind his head. "I'm going to just set all our books on fire."

Maria looked up from her work, seated not far from him in the study. Teresa, Julia, and all the rest were content to either amuse themselves or follow the curriculum that she had provided. Some were so young as to still be with devoted nannies. Yet for whatever reason, her eldest brother remained intractable. At fourteen years of age, he was shooting up like a weed, and rapidly gaining the rangy muscle that came from the roughhousing trouble he got into with his friends.

Just to show that she was still in command of the situation, Maria did not hasten to reply. She finished writing her current sentence, cleaned off the nib of her pen, and delicately returned everything to its proper place. "We both know you're not going to set our books on fire."

"Watch me do it. I'd be saving everyone a whole lot of trouble. I already know how to talk, count, and lace my boots; what's the point of the rest?"

It occurred to Maria that although she had defended many scholarly notions, never once had anyone asked her to justify the very existence of scholarship. The matter left her temporarily tongue-tied. She tried another tactic.

"Your mother is giving birth right now," she pointed out to him. "Don't you think it's a little selfish to whine that people expect things of you?"

"I'm not like you," he grumbled sullenly. "I'm not smart. Hammering facts into me is just a waste of everyone's time."

A momentary flash of resentment bubbled up inside of Maria. It had been decided very early in her life that she would be an icon of an entire movement—a living justification for a woman's right to an education. She had to be as wise as Athena and as learned as Hermes Trismegistus. She had given her entire life to the pursuit of learning, to better please the God who had given her the gift of intellect. She enjoyed learning, but learning demanded everything of her. And here was her brother, annoyed he had to learn the most basic Latin and long division, the absolute bare minimum scholarship necessary to prepare him for assisting his father's business.

"It's your duty," she told him, with all the feeling she'd so recently decided not to have.

"Sod duty," he snorted, putting his feet up on the table and crossing his boots at the ankle. "Who gives a toss about what other people want me to do?"

This was more than Maria could bear. She took up that old reliable teacher's aid, the ruler, and thwapped Savio's feet. "Off the table."

All of Savio's braggadocio vanished, replaced by the whining she remembered in him as a child. He yanked his boots back and clutched at one foot. "Ow!"

"I'll be back to check on this later and I want to see every last line complete. Do you hear me? All of them!"

"Yes, ma'am," Savio grumbled, holding up his hands to preemptively ward off any further assaults.

Fuming, Maria left the ruler on the table and stalked out of the room. She knew Savio would never be an earnest, enthusiastic scholar. But his antipathy for the subject matter stirred up her resentment, and she knew that if she stayed she'd say nasty things.

In the next room, she looked in on Julia, Livia, Lucrezia, and Teresa, all of whom were studying quietly, just as she'd asked. She could rely on Teresa to keep the younger girls in line, at least.

At the foot of the stairs, she noticed a familiar man. It was one of the physicians who'd helped see to her seizures. He wasn't a full doctor, but a doctor's assistant, even though he was starting to get a bit up there in years.

She asked him: "How's it going?"

He looked down at Maria and grinned. "As easy as always. Your father brings in a whole army of help every time your mother's pregnant, but he needn't really go to such lengths. I suspect Oriana would be all right even all on her lonesome. What is this, her thirteenth child?"

Maria didn't have the heart to tell him that Oriana was not her mother, or that this fact was precisely why her father insisted on having so much help on hand. "Something like that," she told the man, suddenly melancholy.

He said something else, but she didn't hear it. She drifted away and eventually realized her feet had taken her to the same room where she'd prayed with the Princess of Austria. It still saw very little use, but remote and quiet as it was, it remained the very best place in the house to pray.

Maria did so now, considering the old scarred-up Byzantine icon. After the customary Pater Nosters and Ave Marias, she asked for forgiveness for her impatience with her brother, who clearly had his own trials to overcome.

For her whole life, Maria had never once doubted the existence or the goodness of God. Not everyone seemed to be so blessed. Many folk had a tortured relationship with their Heavenly Father. In Maria's case, it was her more terrestrial father who insisted on giving her trouble.

But all the same, God commanded His faithful to honor their father and mother. Maria knew perfectly well how she could please Pietro. But sometimes she wondered if she was doing enough to please her departed mother. Anna Brivio had the benevolence of the most altruistic nun, and there was a year when Maria believed the best thing she could do was take the vow of Holy Orders herself. Her father had gravely forbidden it, and certainly his symposium compatriots found the idea equal parts disappointing and mystifying.

Knowing that God watched over her made Maria feel like all her efforts were that little bit more worthwhile. That her diligence would someday matter, even when no one else saw it. She supposed that some folk resented that God did not more noisily and directly answer their prayers, but perhaps they should have paid closer attention to the Bible. When God felt compelled to personally intervene, things were usually going very, very badly in the world.

She could not shake the unhappiness that lived in her heart. It happened every time a new child was born. After it was done, she was always full of joy to see the new baby—but the hours before it happened made her think of her mother. Sometimes, as she got older, she worried that she no longer really remembered what her mother was like, and instead only remembered a memory, filtered by repetition until it only vaguely resembled the truth.

Sitting there, mind upon God and her family living and dead, she suddenly felt all the hairs on her neck begin to rise.

Maria could not shake the feeling that someone else was there in the room with her. Once, she had seen a cat slowly move its head to track something unseen, as if it could see a ghost's slow progression across the room. Maria began to realize she was doing exactly the same thing. Without thinking, she watched nothing at all, and heard nothing at all, eyes moving in a slow line from the door to the empty chair beside her.

She was a rational woman. But nothing she felt in that

moment was in any way rational. Instinct propelled her to leave the room at once.

Footsteps hastened by some intangible anxiety, she moved through the house and back to the stairs, where the doctor's assistant had left.

Her brother Francesco was going up the stairs, and for some reason, she had a horrible feeling about it.

Maria hustled up after him, holding up her skirt partway so she could take the steps two at a time. As she got high enough, she heard the crying of a newborn child and the bustle of the physicians. Francesco, no doubt, was eager to be the first among siblings to lay eyes on the newborn babe.

From down the hall, Maria saw the moment he reached the doorway, and his joy turned to horror. He immediately began to wail.

Dashing toward him, Maria closed the distance and scooped him up. Immediately, she put a hand over his eyes. But she couldn't help but look upon the scene herself.

Blood was everywhere. Maria remembered the smell of it. A metallic, coppery malaise that put her immediately in the throes of nausea. A midwife held the red and screaming newborn child. The white bedcovers had turned to scarlet—Maria could scarcely imagine so much blood was ever inside a person. Two men held down Oriana's arms, while a third dug into her midsection with some horrible steel implement, twine from another sutured wound discarded nearby. Oriana bit into a wooden paddle, her cries of pain muted to a primal growl, as she endured whatever they were doing to her without the benefit of anesthetic.

"You don't need to see this," she told Francesco, but she was speaking to herself. Images of one dying mother overlapped with another in her mind, threatening to blot out the world. She retreated from the room, speaking words of consolation, not really knowing what they were. Francesco howled, and the other children lined the hall, drawn to the doorways by his insistent, near-screaming cries.

A dozen insistent eyes looked upon Maria, seeking guidance.

"Mother is having a hard time," she told them, nearly buckling under the weight of the understatement. She tried to endow her next words with the power of conviction. "But she is fighting. We need to be strong for her. All of you come with me—we're all going to pray and ask Saint Raymond for his holy intercession."

While the children prayed, a silent tap on Maria's shoulder saw her ushered from the room.

It was the physician's assistant, all business, sober in the way of the best doctors. "We had to perform a Caesarian section," he whispered to Maria. "Do you know what that is?"

"Yes," whispered Maria.

"The procedure was a success."

"Good," whispered Maria, without feeling.

"You are young, but you are an old and sober soul, so I will be honest with you. Her chances are not the best, but there is still a fighting chance. So we will all of us be looking over her."

"I will take care of the children," Maria promised, speaking not to him but to God.

"See that you do," he murmured softly. "Your father is inconsolable. I've given him a sleeping tonic. When he wakes, I will tell him you have everything in hand."

Maria, looking upon her brothers and sisters, dearly hoped she did.

Chapter Twenty-One

Oriana battled for her life in the days that followed. Maria battled to keep the household running. She saw to the children's lessons, managed their meals, and gave them all the encouragement they needed, even when she felt more in need of it herself. She might not have had to be so responsible were it not for a certain person's absence.

"My father has not left his room, or hers, since this began," she told the head servant, standing in the otherwise empty kitchen. She had steadfastly resolved herself to her new role. "I am the eldest child, and as such I intend to take control of household matters until current troubles are resolved."

The head servant, a gray-haired man named Giorgio, wore small, pinched-looking spectacles. "With respect, signora, Savio is the eldest son and would thus have the right of precedence."

"Savio is still a boy, and even if he pretends to be a stoic, in private he's crying over his mother. We don't need to put duties on him."

That put a solemn look on Giorgio's face. "I suppose you're right. But I do have six years' experience in my position. You may leave managing the servants' work to me."

She had already planned to do as much. What she'd wanted to see were their master schedules. And the other children's. She was certain such things must exist.

But then, while she'd lived her whole life under the tyranny of schedules, not everyone else cared for such strict organization. All of that structure hadn't sheltered her from trouble, either. Perhaps she should take current events as evidence there were some things you could never plan for, no matter how regimented your life was.

"I'd like to see my father," she told Giorgio.

Giorgio hesitated to reply. "I would advise against that."

She could only imagine how difficult it was going to be. "Let him know I'll be coming up in half an hour."

Giorgio found this an acceptable compromise. "I will do my best to . . . resuscitate him, my lady."

Maria intended to spend the next half hour in prayer. Every priest and nun she'd ever met swore by the power of prayer. And though it might be a jealous desire, she had only one want in her heart—that God not take away her mother for a second time. Even Job only had to lose one family.

She went to the faraway room that contained her mother's icon—but to her surprise, it was not empty. Julia was there, fussing over her favorite doll. She was not yet seven, and while several of her siblings were afflicted with ruddy, tear-reddened faces, Julia had remained as calm as you please.

Julia looked up at Maria and asked: "Do you think Mamma is going to die?"

Maria felt like she'd been slapped upside the head. Only a child could ask the question so directly. "I don't know" was all she could say.

Julia spoke her next words to her doll instead of to Maria. Perhaps that was easier for her. "I went upstairs to say goodbye. But Mamma told me I shouldn't get ahead of myself, and she'd be around a long time yet."

Maria felt a stinging heat at the corners of her eyes. She refused to acknowledge the tears. She wouldn't look weak in front of her sister.

"We don't know what's going to happen," Maria told Julia. Maybe no one ever really did. "All we can do is hope."

The doctors wouldn't let more than one person into Oriana's room at a time. They'd admitted the children in reverse order of age for short visits, supposedly to keep Oriana from straining herself emotionally or physically. A priest had come to say the final sacrament yesterday, and though a fair amount of time had passed since then, he had not returned. Maria dared to hope that this was a good sign.

Julia didn't have an adult's vocabulary, not like Maria did when she was her age. "I'm hoping pretty hard" is what she said, as calmly as she'd said everything else.

Maria decided to leave before she really did cry in front of her sister. With a gentle word of encouragement, she slipped out, found the nearest empty room, and furiously rubbed at her eyes. Only after a few minutes' steady breathing did she feel prepared to soldier on.

She visited each and every one of her siblings in the minutes that followed. The prevailing mood in the house remained grim. Some of the children tried to distract themselves with half-hearted work or play, while others were wholly consumed with grief. Teresa would not even speak to her, absorbed in highly technical practice at the harpsichord.

Eventually, Giorgio came to take her to her parents' rooms.

To her surprise, the place was extraordinarily tidy. Pietro, slumped in a chair that seemed suddenly too big for him, was likewise immaculately dressed. This, no doubt, was all Giorgio's doing. Deep, dark circles under Pietro's eyes spoke to his grief. It was entirely possible he had not really slept since Oriana's trial began. A series of empty wine bottles on a side table and a certain lingering redness in Pietro's nose indicated that he had not gotten through by force of will alone. Maria had never known her father to drink very much—two glasses, even, was a rarity for him.

"Recent events," said Pietro slowly, "have me reflecting on my failings as both husband and father."

There was a speech he wanted to give. Maria's toes tingled unpleasantly, urging her to be somewhere else. "I just wanted you to know that I'm taking care of everything with the other children."

"That's good," said Pietro, "very good. You've always been . . . ." Words escaped him. "A very good daughter."

Maria did not know what to say, either. "Thank you."

Silence divided them for an uncomfortable interval until Pietro spoke again.

"I always wanted what was best for you. I hope you understand that. I wanted to help you achieve your dream. But Oriana told me last night that I was the one who chose that dream for you. I suppose she might be right. And the cost of it—God forbid you might get sick tomorrow, too. Then what will all of it have been for?"

"Oriana is still fighting," Maria reminded him. "She's getting better. I'm sure of it."

She was sure of nothing of the sort.

"And then I selfishly paraded your genius in front of all my acquaintances like it was somehow my own doing, and not yours. I pushed you to exhaustion, telling myself it was all your idea. I went too far, and I want you to know that from now on, you'll be the one to decide what you do and when."

Maria thought of Julia and Savio and Teresa and all the other children, all showing their grief in their individual ways. However much she loved learning, trumpeting her erudition never helped any of them.

"I'm done with appearing at public functions," she told her father bluntly.

"That's fair," he muttered, rubbing his face.

"And the children need more help. I want to help them. Someone should be there to teach them, educate them. Someone who really understands them."

"You're doing it again," Pietro said, suddenly irritable.

"Stamping down on your own wants to help other people. You've sacrificed enough. You should do what *you* want."

"And what if what I want is to help my family?"

"You should start your *own* family. I stopped whatever was happening between you and that boy and I've been too much a coward to admit I was wrong. If you want to get married, I'll support that, too."

Recent events had driven home to Maria the frightening risks that might accrue to motherhood. "I would sooner be a nun," she said, surprised to find she meant it.

"I cannot approve," said Pietro.

So there were limits to his new permissiveness after all.

"This is all extremely premature," said Maria. "I'm going to go ask the doctor if it's safe for me to see Oriana."

Pietro grew harder to hear the longer he spoke. "They all but forced me out to let her sleep. A thing I cannot abide to do myself. I wonder . . . ."

He closed his eyes to select his next words. Eventually, Maria realized that exhaustion had caught up with him, and he'd fallen asleep in the chair. His chin lolled to one side, head sunk at an uncomfortable angle.

Maria tucked a cushion between his cheek and the chair, leaving him to rest.

"Fifteen minutes only," said the ancient white-haired doctor. "Say nothing to overly excite her humors. She is in a delicate balance."

"I saw the worst of it, so I know," Maria told the man.

They stood together just outside the door. She was a little

closer to him than she needed to be, but she wanted to project confidence. She felt that if she acted the part long enough, truth of being would follow.

"Fifteen minutes," said the doctor, holding up a finger.

"Fifteen minutes," Maria repeated, opening the door.

She was not sure what she expected—for Oriana to have aged ten years, or to once again be confronted with the stench of blood. Instead the room was fresh and tidy and filled with the sharp scent of wild herbs, these no doubt meant to ward off the "bad air" often thought to cause disease.

Oriana sat covered up in bed, smiling pleasantly. One could almost imagine her well, if not for the absolutely ghastly pallor of her face, or the fact they had taken her baby away from her. She had lost a lot of blood, and the body could not restore it quickly. Her voice came out weak and small. "Hello, my dear Maria."

"Hello," Maria spoke back, trying to be brave. "I've been doing what you asked. It seems to be going all right."

Oriana laughed brightly. For a moment, she looked wholly well—but the exertion caught up with her, and she all but collapsed back into the cushions. "I suppose I won't be getting up just yet."

"You're better than I expected," Maria had to admit. She didn't want to be too positive. She knew that, too, could come off as worrying. Everyone lied to the dying.

"Feeling better all the time, but I'll admit I'm in an enormous amount of pain," said Oriana, like someone complaining about the weather. "I won't be hurrying to have another baby, I'll tell you that much." She dared to ask: "How is my newborn, Sofia, doing?"

Maria saw no reason not to be honest. "She's sleeping a lot. And she's crying a lot."

"It's an amazing thing about being a parent. You always forget about the screaming and the teething and the spitting and all the rest of it. All it takes is seeing your baby asleep, looking like an angel, and you think: What I wouldn't give for another."

What you might give for another could be your life, Maria thought, but did not say. She felt guilty just for the thought. To her, it seemed a terribly awful one.

Impulsively, Maria gripped Oriana's hand. It felt cold between her fingers. Oriana squeezed back, a tenuous strength still present in her hand.

"I'm sorry," Maria said.

Oriana looked bemused. "For what?"

"For being . . . me. I haven't always been easy to deal with. But you always did your best." Maria had to close her eyes to speak her next words. "Thank you for being my mother." Even though, for the longest time, she'd tried not to let her.

Oriana's smile could rival that of the saints in art. "Ah. You're fine, Maria." She brought up her other weakened hand to clasp Maria's between both of hers. "You're fine, just as you are."

After that, Oriana wanted to hear all about how her rose-bushes were doing.

Chapter Twenty-Two

With some effort, Maria marshalled the house into working order. She'd always had a talent for memorization, and she knew the temperaments of all her siblings from years of quiet observation. Constructing a daily tempo for the house grew easier and easier the more she did it.

Days passed, and though Oriana struggled, she still lived. Pietro, with his worst fears unrealized, snapped out of his stupor. All things seemed to be getting back to normal.

So it was on that morning that Maria woke up, consulted her schedule, and found that she did not want to do any of the things written on the page. A week ago, she would have forced her way through it and thought it virtuous. Today, Maria turned the paper over and thought about what she might want to do instead.

Immediately she caught herself trying to construct a grand, extensive plan. There would be none of that, she decided at once. She picked up a wide-brimmed hat and left the house.

She wasn't sure where she was going. The idea made her

faintly dizzy. She'd just told Giorgio that she would be back later, and left.

What a simple thing. But it was only the second time in her life she'd decided to go out without a plan, and the first with the sun up in the sky.

Despite the light on her skin, the winter cold turned her breath to vapor. Bundled up for the weather, however, she found she did not mind at all.

The world in winter had a different cast to it. Even the color of sunlight seemed somehow more pale. There were much colder places in the world than Milan, but here and there a touch of frost lingered upon bushes and planters, while tiny rivulets of water had frozen on the undersides of iron bars and poles.

Much as she often did, Maria realized she had never really explored the city. Nor would she today. She felt a specific need to visit a specific place, to satisfy a curiosity that had lately lived within her heart.

At the convent of Santa Maria delle Grazie church, Maria found immediate welcome. At her request, she was delivered to the common room attached to the sisters' quarters. A great fire roared within.

Mother Angelica looked almost like a turtle, trying to shrink down into her wimple and habit. Only her hands were raised, to take in the heat of the fire. The winter cold was less kind to the elderly.

Maria was not used to doing things on the spur of the moment. She leaned on formality. "Reverend Mother Abbess, I hope you will favor me with an audience."

Mother Angelica slowly looked up from the fire. The usually stern old woman's expression slowly gave way to a mischievous smile. "Goodness gracious, if you wish to confess your sins, you are in the wrong place. You will need the brothers for that."

"A long time ago you showed my mother a certain famous painting. I was too young and stupid to appreciate it. I would like to see it again."

Mother Angelica very slowly rubbed her hands together. "You are many things, young mistress Agnesi, but your problem was never that you were too stupid. I have seen it before with initiates: Your problem is that you are too smart."

Too smart. This was not an idea that anyone had articulated to Maria before.

Nor did Mother Angelica elaborate on her thought process. More lithely than her stooped posture would lead one to expect, she sprang to her feet. "Well, let's be about it, then."

Maria hadn't expected this. "Right now?"

"It's the dead of winter. When else?" Mother Angelica walked to the hallway. "Sister Helena!" she hollered. "Fetch the keys!"

Maria had already gotten to know Sister Helena. She was the youngest initiate, the one with the big brown eyes she had met on previous visits. Helena came trotting up now, with an almost comically overabundant ring of keys. It rattled in her grip.

"Oh, Maria. You're not here to do more volunteer work, I take it?"

"Not today," said Mother Angelica, before Maria could find a decent answer of her own. "We're to show off the Leonardo."

"Again?" asked Helena. "Isn't there a rule it's only to be shown so many times a—"

"The wonderful thing about being in charge is that I am able to amend the rules." Amused with herself, Mother Angelica told Maria: "The brothers call that 'pastoral practice.'"

Maria dipped her head in gratitude, not trusting herself in repartee with Mother Angelica. This was a side of the woman she'd never seen as a child.

Crossing out of the nuns' quarters and through hallways and annexes, they soon reached the dim, sealed-off room that contained Leonardo da Vinci's dying masterpiece.

It looked, if anything, slightly dingier than in Maria's memory. She was not sure if it was a product of the pale winter light or the intervening years, but it seemed all the more faded. There were more sumptuous paintings all through the city, both new ones and old ones.

And yet . . . .

Looking upon the face of Christ and his apostles, Maria *felt* something. She was not quite sure what she felt, exactly. Was it pity? Sympathy? A vague feeling of resignation? She could not put her finger on it, but perhaps this was what separated the true master from the merely talented: the ability to endow art with emotions not readily defined.

"It's crumbling," Maria said, suppressing the urge to reach out and touch the paint. "Why is it in such bad condition?"

"Leonardo da Vinci was obsessed with his work," said Sister Helena. "He would work on the same piece for years. Supposedly he would wander the streets for weeks just trying to find the right face models. According to the records we have from past brothers, when Leonardo was asked to hurry up this painting, he threatened to give Judas our abbot's face."

Maria could admire that level of stubbornness. "But how does that explain the crumbling?"

Mother Angelica's voice came out raspy. "He developed a new method of painting directly on the wall, without a need for canvas." She spoke emphatically: "It does not last."

The words struck Maria harder than they should have. *It does not last.*

Her mother hadn't lasted. Oriana had survived her surgery, but she would not last, either. When she died herself, her memory of them would not last. People made masterpieces to leave an immortal legacy, but what did it mean when a master's greatest work soon flaked away to nothing? The laws of mathematics, perhaps, were eternal. But mathematics had told Maria nothing about how to actually live her life.

Feeling oddly dizzy, a question came unbidden to Maria's mouth. "Mother Angelica, how does one choose whether or not to be a nun?"

Mother Angelica was taken by surprise. She cleared her throat, almost wheezing. "We speak of the process as 'discerning a vocation.' You're familiar with the phrase?"

Maria nodded. "I've thought about it off and on."

"The most important thing is to regularly set aside time to sit and pray and be honest with yourself about whether it is what you want. If it is what you feel called to do. When we search our hearts for our own desires, we will often discover what God intends for us."

Maria could only admit that she had no idea what God intended for her at all. It was like Oriana had said: Maria had always let other people show her what they wanted, and tried to figure out how best to fulfill expectations. She had no idea what she wanted for herself.

"I'd like to be alone with the painting for a minute, if that's all right," Maria murmured to the nuns.

Mother Angelica, faced with Maria's earnest request, could only agree. "As long as you need."

Maria stayed behind, meaning to pray. But her mind kept coming back to her family, both living and dead.

Eventually she cried, not quite understanding why.

It took time before Maria felt ready to face the nuns again. She wasn't sure if she wanted to be one, but she admired one thing about them all: They had each made a very difficult and significant choice to don their habits, each of their own volition.

Perhaps she truly would enjoy being a mathematics professor. But there had to be more to being a professor than just knowing mathematics. And certainly there was more to living. She quietly resolved to find the answers to all her questions.

When she finally left the convent, the sun was lower in the sky and a carriage was outside waiting for her. She hadn't sent for it.

It had only just arrived. Giorgio exited the vehicle, hustled halfway up the steps, and stopped when he saw Maria.

"Your father was confident I'd find you here," he said, in the urgent way of a man with unhappy news.

"I'm fine," Maria assured him, hoping it was only her father being worried about where she'd been.

Giorgio gestured at the carriage. "It is best that you come immediately."

Even a week of giving orders had left Maria with greater confidence in taking control of a conversation. "Best also that you explain immediately."

That took Giorgio aback for a moment. "It's about your mother," he told her, holding open the door.

This was exactly what Maria had feared. She felt her stomach fall out from under her, but with her eyes only recently dried, neither sadness nor fear could find a hold on her. There was only sudden, grim acceptance. "Is she finally cleared to get out of bed?"

"She was recovering from surgery, but—"

Maria demanded: "Tell me directly."

"It seems that despite that recovery, she has suffered a late-manifesting infection of the blood."

"But she was fine! She was getting better!"

Giorgio could only hide behind platitudes. "It seems God had a different plan."

Surgery always carried with it the risk of infection. Science did not know the root cause of such fevers, but every incision was a roll of the dice. The procedure Oriana had undergone bore a higher risk than most. If fever had set in, then the outlook was already dire. Modern medicine still had no tools to reliably treat or prevent such a thing.

It was tantamount to a death sentence. In the end, Maria would need to bid farewell to her mother for a second time.

Robust to the last, Oriana battled stubbornly for her life, but this time there would be no recovery. Maria had once thought her stepmother a fool. Only too late had she come to understand her strengths.

Soon, Oriana fell into a sleep from which she would not wake. Only Pietro and the doctors saw the moment of her passing.

The family had already mourned Oriana while she was still alive. Now that she was well and truly gone, what descended upon them was a more quiet kind of grief.

Alone and empty, Maria desperately hoped she might yet understand what God meant for her to do.

Part Four

FINDING A CALLING

Chapter Twenty-Three

"You will all see on your slates a series of mathematical problems," Maria announced, clacking her chalk twice upon her own slate for emphasis.

She stood at the front of what had become the family classroom, a place of her own design. From the desks to the individual handheld slates, every last detail was a thing Maria chose herself. She felt especially particular about the slates. In the age before blackboards, such handheld tools remained a key instrument of group instruction.

Julia made a low noise of dismay upon seeing what she was expected to solve. The other children were already puzzling out solutions. They knew from experience that no amount of complaining would satisfy Maria—only an earnest attempt at results.

One of her acquaintances outside the family had thought it excessive to build a classroom inside their house, but Maria now had no less than nineteen brothers and sisters, and she had long ago made her intention clear: She would see to their education personally.

The oldest children in the family no longer had need of tutoring, but the classroom remained in use.

"It's not fair," said Julia. "I shouldn't have to solve the same thing as someone with years more practice." She glanced pointedly at Francesco.

"Well, I'm glad to hear that you are no longer looking over his shoulder to get your answers," said Maria, with a warmth that she hoped took the accusatory edge off her words. As a teacher, she couldn't abide cheating. "If you did, you'd have noticed that I made a unique set of problems tailored specifically to everyone's age and ability."

Julia made a little grumbling noise as some of her brothers laughed.

"I'll give you twenty minutes," said Maria. "Remember to show your work, Francesco."

Francesco showed great promise as a mathematician. He had that quality Maria had realized was rare a little too late in life: an intuitive sense for calculation. If he only applied himself enthusiastically, he might be a great professor or intellectual, but his heart remained fixed on the battlefield. He still wanted to be a soldier, God help him. Men were dying left and right in a stupid and pointless war, and all he wanted to do was throw his own life away.

Maria watched him scribble with chalk. He wore a dissatisfied, put-upon frown. He had to have known she challenged him more than the others, and he clearly felt it was unfair.

Hovering there wasn't making it any easier on them. "You have twenty minutes," she declared before stepping out of the room.

Ever since Oriana's passing, Maria had taken on more and more of the duties of running the household. She'd found herself both adroit and content in the role. But it did mean juggling several different responsibilities.

Without delay, she cut a straight path to the kitchen.

There, Giorgio was overseeing the cooks. His hair had lately begun to change from gray to white. He now looked like a distinguished older gentleman and some of his children were beginning to have children of their own.

Maria asked, "Did we finally get those spices we were needing?"

"Yes, of course," he replied smoothly. "And the game birds and the new utensils, and the necessary table settings to reflect your father's current ideas about developments in textile fashion."

She could always rely on Giorgio. "Very good. Remember, there will be a full family dinner tomorrow evening, with certain of the Brivios attending."

Giorgio looked for a moment like he would give a rote reply. But instead, he looked Maria up and down for a moment. "May I have permission to speak candidly?"

Maria did not answer verbally, but her gesture made her intentions plain.

"It's not right, you needing to be in charge of everything. The education, fair enough. No one's cleverer than you. But the household—you are not the lady of the house. Carlotta is."

Carlotta. Her father's third wife.

"Giorgio, how old am I?"

Giorgio looked aghast. "I could not be so rude as to give a lady's age."

"I am thirty years old, Giorgio. How old is Carlotta?"

Giorgio slowly leaned back. "I could not be so rude as to—"

"Carlotta is twenty-five. And if I am being perfectly honest, I believe I have spent more time taking care of her children than she has."

"She is also currently in Venice," Giorgio was forced to admit.

Other women might have spent a long time nursing resentments about their new stepmother. Maria had already done that once in her life, and she refused to waste time on it again.

"It looks like you have everything in hand here," she said. "I am going to the classroom."

That night, Maria pondered her failures as a teacher. Mathematics came to her as naturally as breathing. Teaching someone with true talent was like grasping them by the hand and taking them on a merry tour of the countryside. Teaching someone like Julia, who had neither talent nor love of learning, was a bit like trying to hammer a round peg into a square hole.

Maria still used the same lamps she did as a child, but she did her best not to stay up until midnight. The flickering oil flame revealed the pages of four different mathematical tomes. Each of them took a different approach to the fundamentals of calculus. Each of them was uniquely wrong or misleading about one thing or another. How, then, to give the children the best possible study material?

She'd bought a second copy of each book. Painstakingly, with the occasional aid of a penknife, she excised the very best pages from each one. Even more painstakingly, she'd cut single key paragraphs from otherwise dull and meandering passages. She had all the elements of the perfect textbook here, if only she could figure out how to reassemble it.

A knock at her office door interrupted her thoughts.

"Come in," she said, startled, standing up.

A young and furious Francesco entered. Taller than her in his late teenage years, he stuck out his chin to further accentuate the difference in height.

"You're angry," Maria prompted.

"The war may have just ended," said Francesco. "A draft treaty is being sent to the Imperial Diet."

He said this like it was bad news.

"Which means that my chance to represent our family's honor is well and truly gone. I hope you and father both feel very proud of yourselves."

For eight years, half of Europe had been dragged into battle over the question of whether or not Princess Maria Theresa should be allowed to rule the Holy Roman Empire. Or at least that had been the question at the start. As usual, men with power had long nursed designs on foreign lands and riches and waited only for a suitable excuse to start throwing away men's lives to take them.

Maria despised war. Its wages were never more than folly.

"Our family was obliged to provide a son to the army, and a son they got. Your father needs you here to help with the business."

"He didn't and he doesn't," Francesco fired back. "Savio went off and volunteered before you could stop him and you've used that as an excuse to control me ever since."

"Yes, and how did that work out for Savio?"

Francesco averted his eyes. Savio had come back from Silesia blind in one eye and missing the better part of an arm. Everyone pretended he was the same, but there was no bringing back what he'd lost. Eventually he had left for an extended stay at the country estate of his wife's family.

"That's why I need to go," said Francesco. "You don't understand what's at stake."

Typical masculine stupidity. Maria breathed out lengthily. "Of course I understand what's at stake. Better than you, I daresay, since I know our empress personally."

That took Francesco aback. He'd never known Maria to leave the house for anything except for church and charity.

Maria got up and began rummaging through her old papers. Even at age thirty she still hadn't constructed a truly organized filing cabinet. "In fact, for a time, I regularly exchanged letters with her." Back then, she had been too young and naive to appreciate the gravity of the honor, or the promises it implied.

Eventually, Maria found the old letters. Not without a certain pride and satisfaction, she set them out on her desk, along with the drafts of her replies.

"It's true," said Francesco, eyes wide as he touched a fingertip to one of the letters. "It's really her signature and seal."

CHAPTER TWENTY-THREE

Maria smiled. "Do I seem like someone who's in the habit of lying?"

Francesco turned his head away. "No, I just . . . ."

"Sane people do not start wars, and if they must fight them, they do it to keep their people safe. I have no doubt that the empress feels exactly the same as I do." That was a slight exaggeration; they had never written about war. "If you truly, desperately want to join the army, that is a conversation to have with your father, not me."

Francesco scowled. "No one can have a conversation with him about anything these days."

"That's not true," she lied.

"I'm going to bed," Francesco announced, leaving with no further ado.

Maria had not really spoken to her father for weeks. Speaking to him these days created no small number of difficulties, but on the plus side, his sullen distance did nothing to stymie her. Their arrangement was simple. She ran the household, he ran the business, and she studied only at her own pace, for her own amusement.

Maria had resolved to try to live life in the way she found most gratifying.

Was it time to write again to the empress? Would the princess have time for such a letter?

She dipped her pen into the ink, considering the possibilities. The urge to write was upon her, but she had no interest in burdening the woman already burdened with war.

Her eyes returned to the scraps and cuttings and loose pages of mathematical treatises that had now all been stacked in the corner of her table. There was always that project. She felt certain that she just needed one last piece to fall into place before she'd have it all figured out.

Perhaps she had been thinking too small. That was the problem, she suddenly decided. All her life, she had been obsessed with absorbing other people's words.

What were *her* words?

Maria knew her sisters far better than men who had died one or more centuries ago. If she wanted them to have a textbook, well . . . she might as well just write it herself.

Chapter Twenty-Four

"You wrote a whole book?" Teresa asked Maria, incredulous.

The two of them sat next to Oriana's old rose garden, drinking tea. Maria had lately grown fond of the practice. Like her father, she found wine had too strong an effect on her mind.

"You make the project sound so grand," Maria said. "I just started on page one and I kept on going until I was done, with lots of starts and stops in between."

Teresa wore an extraordinarily fashionable wide-brimmed straw hat, the latest thing in headwear. Its slight tilt nearly shrouded one of her eyes. The pale blue ribbon tied around its center only accentuated its rustic appeal. In France they were apparently calling them *bergère* hats, and they were the very peak of fashion.

"Downplay it all you like, but I couldn't imagine putting so much work into any one project." Teresa puffed lightly on her tea, holding it close to her lips without drinking.

"You won't burn yourself," Maria assured her. "And what do

you mean, you can't put so much work into a project? You slaved over the composition of *Il Ristoro d'Arcadia* for what must have been a whole year."

"I suppose," said Teresa, as averse to direct praise as her older sister.

"It debuted at the Royal Ducal Theatre with nobility in the audience."

"I suppose," said Teresa again, still avoiding eye contact.

"It was well received and I saw it, too, and you should be very proud."

Teresa set down the teacup without drinking from it. She braced her hands atop the outdoor dining table. "Maria, do you remember when you recommended my work to the princess?"

"Yes, ages back. She mentioned that she'd be happy to hear you play someday." Maria hadn't thought this to be a platitude.

"I have my heart set on the Viennese stage. With the war done, and having debuted at a major venue, I believe it's time for me to try my fortunes in the capital."

A little bit of her old pervasive anxiety quivered through Maria at the thought of going off to Austria. It felt as far away as the mythical kingdom of Prester John. "You know I haven't heard from the empress since before the war began, yes?"

"Yes, and now it's over." Teresa grinned, full of the infectious confidence that came to her so easily. "What about you? Don't you feel ready to be a professor? After all that fuss, you never even applied to university."

"I'd rather be a nun," Maria said earnestly.

"That again?" Teresa pretended to gag.

"What's wrong with being a nun?"

"What's stopping you from *being* a nun?"

"What's stopping you from getting married?"

"What's stopping . . . ?" Teresa trailed off, incredulous. "Me, getting married? How old are *you* again?"

"A lady does not give her age," said Maria, thinking of Giorgio.

"Yes, well, last I checked, we grow older at the same pace, so I've got a good idea."

Maria nursed her tea to absolve herself of the need to retort. Only after a short time had passed did she speak again. "The book isn't revolutionary or anything. It's simply a guide for the instruction of new students in calculus."

"I can't say I envy the little ones, having you as their teacher. I got off easy."

"I'm not so hard on them. And some of them aren't so little."

"Well, I can't say our father is doing you many favors forcing you to take care of them."

"He's not forcing me. It was my idea." Maria thought back to her conversations with Mother Angelica about whether or not she ought to take a nun's vows. "It simply feels like what God wants me to do right now."

That bothered Teresa for some reason. She sunk back in her seat, sighing. "You say that with such real conviction, Maria. Meanwhile I've never felt certain God has paid attention to a single one of my prayers."

Maria echoed the sigh. "I could recommend you to my spiritual director, if you think that would help."

"No more religion," Teresa said emphatically. "And just between you and me, I hear that Carlotta might be coming back tonight."

Well, at the very least, that might make her father easier to deal with.

A cloud lingered over Pietro, as it always did when his wife was not in town. Though he had found success as a young man, age eventually caught up with him, as it did with everyone. Oriana's death had put at least ten years on him. Wrinkles and white hair did much to change the way he looked. He was now over sixty.

His latest wife was less than half his age.

"I hear Carlotta is set to return soon," said Maria, visiting the room Pietro had lately taken to moping in. It overlooked the street, allowing him to stare out in appropriately gloomy and introspective fashion. He did so now, chin resting in his fist.

"If she should choose to return at all. It's because of me that she takes all these holidays and pilgrimages, it must be." Pietro's voice came out low and without inflection.

"I think that's perfectly inaccurate. She's always very happy to return. It's simply the lifestyle she's accustomed to as the daughter of a diplomat."

"Happy to return only because she knows she will soon depart again. She considers me a distraction at best."

A daughter should not need to be the emotional bulwark for her father, Maria thought to herself, trying not to be too impatient with him. Conversations like this never got anywhere.

CHAPTER TWENTY-FOUR

On the other hand, he always returned to form when Carlotta at last arrived.

"If she holds you in such disregard, it seems unlikely you would have had multiple children."

"You should get married," Pietro said, not for the first time. It was an old and losing battle; at this point, Maria knew she was an utterly unmarriageable "old maid."

"I believe that would be slightly challenging," said Maria.

"Nonsense. Find a widower, somebody mature and clever who would appreciate your gifts. You're still young enough to have children. It would bring you happiness."

He made it sound so very simple and straightforward. Maria did not know a single man in her circle of acquaintances, or her father's, who had quite so many children as he did. Happiness eluded him regardless.

"I also wanted to let you know that I've agreed to take on more students," Maria said.

That got him to look away from the window. "What? More students? You said the youngest weren't—"

"No, you misunderstand. Students from outside the family. It seems the children are outperforming all of their peers, and my old reputation is still worth something. Some of their friends' parents have asked if their children might join my courses. If you'd like, I've prepared a list for your approval."

No doubt he had all sorts of ideas about whether they were of the right social strata, or of sufficiently prestigious families.

But an enervated Pietro only made a cursory glance at the

paper. "No, that's all right," he said, turning his eyes back out the window. "I trust your judgment."

By midday, the family classroom had grown to contain no less than twenty-five students. They were all of various ages, though the greater problem proved not to be variation in skill, but rather getting them to stop talking to each other.

Maria had considered bringing out the new textbook she'd designed—it had been a work quite some time in the making—but she decided it was better to wait. She left it in the library, pondering over how much work it would be to get copies made for all of these students. Would it be better to copy it out long-hand? What was the smallest print run one could commission, anyway? She knew nothing about publishing.

But today was not a day for mathematics. Today was the day for French. Be it the most basic verb forms or the most advanced constructions, in language there was always something more to do. For some of her more promising students she had even gone so far as to combine disciplines—giving the books *in* French on other scholarly topics.

Everything went very well. There was just one small problem: Midday gave way to afternoon and marched relentlessly on toward evening, but there was no sign of Carlotta.

Long after the children went home, the young lady of the house still had not returned. Maria dreaded to see what this would do to her father's mood.

❧

That night, Pietro did not attend family dinner. Fearing another episode of gloom, Maria sought him out—but he was not so easily found. The house was large, and she did not find him in any of his customary haunts. Instead, he had holed himself up in the library.

Inside, he greeted Maria with a huge, enthusiastic smile. "Maria!"

This was not at all like him. Had the stress grown too much?

"That is indeed my name," she said, mystified.

"Don't give me that look." Pietro pounded a hand on the book beside him. "You've been holding out on me!"

Maria had to study it for a whole five seconds before she understood what she was looking at. "You've been reading my book."

Pietro's hands had an animating enthusiasm that had of late proven elusive. "It's brilliant! Absolutely brilliant."

Maria immediately found herself filled with the desire to be somewhere else. "Hardly. It's longwinded, inelegant, and doesn't have a single original idea."

"The business about the one curve—the *versoria,* you called it? I'd never seen that before."

Why did this sound so much like her conversation with Teresa that morning? "Nonsense. Pierre de Fermat had that one all figured out years ago. All I did was describe it."

"Selling yourself short as usual. What you've created is nothing short of a masterpiece. It's like an elegant summation of all the world's mathematical knowledge."

"You're swooning over a teaching aid. It's just a tool for me to help better describe things to my students."

"Yes, but we're all of us students at some level or other, aren't we?" Pietro, practically thrumming with enthusiasm, struggled to posture at nonchalance. He steepled his fingers together. "I'll admit there were parts I struggled with myself. It's been decades since I had a look at really abstract calculus. I have a friend at the local university, and I was wondering if you'd be all right with me taking the book for him to review."

Maria had seen this play before. "No." The word came out of her mouth sharp and firm. "Absolutely not. I have no interest in showing off. I made it for a purpose, and I'll use it for that purpose. No more intellectuals fawning over my work."

Pietro's happiness slowly and visibly receded from his face. Resigned, he sunk back into his seat, sighing melodramatically. "Fine," he said at last. "Fine. I won't take him the book."

He massaged his temples as he watched his daughter leave the room.

The girl had no idea just how smart she really was, even after all these years. Her book, with a bit of refinement, could become an international standard. He'd never seen calculus described with such persuasive clarity.

Her being like this was his own fault. He knew that. He'd pushed her until she got sick, and it had put such scars on her that she still distrusted her own excellence—which was only to be expected. The pursuit of excellence had brought her more pain than joy. Fame and prestige meant nothing to her; she saw only the stresses that fame demanded.

He was on his feet now, pacing. Oriana had made him promise to let Maria do what she pleased with her life. To not make his dreams her dreams. But he couldn't tell if Maria was still living in his shadow, even now—by running away too far in the opposite direction.

Ultimately, he decided, she should at least be allowed to know how brilliant she was. She should be allowed the opportunity to see her as others saw her. Only then could she truly make a clear-eyed decision.

Maria talked often to the children about learning what God wanted them to do with their lives. Pietro believed ardently that He would not have given her such an extraordinary mind just to spend life in a cloister, or to live in her own house as if it were a cloister of a different kind.

Resolved, knowing with grim certainty that neither Anna nor Oriana would have approved, he took out some paper and began to transcribe the cleverest bits of Maria's book.

After all, he'd only promised not to take the book. He never said a thing about her ideas.

Chapter Twenty-Five

Six teenage children in tow, Maria entered the Ambrosian Library, where she still held a membership after all these years. Blessedly, the dour librarian who had once bedeviled her was long gone. Instead, it was one of her very few friends who received her.

"I was delighted to receive your request," said Sister Helena, once a young initiate and now a full sister in her own right. "It's so hard dragging you out of the house."

"I keep busy" was all Maria could say, though she knew it a failing.

Helena knew better than to complain. "Anyway, this should be fun. Usually it's a bunch of stuffy dignitaries who get to see the private collections, so it's nice to see some enthusiastic young learners."

"Say hello to Sister Helena," Maria quietly instructed her siblings as they moved past the main library and into the back hallways of the building. She hoped they proved as enthusiastic as Helena gave them credit for.

Julia could not long contain her surprise. "Your old friend at the library is a nun?"

"Technically not a nun, but that gets very specific and you didn't come here for theology," said Helena, beaming at all of Maria's assembled siblings. "You weren't kidding when you said you had a big family."

"There are fourteen more of them, actually," Maria had to admit.

Helena gasped. "Fourteen . . . *more*? How could . . . ." She trailed off, agog.

"My father remarried twice. I believe Mother Angelica would have suggested he 'feels called' to raise a very large family."

"Twenty . . . twenty-one children? How does he have time to get anything done?"

Maria watched Helena's efforts to open the door at the hall's end, debating whether she should say it was all thanks to her tireless efforts. It might be taken as boasting, or as complaining, when really she meant it as neither. It was just the way things worked out.

Francesco cleared his throat impatiently. "I was told there would be art."

Lucrezia, who lately fancied herself a painter, blinked her heavy-lidded eyes. "Is it true you have a set of originals by Tiziano?"

Finally mastering a stubborn lock, Helena pushed open the door with a creak. "We most certainly do. Our pinacoteca would not have been possible without the tremendous donation of Cardinal Federico Borromeo's complete collection, and we have everything from the *Adoration of the Magi* to original Leonardo manuscripts."

Maria, sensing her time to play the part of teacher had come, stepped ahead of the children. "Now, remember what I was explaining about the art of the Venetian School . . . ."

Only after a complete tour did Helena finally consent to let Lucrezia set up her easel and attempt a sketch in imitation. With the other children looking over her shoulder or distracted by other parts of the collection—Francesco, for instance, grew quite fixated on trying to decode the gothic lettering of an illuminated manuscript—it allowed Helena and Maria a moment alone.

Maria had to thank her. "Private showings like these are usually reserved for very important folk, so I'm quite grateful that—"

"Oh, come off it. You *are* very important folk. Even if you don't realize it."

"I'm just a teacher," Maria insisted, wondering why she said it with such force.

"Yes, yes, just a teacher." Helena had no interest in retreading that debate. "Remind me, how many years did it take you to work up the will to step in here once I took a volunteer position with the society?"

Maria didn't see how that was relevant to anything. "Just one."

"A whole year! And you'd been paying dues for years before that and not using the membership, just because some silly thing happened here once with a boy."

Maria felt her neck and ears growing hot. She studiously

avoided eye contact with Helena. "How do you know about that?"

"Let's just say I grew curious about why a woman who loves books should be terrified of our city's very finest library, and made certain inquiries."

Helena was not the only one who made inquiries. Maria, wishing to leave the whole business forever behind her, had eventually discovered that Carlo no longer attended the library, and that his brother Mario had inexplicably packed up and left for Savoy in the west and presumably taken the family along.

Such estrangements happened frequently. Maria did not pine for Carlo, even if she sometimes grew curious about what might have happened if they had been free to pursue romance. Other young men here or there had caught her eye since, but over the years she had never felt called to marriage.

Nonetheless, the memory of it all darkened her mood.

"You're off in your own world again," said Helena, nudging Maria with her elbow. "Look, my point is that you let things live too large in your memory. You hated the pain of rejection, so you avoided the place where it happened and all attention from men to keep yourself safe from that pain."

"I hardly think that's fair," said Maria.

"You hated being your father's pet genius, so you quit giving public lectures. I can't blame you for wanting to stay away from things that make you uncomfortable. But God's wish—"

"I thought we didn't come here for theology," said Maria, surprised with herself. That was a far snappier retort than she usually ever considered.

"God's wish is that we become more like Christ, and the path to Christ lies on the other side of suffering. You must embrace the pain and pass through it."

It was a very devout thing to say. Maria, being devout, could find no fault with it. That did not mean, however, that she had to agree, or be happy about it.

"Fifteen minutes," Maria called to the children impatiently.

"But I've only just started," Lucrezia almost whined, hard at work on her imitation of the bygone master.

Returning home, Maria let the children stream inside ahead of her. Her legs felt little better than lead as she crossed the threshold and shut the door behind her.

"Maria!" came Pietro's voice, filled with uncharacteristic cheer. "Come here, will you?"

Maria trudged to the sitting room. Inside, her father sat in one of two overstuffed armchairs, the other occupied by a man Maria had never seen before. A distinguished older gentleman, his suit coat showed the kind of elegant imported brocade that had lately become fashionable.

The gentleman asked Pietro: "This is her?"

"There's someone I would very much like you to meet." Pietro beamed his brightest smile.

Maria could feel her stomach drop so deep, she was amazed she didn't turn inside out. Her father had been speaking to her about marriage, about children, about finding some kind of widower. Had he decided to try to arrange this with one of his acquaintances?

Struck still, Maria could only stammer. Flailing for a coherent reply, her eyes eventually affixed to what the man held in his hand. It was a book. The very same book she had spent so much time writing.

"Allow me to introduce myself. I am Ignacio Vicari, the head mathematician at the University of Bologna. Your father was kind enough to show me some fragments of your treatise."

A dozen objections warred for primacy in Maria's mind, but one thing stood out to her most. "Bologna? You came all this way in person?"

"Yes, and I'm afraid I had no choice. I wrote to your father for a full copy, but he steadfastly refused. Said he made a promise not to send it out."

"That was very lawyerly of you," Maria muttered to her father, feeling slightly betrayed.

Pietro, for his part, at least had the grace to look abashed.

The visiting professor either did not apprehend the nuances of the situation or had chosen to brazenly ignore them. He repeatedly patted the cover of the book. "I've been reviewing this since my arrival this morning, and it is even more elegant in the long form than it was in excerpts. It's absolutely splendid. My dear, let me tell you, I have not been this excited by a book in years."

"You're being too kind," said Maria, believing it. "It's only a teaching tool. I give lessons to my siblings and a few of the other children who live nearby, and I wrote it for them."

"Well, I daresay they must all be brilliant. I've never seen someone so concisely interweave both differential and integral calculus. They are usually treated as completely separate disciplines, but you have shown persuasively that they go hand in hand, and shown step-by-step why it is so. It's the finest teaching tool I've perhaps ever seen."

"Well, it's not finished yet," Maria said, self-consciously adjusting her sleeves. It was not only her father who could be lawyerly with words. She knew her statement was only true in the strictest sense. She had a few minor corrections and additions to make, but the vast majority of the text was final.

"All the better," said the professor. "I've come here to tell you it would be my pleasure to help you prepare it for publication. As an official university offering. Were you not the young woman who gave that famous speech in defense of women's education?"

"Yes, that was me," Maria was forced to admit.

"You have proven that speech to be not just a challenge to orthodoxy, but also a prophecy of your own future. Your work already exceeds that of some of our staff. You absolutely have a future—no, let me say, a *destiny* in academics."

Pietro gently folded his hands together, beaming his biggest, proudest smile. Once upon a time, Maria would have done anything to bask in its glow. Now it made her irritated.

"You are very kind, and you have given me very much to consider," she told Professor Vicari. "I can't make a decision so significant so quickly."

The professor grossly misinterpreted her words. "Ah, already working with someone else, are you? Or perhaps you've got multiple offers for partnership? Allow me to ensure you my name would not appear in the text. The achievement would be wholly yours. In fact, I would be happy to show you some of our past work; I took the liberty of bringing it with me from Bologna."

"I'll send word when I have time to look," Maria promised him. "But I must discuss this with my father now."

"Yes, of course, of course. A great pleasure. I hope to see you again soon."

Maria waited until he was gone before shedding her polite smile and turning a much more grave expression upon her father.

"Don't look at me like that," said Pietro.

"I told you quite plainly. I am happy living my life the way I do now. I have no interest in academia."

"You're lying to yourself."

"And you lied to me. You promised you would not send out the book. And do not prevaricate in your businesslike way—you know precisely what I meant, even if I did not phrase it as a contract."

Pietro, maddeningly, still wore a look of satisfaction, basking in the residual glow of seeing his daughter so highly praised. "I have told you more than once before that I have made many mistakes as a father. I meant that, and it is true. But this was absolutely not a mistake."

Maria, standing, looked down at her father in naked disapproval.

"You're the best daughter I could ask for. Kind, dutiful, brilliant. And extraordinarily giving to your siblings. But you should be allowed to do what *you* want to do."

For the first time in years, Maria shouted at someone. "I

have told you already, and you will not listen—I am *doing* what I want to do!"

Not once in her life had Maria taken such a tone with her father. For a time, it struck Pietro silent.

The sound of the family's old standing clock, the one they'd had ever since Maria was a child, ticked loudly in the room.

When Pietro spoke, he spoke very quietly indeed. "You are lying to yourself."

Maria felt like she had been slapped. "And what is that supposed to mean?"

"I am not clever enough to write this book. But I am clever enough to understand it." Pietro picked it up and gently turned its pages. "You tell yourself you wrote this book for your brothers and sisters, but they are all too young to understand it. Not clever enough to understand it. Except perhaps Francesco, and he's the same as you. He insists on running away from his talents."

There was a kernel of truth in all that nonsense. Despite months writing the book, Maria had yet to find a way to integrate a single line of the text into her lessons. She had not even realized it until that moment. The realization angered her.

Maria silently cursed Carlotta for not coming home and distracting her father.

"God gave you a gift, Maria. You should share it with the world."

"I am done with chasing after academia. I wrote this to unclutter the attic of my mind. That's all."

Pietro sighed lengthily, age showing on his face, which had

lately begun to accrue more wrinkles. "You are a grown woman. You can make your own decisions. But I know that this is what God wanted for you to do."

Maria took the book from him and tucked it under her arm. She had heard enough talk of God for one day. A faint ringing in her ears, a faint nausea in her stomach, she retreated to her bedroom. There, she distracted herself with the lines and curves of equations until she forgot about the pressures of the world.

Chapter Twenty-Six

Despite her father's appeal, Maria persisted stubbornly in her role as neighborhood teacher. Weeks turned to months, but his words nonetheless needled her. He'd spoken one undeniable fact: She never did find a proper use for her treatise in the classroom. For some of her students, even long division proved a trial. She couldn't hope to teach them calculus.

The morning found her at her writing desk. As a child, Maria would spend even Saturdays in study, but she could not manage such a pace with so many young learners. There was much more to being a tutor than simply standing before a room and declaiming knowledge. Those lessons needed to be prepared, student work needed to be reviewed, and solutions had to be concocted for the weaknesses of each individual learner. Understanding everyone's personal style was a bit like solving a puzzle, and teasing out the solution always felt rewarding.

Alas, she despaired of ever getting Lucrezia to hold numbers and letters straight in her head. Reviewing the girl's work, it seemed like characters on the page invariably got jumbled out of order every time she did anything with them. Maria resolved to have a word with some of the volunteer teachers who did work through the convent to see if any had encountered a student with similar problems.

The sun had scarcely moved halfway to its zenith when Giorgio knocked on her open door. "There is a visitor here to see you."

Maria immediately worried it was that professor again. "For me?"

Giorgio nodded very slowly. "He insists that you come to see him immediately."

The mystery of Lucrezia's fuzzy numbers could wait for a later hour. Maria got up and moved to the stairs. She let her shoes clack a little louder on them than usual.

Standing in the house's foyer was a dangerous-looking man with a brick of a jaw. Maria had never seen him before in her life. His shoulders seemed almost too wide for his body. Unmistakably a soldier, he wore the white-and-red uniform of the Imperial Army.

Maria's mind turned to an entirely new set of fears. Had Francesco finally made good on his threats to run away and join the military?

The man boasted the ramrod posture common among the most disciplined soldiers. He spoke in gravelly German. "You are Maria Gaetana Agnesi, eldest daughter of the house?"

She had to admit she was.

"You are summoned to the palace of Milan by order of the Archduchess of Austria, overnighting this evening in Lombardy. You have fifteen minutes to prepare."

Maria hadn't expected much when she sent off the letter she'd discussed with Teresa. She also couldn't help but notice that Teresa had not been summoned along with her.

It occurred to her rather quickly that the longer this man stayed in the house, the more likely Pietro was to notice his presence. The last thing she needed was for him to muscle in on matters, especially if he was in one of his darker moods.

"No sense delaying," she said. "Let's be off immediately."

A carriage had been provided. The soldier said very little in response to her inquiries. Evidently, military affairs proceeded on a strict need-to-know basis, and he had simply been ordered to pick her up. On the subject of *why* she might be summoned, he proved not at all helpful.

The carriage ride was long enough for her to develop any number of ideas. Perhaps she was to be leveraged in forcing the family to pay off imperial war debts, as the Brivio family once had. The notion that Empress Maria Theresa Walburga Amalia Christina of the most revered House of Habsburg just wanted her over for tea seemed vanishingly unlikely.

The one time she'd met the woman was the better part of twenty years ago. She didn't really remember all the details. How much etiquette would be expected of her?

As when the empress's late father had visited years before, the palace swarmed with foreign soldiers. This was no surprise. A monarch did not travel without their personal guard. Initially, the presence of so many firearms worried Maria, but her muscular chaperone cut a path straight through all the musketeers to the decadently painted audience chambers that lay within.

Maria found herself deposited within a too-large sitting room in which resided only a lonely sofa and chair. No doubt the wasted space was meant to both reinforce the scale of ducal wealth and intimidate the visitor for good measure.

Not quite brave enough to immediately sit down, Maria busied herself with looking at the heavenly splendors depicted on the ceiling. The slow rotation required to take it all in inevitably brought her hip into contact with the furniture.

Choking back a rude exclamation, Maria looked around slowly to make sure no one had seen her moment of peril. In fact, there was no one present to see her. Her minder had slipped off while she'd been distracted by art.

A doorless archway at the far end of the room led deeper into the palace complex. She told herself she would behave herself and stay put, but boredom has a way of testing one's resolve. The longer the minutes dragged on, the more curiosity compelled her to go and have a look. Inevitably, look she did.

The moment proved serendipitous. At the end of a long paneled hallway, Empress Maria Theresa hissed at a shrinking servant. She was trying to be quiet, but between the excellent acoustics and her naturally loud voice, the sound carried well.

She demanded: "My husband is *where*?"

Forehead visibly sheened with sweat, the servant held up his empty hands. "V-v-visiting an old friend and confidante of the House of Lorraine is what he told us. You must understand, he is the emperor and we did not think to question his—"

"You will go and find him, and you will find whatever young lady he's with, and you will bring them both in front of me. *Now.*"

"Your Highness, that might prove slightly—"

"I don't care if you have to use the grenadiers! Go and get it done!"

Wilting under pressure, the man bowed in the formal, courtly style. "Yes, Your Highness."

By the time the Holy Roman empress arrived in the audience chamber, a slightly worried Maria had already retreated into one of the empty seats. With royalty now present, she just as quickly sprang back up to her feet to curtsy.

The empress weathered the courtesy and deposited herself in the armchair. Even her thoughtless flop had a certain imperial grace. This was no small feat, as rich living across the intervening years had left her with a much wider frame than Maria remembered. All the displeasure over her husband's escapade had vanished from the empress's face, replaced by simple and genuine warmth.

"Ah, Maria Gaetana, we meet again. Look—we've both of us gotten dreadfully old."

The familiarity felt strange to Maria. A pleasant kind of strange, but strange nonetheless. "You do me great honor simply to remember my name, Your Highness."

"Yes, well. I've got a whole fleet of people whose job it is to remind me about these things." She made a dismissive little gesture with her fingertips toward the halls beyond. "Not that I'd forgotten you, mind. I would be remiss to forget one of the great geniuses of our generation."

"I'd hardly go so far as to call myself a genius. Just an early bloomer."

"Ah, but what a bloom! You were—are—an inspiration to all women."

Maria fidgeted in her chair, about to retort, but the hand of the empress stalled her words.

"There is a limit even to Christian humility," the empress told her, eyes sparkling. "I will not allow you to denigrate yourself or your talents in my presence." A little too amused, she added: "As your empress, I demand this."

Some people had an instinct for politics. Maria had never been adept at reading people's expressions. For all she could tell, the empress really was interested in nothing more than catching up.

"I am truly sorry, Your Highness, but if you are here to praise my pursuit of academics, I admit you may be disappointed. My interests have changed somewhat since I was a child."

"Is it not always so? So, no longer a mathematician, then." There was a certain light in the empress's eyes that Maria did not quite understand. "What holds your passion now?"

"I take care of my family," Maria said, unable to be anything but honest.

"Ah! My fleet of people, it seems, were remiss in not mentioning anything about your marriage."

Maria felt more and more at sea with every exchange. "No, no, not married. I have no children. I meant my brothers and sisters. We lost . . . my mother, and their mother . . . and there are twenty of them, so . . . I sort of took charge."

"If my father had produced so many sons and daughters, history would have been very different," said Empress Maria Theresa, suddenly grave. "All those young men dead, Silesia gone . . . ." She shook her head. "But never mind that. Time and toil will settle all woes. Know instead that I am in the fullest and warmest support of large families. If I could die surrounded by dozens of grandchildren, nothing would give me greater joy. Franz and I are hoping for our tenth child."

Maria thought back to the heated exchange in the gallery. "You must love your husband very much" is what she said out loud.

One would never imagine the thought of infidelity had crossed the empress's mind. Her smile could rival a saint's. "Oh, more than I could ever describe."

Oddly, she seemed to mean it with every fiber of her being. Theirs was surely a complicated relationship. "It must be challenging to be both mother and empress."

"Oh, at first. At first. I let all the fools and sycophants my father surrounded himself with run things, believing them wise. I was younger than you are now when I took the throne—much younger. Their advice caused the deaths of thousands. To be pregnant is a battle itself, but to be pregnant at war, give birth between battles, and yet sit on the throne . . . well. I taught them what I was made of."

Made of a stronger substance than I am, thought Maria, who had taken three decades to fully overcome her fear of stepping outdoors.

The empress straightened her posture. "Circumstances have forced me to rapidly become a fine judge of character. Let me tell you, Maria Gaetana Agnesi, though you speak little and doubt much, the spark of intellect is in your eyes. You are familiar with Laura Bassi?"

This much Maria had expected. "Yes. We met once by chance. A 'scientist,' she called herself."

"Yes, and one the world cannot deny. The very first woman in the world to earn a doctorate in the sciences, since recognized by the pope himself, a thing that happened a scant few years after you called for women to be shown into the academy."

Maria had been forbidden to criticize herself, and with effort, she held her tongue.

"No, it is not a thing that happened because of you alone," the empress continued. "But your efforts mattered. Her efforts mattered. As did those of everyone who helped you and her and dreamed of a different future. From my position, I see that very little happens without collective struggle. You have helped women to be taken seriously as intellectuals, and to me, that means something."

Maria bowed her head. "I . . . thank you, Your Highness."

"Even if you never draw another graph, you have already done enough."

The words felt loud in her ears. *You have already done enough.*

"There is another thing I've done lately," said Maria. "A small mathematics project. Some people think it might be of some value."

The empress smiled. "I also have people whose business it is to understand mathematics. We might have this conversation in a half-dozen languages, but I have never been fluent in numbers."

"I suppose it's the one thing I've always been very comfortable with. When I was a child, and I got very nervous about something, I used to do equations in my head to give myself something to think about besides how nervous I was."

"You're a very strange person," the empress stated good-naturedly. "But so it ever is with genius. Send me a copy of your whatever-it-is, won't you? A woman in my role must always stay humble. And who knows? The common women of our empire might be once again inspired."

The creaking of doors interrupted their meeting. Respectively abashed and worried, a stout older man and a slender young woman were led into the audience chamber by a full escort of imperial guards. Both man and woman wore the most sumptuous finery. There was no doubting the man's identity.

The empress beamed to see her husband. "Oh, *hello,* Franz. This is the clever young lady I told you so very much about."

"Your Highness," Maria greeted Holy Roman Emperor Franz Stefan the First, King of Germany, Archduke of Austria, Grand Duke of Tuscany, and erstwhile duke of Lorraine and

Bar. She could not help but notice that the empress completely ignored the woman at his side.

Franz Stefan looked like a child caught at mischief. Dour, he crumpled his hat between his hands. He recognized Maria. "The mathematician."

"Yes, the mathematician," said the empress. "Much clever-er than your *old friend,* I'm sure. Maria, darling? Your sister Teresa—she performs original works for the concert hall, yes?"

Maria, sensing a certain volatility in the empress's expression, began to stray ever so slightly in the direction of the exit. "Yes, Your Highness."

"Tell her we would be most delighted if she attended on us this evening for a private performance. Women in the sciences, that's all well and good. But in Austria, we are most passionate about the arts."

Maria knew a dismissal when she heard one. She was halfway to the palace exit before the shouting finally began.

Chapter Twenty-Seven

You have already done enough, the empress had told her. Oddly, Maria found those words the highest motivation to do more.

That evening, she stood alone in her room and stared down the draft of her book on mathematics and calculus. Somewhere in the palace, Teresa was playing for the pleasure of the imperial family. Maria supposed that reflected the difference between their two disciplines. Music was a communal experience, practiced most genuinely in front of an audience. Mathematics, meanwhile, was invariably an inward-looking process, worked out between mind and paper.

Slowly, Maria flipped through the pages, past her explanations and meticulous graphs. Her father, for all of his unwelcome prodding, had been right about one thing. Maria knew that the very best work in her book had everything to do with the *versoria.* "The rope which turns the sail" was the best translation she could come up with for the Latin term. Luigi Guido Grandi, a monk, had written of it extensively in his treatise, but there was something inaccessible and insufficiently persuasive about his description. He had been one gateway for Maria to Leibniz, and Leibniz was a man of seemingly inexhaustible ideas.

Maria had often struggled with the notion that she had no ideas of her own. After sitting in front of the empress, she felt her perspective had changed. Looking back at her life now, she realized her problem was more that she had no *faith* in her ideas.

People always called her a genius, and she always rebelled against the label. Why was that?

A genius learns things faster than everyone else. As a child, Maria gained a child's knowledge effortlessly. Without effort, she drank in the adulation of adults. When she moved on and learned adult wisdom, the praise she received only increased. By the time she'd grown up, she'd internalized the idea that if something didn't come to her naturally, if it took struggle, then she'd already failed, even if in the end she understood.

She'd struggled over this book. Writing, rewriting. Throwing material out, starting sections over again. It made her feel like an idiot. Every revision revealed to her more plainly the idea that she was a fraud. But what did that matter if the reader was enlightened in the end? She'd been blinded by her own vanity.

Pen in hand, she sketched out the graph of a derivative equation. The *versoria* was nothing more than an expression of inverse trigonometry. Using the arctangent function, she could show everything about it visually, breaking down a complicated abstraction into clear component parts. At evenly spaced intervals, the curve swept up elegantly from the central axis.

Many years ago, Vittorio Bellone had castigated Maria for

failing to show her work. She hadn't thought about him in years, but she suddenly felt compelled to let him know what she'd done. After all, in the end, she hadn't just shown her work. She'd shown the work of all the geniuses she'd obsessed over for half her life—better than they had themselves.

Maria felt the emotion that had eluded her so often in life: confidence.

"It's ready," Maria told her father.

"What?" A confused Pietro stirred from his repose in the garden. As he grew older, he needed more and more naps to keep up with his young wife. Carlotta had deigned to actually stay home for the summer season, and Pietro always surrendered to his compulsive need to spoil her. That was fortunate, really. Maria felt certain that if he'd been looming over her shoulder, the project never would have gotten done.

"My book." She'd rewritten it from start to finish for corrections, and then again to ensure the most perfectly legible handwriting. It had taken a full month. She placed the finished text in her father's lap. "I've finished it."

Pietro wanted to say any number of things. It was plain on his face. Maria thought about seeing how long he'd be able to keep up the charade of not wanting to pressure her, but ultimately, that would have been dreadfully unkind. She informed him: "You may have it copied and sent to the university."

Pietro's mouth hung open for a moment in shock. And then, he laughed. Holding the book above his head like a priest performing the eucharist, he let out a loud, triumphant laugh. "Wonderful! Wonderful! Oh, I can't wait to read it!"

"I have a condition," said Maria.

Pietro brimmed with vigor as he flipped through the pages. The years seemed to vanish off his face. He skimmed too quickly to admire the actual words on the page, but even skimming threatened to damage his heart from sheer force of glee. "Name your condition."

"I want you to send a copy to my old tutor, Professor Bellone."

That stopped Pietro. "The one who insulted your mother?"

Maria was dumbfounded. Was that what he believed had happened?

"Yes. Him."

Pietro grimaced momentarily, but as he came upon the section dealing with derivatives, the book stayed still and open on his lap. Skimming interrupted, he was briefly immersed in graphs. "This is a big change, you know. What happened?"

"An acquaintance of mine persuaded me that the world needed to see my work."

Pietro flipped the pages back to the beginning. "You dedicated the book to Empress Maria Theresa?"

"She was very persuasive. Without even meaning to be, I think."

Pietro stopped again. Clearly he had not connected "acquaintance" to "empress." At least, not until his daughter had spoken. "*She's* your acquaintance?"

"Well, yes, in a matter of speaking," said Maria.

"You saw her again? When? Is she here? Did I sleep through it? Where is she now?"

Amid the barrage of questions, Carlotta meandered out into the garden, dressed in a diaphanous green gown made from Pietro's very best fabrics. A short woman of barely five feet, with rare red-colored hair and pale eyes, it was easy to see how he'd become so enchanted with her. In her tiny, high-pitched voice, she inquired: "What's all this shouting about?"

With the strength of a younger man, Pietro sprang to his feet and lifted his diminutive wife by the waist. "It's wonderful," he told her, spinning in place. "Absolutely wonderful! Our Maria's going to be famous!"

Not so long ago, Maria could not have imagined a worse fate. Perhaps she might yet come to regret her decision. But for now, she allowed herself to bask in the glow of her father's approval.

Vittorio Bellone had the most dreadful hangover.

"You're pathetic," said Professor Romano, not for the first time.

On a better day, Vittorio might have complained. Sequestered in his office with the windows drawn and covered, *still* feeling the piercing discomfort from the light leaking through the open door, he could not especially disagree.

"Professor Romano . . ." Vittorio managed, trying his best to hide his state and succeeding not at all.

Old, bald Professor Romano proved relentless. "You've

been working here for decades, and you've made no meaningful contributions to the existing literature whatsoever. And yet you spend your days off work drinking yourself into a disgusting stupor. I would call you lazy, but perhaps you have just made peace with the fact that you will never do anything of academic value."

Vittorio had perhaps been a touch remiss with his research of late. "Did you come here to congratulate me on my accomplishments in the field of recreational drinking or did you want something?"

"Tenure," Romano spat out, like the word was a slur. "I am sure they regret the day they thought you worthy of the honor. But here. Something came for you." He plunked a parcel on Vittorio's desk.

"Thank you," said Vittorio, closing his eyes as he massaged his temples. "I will get to it presently."

"Tenure," Romano griped again, retreating back into the university halls.

Everything had gone wrong for Vittorio after he lost the Agnesi assignment. All his private clients found him no longer sufficiently prestigious for their well-moneyed children. Undeterred, Vittorio had taken the considerable money he'd saved and chartered a trade voyage to the Spice Islands, hoping to reap the rich rewards of long-distance trade.

God had other ideas. The Barbary pirates had assaulted the ship when it returned to the Mediterranean, making off with the entire cargo. It was lucky that the crew had not been enslaved. Unfortunately, for a small-time investor like Vittorio, the whole affair had been an all-or-nothing gamble, and so his good fortune had evaporated with no prospects for renewal. He'd had to subsist on professor's wages ever since.

After a long interval of headache, Vittorio opened the parcel. Within he found a book and a letter. The title of the book: *Analytical Institutions for the Use of Italian Youth.* The author: Maria Gaetana Agnesi.

To my first and very best teacher, the letter began.

Vittorio found himself suddenly too misty-eyed to continue reading. Must be the liquor, he told himself.

The next day, Vittorio came to the university with fire and purpose for what felt like the first time in years.

Romano's desk was littered with the ramblings of philosophy students. The look he afforded Vittorio was suspicious. "You seem strangely motivated."

"I've just read the most remarkable book," said Vittorio. Smiling felt strange. He'd done so little of it lately. "It's a textbook that'll change the way mathematics are taught all across the continent."

Romano chortled. "Then I'm sure you had nothing to do with it."

"No. Nothing at all." Vittorio simply couldn't stop smiling. "But Jove as my witness, I'm going to see it on the desk of the pope himself."

Chapter Twenty-Eight

"A publication of the University of Bologna, it is a work in two volumes. The first volume expounds upon finite quantities, the second upon infinitesimal calculus. Here we see the work of a most cogent and incisive mind, a digestion and reformulation of the sum total of human mathematical knowledge. Mark me . . . ."

The speaker droned on, turning Maria's introduction into a speaking engagement all its own.

She stood there beside him, facing a salon of the wise and the wizened, wondering why she'd forgotten how much she'd hated this sort of thing. It had once upon a time quite literally driven her to seizures.

Of course, nowadays she actually slept. Maria no longer felt that desperate need to prove herself. Nor was she quite so afraid of new faces and new places.

People needed space and time to grow, she told herself. She had grown, and she could do this.

"You are all very kind," she told the crowd, touching a hand to her chest and weathering their applause. "As a young learner, I spent years exploring the writings of the great geniuses. This book was my attempt to make that journey easier for the next generation—my young brothers and sisters most of all . . . ."

The talk went splendidly. Somehow, these days the words just poured out of Maria naturally, like the Holy Ghost was helping her every step of the way. Perhaps He truly was. She'd been praying more and more often.

It didn't stop her from wilting into a sofa back home when it was all said and done. She put a cold rag over her eyes, like one of her doctors had recommended she do back when she suffered from seizures.

Her father cleared his throat delicately from the doorway. "Everything all right?"

Maria didn't get up or nod. The coldness of the cloth and the water's slow evaporation had the desired therapeutic effect. "Just trying to take good care of myself. I think it went well, don't you?"

"It went splendidly." Pietro no longer acted the pedant and parsed out her speeches for improvement, like when she was a child. He, too, had grown a little. "I just wanted to let you know you've received some invitations. Your book is getting around."

"I'd as soon not travel."

She heard the rustling of pages as her father turned through the post. "What if it was travel to Venice? Or Paris? Or Vienna?"

That was too much to ignore. She peeled the cloth off her eyes and folded it up even as she rose. "As far away as Paris?"

Pietro looked older all the time, but he still had all his teeth. His grin revealed them. "In fact, there's been more than one inquiry about translating your work into French. How's that, eh? Italian learning at the forefront, and you leading the charge."

Maria had to admit it gave her a certain satisfaction. The simple pleasure on her father's often-gloomy face likewise filled her with a simple joy.

"A fine idea, but I'd like to meet the translators first. But on the other hand . . . I am not sure I have it in me for very long journeys. The thought of having to sleep in someone else's bed . . . ." She shook her head. "It'd be hard."

Pietro placed the assembled papers on the table. "Well, have a look at your leisure. You're a grown woman and I trust you to make your own decisions."

Maria thanked him and sat down to review the adulation heaped upon her. There were a great many invitations, a number of them to places her brothers and sisters would likely have loved to visit. But Maria was not naturally inclined to the unfamiliar.

Moreover, she had to be honest with herself: She loved learning, but she hated public speaking.

If she were to leave Milan for the first time in her life, it would need to be for just the right offer, phrased in just the right way.

As there were Heaven and Hell, in the Vatican there were the Sacred and Profane Museums. These were the creation of Pope Benedict the Fourteenth, born Prospero Lorenzo Lambertini, a man who loved knowledge as dearly as he loved God. In their halls, the holy and secular treasures of the Church were soon to be put on display.

Among all the popes in living memory, it was Benedict who had proven the greatest friend to science. Rumor held that he had even conducted dissections of the human body personally and proclaimed it an exploration of God's design.

Vittorio Bellone had cashed in a great many favors for the right to see the pope, but if he had not been a professor at the pope's own university, he might not have found it possible.

Shadowed by orderlies and pike-carrying Swiss guards, the pope entered the foyer of his great museum project. Their feet echoed on cold marble tile, the sound amplified by the emptiness of the rooms. The plinths were all as yet bereft of exhibits.

"I am an extremely busy man," the pope told Vittorio, not unkindly. The sound of chiseling and hammering could be heard from the laborers further within. "So busy, in fact, that I do not set my own schedule. As such, I have no idea why you are here."

For all his years, the pope had no shortage of vitality. Vittorio was obliged to hustle to keep up. He decided to begin with that ecclesiastical classic: flattery. "Everyone says that you're a brilliant scholar."

The pope dismissed this praise by quoting not scripture, but the ancient Greeks. "'The oracle at Delphi said that I was the wisest of all the Greeks, for I alone know that I know nothing.'"

"Be that as it may, I'm told you're always looking for new scholars and scientists to sponsor."

The pope sized up Vittorio. "If you're looking for a grant, you've come to the wrong place. This museum is eating a golden hole into an already vanishing budget."

Vittorio, having just walked through the staggering wealth of the Vatican to get here, found that slightly hard to believe. "You misunderstand. I'm not here for myself. I'm here on behalf of someone else."

"Some student of yours?"

Vittorio knew he would only get one chance to spark the papal interest. He cleared his throat. "I watched with interest as you awarded honors to Laura Bassi."

The pope stopped, considering this. All of his retinue stopped as well, like a single well-oiled machine. "It was not a uniformly popular decision, showing such favor to a woman."

Vittorio produced Maria Gaetana Agnesi's book. "What if I told you there was another girl of the same generation who has grown up to equal brilliance in another field?"

The pope's expression was perhaps best described as skeptical.

Maria had decided to sleep in that morning. After her third public appearance that month, she felt she owed it to herself to relax. If there was one thing she regretted most about once again being a figure of scholarly admiration, it was that she wasn't giving her family the attention they deserved. Many of her teaching duties had already been passed on to others, and it inspired a certain guilt. But now, older and wiser, she knew she had to spare a little attention for herself.

The poetry of the Romans had ever been her greatest pleasure as a reader. She spent the morning with Aeneas, reliving his long feud with Turnus upon the shores of Italy.

A sharp knock interrupted her reading. After saving her place, she found a deeply flustered Giorgio outside.

"I am truly sorry—your father left instructions you were not to be disturbed, but there are two messengers here to see you and I fear to keep them waiting any longer."

Surely it was not a reappearance of the empress. Maria had asked to be told in advance if ever the imperial family should return to Milan. She would have known.

"Are they important?"

"They are from Vienna and from Rome."

Maria wondered if her choice about where to travel was soon to be made for her. "I'd better change into something more impressive."

When she arrived downstairs, Pietro was regaling the visitors with tales of his last trip to Provence, now many years past. Maria had heard all the stories a dozen times before. She used the distraction to study the visitors.

One of them, a tall and reedy fellow with a tremendous mustache, wore the red-and-white garb of the Imperial Army. The other was short and doughty and bald, with a priest's collar.

Maria had scarcely gotten into the room before the soldier stood to attention. "Young mistress Agnesi, I extend to you the greetings of Her Imperial Highness, Maria Theresa von Habsburg. She congratulates you on the successful publication of your first great work."

The priest looked not at all pleased for being upstaged. He was, however, too polite to interrupt.

"The empress humbles me," said Maria.

"Further, the empress bids you accept this letter and this small token of her esteem."

Maria took the letter, resolving to read it later, when she could properly appreciate it. Even if she had planned to do otherwise, the sudden emergence of the "small token" destroyed any chance of concentrating. Set inside a small open box, it was a diamond ring. With a golden band and a tremendous, sparkling cabochon, it was the richest gift anyone had ever given her.

"Oh my goodness," said Maria, holding it up and inspecting the way it reflected the light. "It's so large."

Not to be outdone, visibly brimming with competitive spirit, the priest stepped forward also. "I have in my hands a complimentary letter from His Holiness Pope Benedict the Fourteenth, along with this small token of his esteem."

Maria's eyes threatened to bulge as she took this next "small token," which proved to be a gigantic, chunky golden medallion strung on an equally sumptuous chain.

"Oh my goodness," Maria said again. She looked to her father for support, but a beaming Pietro only shrugged.

The competition of gifts was far from over. The imperial envoy had gone behind his chair to retrieve a far larger box, which he set upon the Agnesi salon's largest table. Smug as you please, he pulled off the lid, revealing a glass display case studded with an absolutely obscene number of small, glittering diamonds. "The empress is so impressed with the reception of your book that she thought it only fitting you would have a worthy receptacle for it."

The priest pressed another gift into Maria's open hands. "The pope bids you accept this golden wreath, a glittering sister to the laurel, to crown the leading mathematician of her age, in celebration of her genius."

Maria didn't put it on her head. It was entirely too embarrassing. But she had to admit, it did look pretty. She would wear it later.

"Know that the empress would be happy to receive you and your sister in Vienna as sponsored guests of the state," proclaimed the imperial envoy.

But the priest looked most satisfied, knowing he had the best offer of all and had saved it for last. "His Holiness offers you a professorship in mathematics and physics at the University of Bologna. You will be the second woman in all the world granted the honor of such a chair. All you need to do is confirm your acceptance, and he will make the necessary arrangements."

The thrill of triumph coursed through Maria. It surprised her to feel it so strongly. She had turned away from that path. Yet deep down, perhaps it was what she had desired all along.

Anxieties could wait. Replies to the great and powerful could wait. For now, Maria allowed herself—and her father—to bask in the joy of the moment. That night at dinner, all of her family would celebrate.

Chapter Twenty-Nine

Triumph turned soon enough to trepidation. Time had allowed Maria to master many fears, but this was an entirely new development, one that threatened to forever change the comfortable life she'd created.

"It's not something you need to do immediately," her father counseled her. "You can take your time with it. Find the right townhouse in Bologna, get it decorated to your personal taste, spend a couple of weeks in it, and I imagine you'll find the university far less intimidating."

Maria paced around the sitting room, not really seeing anything. She was too tied up in her own thoughts. None of them had to do with material comfort—that kind of luxury didn't concern her. Really, she preferred spartan living.

Pietro coughed, not for the first time that day. Autumn weather was never salutary for his health. The transition to the cold ate at his aging bones. "You will do what God has planned for you. In the end, that is all that any of us does."

This was an unusually pious proclamation from Pietro.

"I just need time," said Maria.

That brought a frown to Pietro's face. "Yes," he said. "I suppose that's all any of us really needs."

Pietro went to bed early that evening. In the morning, he did not rise.

"It is a rare form of consumption," said a sharp-nosed doctor whom Maria had never met before. She had told Giorgio to get "the best," and this was who had shown up, along with a pack of orderlies. "It cannot be cured, only treated. To be perfectly honest, it's miraculous he was able to hide it so long."

Maria sat beside her father's bed, wondering why heaven saw fit to send such a trial upon her now. Pietro had awakened just long enough to be poked and prodded and cough up a worrying amount of blood. The doctors assured Maria she could not catch what he had, but she would have insisted on being present in any event.

"And . . . while I know this may not be the ideal moment, my congratulations on your appointment," said the doctor. He immediately made himself scarce, reviewing his notes of diagnosis in a far corner of the room.

While Pietro slept, Maria reread the letter from the pope several times. She stared at it, conflicted. There was no way she could dare go off to Bologna while her father was on his deathbed. Someone needed to run the house.

"I'd like to see it," said her father.

Maria startled to realize he was awake. "Yes, of course," she said, extending the paper.

"That's not what I meant," said Pietro, but he took the letter anyway. Even wasting away, pride glowed from within him at beholding the work of the pope's own hand. His eyes darted from line to line, far more lively than his weakened grip and clammy skin. "But what a tremendous honor. What a great and remarkable triumph. Maria, if you remember one thing about me, remember that I am and always have been the proudest father in the world." Pietro's voice was small, but steady. He seemed to be fighting the very idea of illness, like force of will could make it gone.

"I would never have received the honor without your encouragement," Maria told him gently, fearing that words spoken too loudly might exacerbate his condition.

She breathed in, breathed out.

"I'm going to accept the position," she resolved. With one chapter closing, another must begin, she thought.

"I'd like to see it," Pietro said again, louder. He struggled to get upright.

"That's enough of that," said the doctor, not so very absent as he pretended to be.

"If my daughter is to be invested with a chair at the pope's own university, then I will see it with my own eyes," Pietro stubbornly proclaimed.

"Papà, you can't travel!"

"It's a hundred and twenty miles from here to Bologna," the doctor said. "The idea is ludicrous."

Pietro's gaze bored a hole through the doctor. "If I stay here, will I survive?"

The doctor may have been the best in town, but he was not the gentlest. "No. I would measure your life in months rather than years."

"Then there is no sense in my staying. And no sense in worrying everyone. We won't tell Carlotta about this. We won't tell the other children. I can't stand the idea of everyone looking at me like a decaying invalid for however many days I have left."

"Signore, with respect, you *are* dying," said the doctor.

Pietro had managed to attain his feet. Maria stood ready to catch him if his buckling knees should give out.

Pietro grated: "God chooses *when* we die. Man chooses *how* he dies."

The doctor turned his attention to Maria. "God bless you, signora, for it will be a trial, but do your best taking care of this stubborn old mule."

Quick on the heels of her reply to the pope, Maria and her father began the journey to Bologna. It was the first time she had ever left Milan.

The noises of the city, the shape of the landscape, even the colors of the countryside had all become familiar background fixtures of her life. In the same way that one grows accustomed to the scent of perfume or incense and eventually ceases to notice it, the small predictable patterns of her Milanese life only became notable by their absence. Sleeping at traveler's inns, she reflected a great deal on how much even an unfamiliar ceiling could do to change one's sense of safety.

She stayed awake more than she slept, worrying about the

sound of her father's breathing, and wondering if she only imagined it as being more raspy over time. She wished she was still at home. She worried about her siblings. She worried about herself.

Bologna greeted their carriage draped in the colors of autumn, trees turned to faded orange. As a child, Maria kept the curtains closed. Now, she took in every detail of an increasingly unfamiliar world.

The twin leaning towers of Bologna announced the city. These two fortifications of old medieval stone peeked over the rim of the outlying hills, reaching up toward the sky. Hundreds of feet tall, they looked down upon a city of tile-roofed houses, both smaller and less grand than Milan.

But there was an energy in the air, a vibrance of activity on the streets. After generations of decline, a pope had come to power who called Bologna home. Past pontiffs had seen this city, one of the Papal States' largest, as nothing more than a source of taxes. Now the taxes had been lessened, the censorship relaxed, and everywhere new buildings were being built.

The University of Bologna was not a new building. By most reckonings it was the oldest institute of higher learning in the world, and certainly the first to call itself a university. The wisest men—and now the wisest women—of Catholic Europe had been drawn there for centuries.

So it was with Maria Gaetana Agnesi, whose arrival had been expected.

A trio of local officials welcomed their carriage, only too happy to extol the virtues of their city and boast of local wonders like the Fountain of Neptune. Maria, worrying for her father's tenuous health, politely declined the grand tour and asked to be shown straight away to their lodgings.

Clearly they had been prepared at the pope's own order. They were shepherded to a guesthouse beside the basilica of Santo Stefano, a complex of churches old and new. From her rooms, Maria could hear the sound of hymns and the tolling of church bells, here in this city both pious and pedestrian, where the Church and commerce competed for hold over the hearts of the people.

The next morning, an unexpected papal emissary arrived at their quarters, inviting Maria to attend a High Mass. Quietly, the pope had come to his home of Bologna, as he often did, to refresh his mind and say Mass. Maria, if she so chose, might accept her appointment at the pope's own hand, to the sound of the choir and the rumbling of organs.

Though Maria had entered into the unfamiliarity of the world beyond her home, the Church remained universal. Everywhere in the world, the Latin was the same and the hymns were the same. She sat together with her father at the front of a gothic, medieval church, one of many unknown chapels across the city of Bologna that she might yet explore. Her natural instinct was to shy toward the back of a Mass, where she could take in everything, but by the request of the pope, she sat in the very front.

He was an old yet vital man, Pope Benedict. She watched him closely throughout the Mass. When the service reached its end, he turned his hand toward her and welcomed her to the stage. From the head of the Church, she received the same praises so many people had awarded her all of her life: a genius, a visionary, an expert, a credit to women and a pious servant of the Lord.

He put in her hand a rolled-up document of honors, clasping thick, rough palms around both the paper and her wrists. Full of pride, the Holy Father proclaimed Maria to the chair of mathematics and natural philosophy and physics at the great university in the city in which they stood.

Maria prayed often, but only rarely did she feel the presence of God. Mother Angelica had warned her not to hope for such a thing, only to welcome it when it happened.

She did not feel it now, either.

Maria rarely indulged in applications of vanity. Staring at her face in the mirror, she found her use of cosmetics garish, her cheeks too bright. She wanted to look her best, but ultimately, this wasn't the right way. She removed it all with a wet cloth and decided to simply wear the face that God had given her.

Today she was expected to make her first appearance at the university. What she might teach, where she might reside, whom she would work alongside—it was all in flux.

"Maria," came her father's voice, croaking from the other room.

After adjusting the sleeves and shoulders of her dress, she went to the bed he had been provided.

"It was wonderful watching you accept the pope's commission

yesterday," he stated quietly, staring up at the ceiling. It wasn't weakness that held him so still, but something else. "But I am not sure if it was right."

Maria quickly opened her mouth to reply, closed it, then opened it again. "I came all the way here. I've been working for this all my life. What do you mean, it isn't right?"

"I always dreamed of seeing you win this honor." Pietro turned his head toward her. "I always wanted the greatest and brightest life for my children. For you, I dreamed of professorship. But I don't know what *your* dream is."

"Of course it's my dream." Maria didn't know what the feeling was inside of her. It wound tightly through her chest, constricting her ribs on every inward breath. "Of course it is."

"I am not so sure." Pietro held a red-speckled cloth loosely against his chest. For now, the coughing had subsided. "I don't think you looked happy taking that commission. I wonder if it's not aspiration that got you here, but sheer force of habit, too cleverly pursued."

Maria looked down at her ailing father, a frown etching ever more deeply upon her face. "I believe what I've heard from countless people: God gave me a gift. And Christ tells us our blessings are to be used and shared."

"You're right, of course." Pietro stood up from the bed, moving from the window to take in the skyline of Bologna. He wanted to say something else. But instead he coughed—a hacking, wheezing, lung-straining cough that saw his handkerchief speckled a darker shade of crimson.

CHAPTER TWENTY-NINE

"You shouldn't be talking," Maria said, holding him by the shoulders.

Pietro turned to face her. Silently, he hugged his daughter with weakened arms. "God gave you a gift, Maria. But it's up to you how to use it." He kissed her on the forehead, like he had when she was a child.

Unable to stand any longer, he sank back into bed, where weariness settled over him like a heavy blanket.

Pietro told her: "Don't do what you have to do. Do what you want to do."

Soon enough he was asleep. Sometime late that night, he died.

At the University of Bologna, a trio of professors awaited their newest fellow chair. Two of them were men, mathematicians both. They were joined by natural scientist Laura Bassi. Yet after three hours of waiting, there was no sign of Maria Gaetana Agnesi.

Her lateness only increased the school's anticipation. It wasn't long before students and doctoral candidates joined the waiting few. What sort of teacher would Agnesi be? What would she research? Was she really as clever as all the rumors said?

In the end, they all went home disappointed.

Maria Gaetana Agnesi would never enter the University of Bologna, not for as long as she lived.

After countless hours of work, Maria had put together an airtight lesson plan. She felt absolutely certain that it was just what her students needed. Papers and slate tucked under her arm, she walked the familiar halls of a Dominican convent.

At the hall's end was the classroom she'd made her own. She knew every student by name. By now, only a few of those students were her own family. But the size of her classes kept getting larger, and the family house simply wouldn't fit them all—nor was it accessible to the kind of student she felt most compelled to teach. Not the ones who rebelled at learning, but the ones who yearned for it. The poor who might be wise, if only life would give them a better chance.

"Today, we'll be starting French," she told them, a loose and easy smile upon her face.

Epilogue

Old as she was, Maria had never stopped learning. After mathematics, she had thrown herself headlong into theology. Lately she had begun writing an entirely new book—about how rational and scientific contemplation could also be a way of knowing God. But it was slow going ever since her fingers had turned arthritic. She often found herself stopping to massage her joints, which did give her time to contemplate what she might want to write next, but did little to ease the pain.

The Agnesi family house had been sold decades ago. Her brothers and sisters all had lives and families of their own.

She had at last discovered her vocation—not in holy orders, as she'd long quietly wondered, but in charity.

Looking at her throbbing knuckles, she finally decided writing was a losing battle. She rose from her simple, time-worn desk and walked the halls of the Opera Pi Trivulzio, the poorhouse that she had used her own money to found.

A certain low thrum of activity was in the place even in its quieter hours. It housed the forgotten elderly of Milan, those who had no money or families to fall back on, or faced the cold rejection of unsympathetic descendants. Tending to them were nuns she'd somehow wound up in charge of. They had a great show of faith in Maria, a woman who'd taken no such vows.

"Ah, the young mistress," an ancient guest of the house proclaimed, thin skin wrapped tightly around his aged bones. Spry as a young man, he lowered into a courtly bow of recognition.

"Oh, stop that, Antonio," said Maria, nudging him playfully. "I'm about as young as rusted bronze." Her hair had just about all gone gray, after all.

Antonio laughed, and an old woman, only newly arrived at the poorhouse, surrendered to laughter also. "If you're old, then what does that make us?" she wondered aloud.

"Beloved guests of our house," Maria proclaimed, continuing off on her rounds.

Unable to long stand idleness, Maria found a forgotten basket of laundry and took it outside to the yard, where she began hanging up sheets and aprons. She never shied away from manual labor.

One of the youngest sisters trotted into the yard shortly after, clutching at the top of her habit. "Mistress Agnesi, you don't need to do that!"

The young sister—Francesca, wasn't that her name?—was probably the one who'd been given this task. Maria supposed that she was worried about being scolded.

"No, I don't need to do it," Maria said, slyly amused. "But I want to do it. Help me finish, won't you?"

Together, Francesca and Maria made short work of the laundry. A certain fresh scent filled the air as the breeze softly rippled the clothing on the line, already soaked and soaped before being strung up high.

Francesca shook her head. "I've never understood where you get all your energy."

Hands on hips, Maria surveyed the laundry and allowed herself to enjoy the satisfaction of a job well done. "It's just one of those mysteries, I suppose."

Not all the work at the poorhouse was as easy as all that. Many of their charges were sick and infirm, and needed special assistance. That day, Maria replaced bandages, changed bedpans, and took time simply to talk to their wards. The simple joy of conversation sometimes did more to salve human suffering than the best medical treatment. Speaking with the elderly always presented unique opportunities: Each person was a rich repository of unique life experience, lived more immediately than what was written down in books.

Books had never left Maria's life, however. That night, she made her rounds again, blowing out all the candles, one after another, save for the one she carried to find her way. She carried it back up to her room, where she lit her old oil lanterns. First to rise, last to sleep—that was the way she found time for herself. Time to spend with her books, and on the writing of her own.

Most days, she took care of the old. Tomorrow was a day to spend with children, teaching at the convent, the same way she had for years. This year, she had an especially promising student. Young Viola absorbed knowledge like a sponge. She'd never had a father to raise her, and her mother had left her to the mercies of the world.

Maria decided not to work on her latest book that night. Instead, she quietly amended her lesson plan, scribbling long into the nighttime hours.

Across from the convent, opposite the poorhouse, Viola sat in an orphanage bedroom, bedcovers pulled up to her chin. All the lights had gone out by order of the nuns, and quiet had settled over the city of Milan.

In her teacher's distant window, flickering candles danced, just as they did on every peaceful night.

About the Author

Eric Martin is a screenwriter and novelist. Currently, he is the executive producer and head writer for the highly acclaimed Marvel and Disney+ streaming series, *Loki*, starring Tom Hiddleston and Owen Wilson. Previously, Eric has worked in series television on *Rick and Morty* and the premium cable television drama *Heels*. In 2017, Eric published the historical fiction novel, *Saving the Republic*, based on the life of Roman statesman Marcus Cicero. Eric has a bachelor of art in film studies from the University of California and a masters of fine art in screen and television writing from Pepperdine University. In his free time, Eric enjoys studying history, climbing mountains and running. For some reason, he has run ten marathons and completed his second ultra marathon in 2021. His favorite food is water.

ALSO FROM THE MENTORIS PROJECT

America's Forgotten Founding Father
A Novel Based on the Life of Filippo Mazzei
by Rosanne Welch, PhD

A. P. Giannini—The People's Banker
by Francesca Valente

The Architect Who Changed Our World
A Novel Based on the Life of Andrea Palladio
by Pamela Winfrey

At Last
A Novel Based on the Life of Harry Warren
by Stacia Raymond

A Boxing Trainer's Journey
A Novel Based on the Life of Angelo Dundee
by Jonathan Brown

Breaking Barriers
A Novel Based on the Life of Laura Bassi
by Jule Selbo

Building Heaven's Ceiling
A Novel Based on the Life of Filippo Brunelleschi
by Joe Cline

Building Wealth
From Shoeshine Boy to Real Estate Magnate
by Robert Barbera

Building Wealth 101
How to Make Your Money Work for You
by Robert Barbera

Character is What Counts
A Novel Based on the Life of Vince Lombardi
by Jonathan Brown

Christopher Columbus: His Life and Discoveries
by Mario Di Giovanni

Dark Labyrinth
A Novel Based on the Life of Galileo Galilei
by Peter David Myers

Defying Danger
A Novel Based on the Life of Father Matteo Ricci
by Nicole Gregory

Desert Missionary
A Novel Based on the Life of Father Eusebio Kino
by Nicole Gregory

The Divine Proportions of Luca Pacioli
A Novel Based on the Life of Luca Pacioli
by W. A. W. Parker

The Dream of Life
A Novel Based on the Life of Federico Fellini
by Kate Fuglei

Dreams of Discovery
A Novel Based on the Life of the Explorer John Cabot
by Jule Selbo

The Embrace of Hope
A Novel Based on the Life of Frank Capra
by Kate Fuglei

The Faithful
A Novel Based on the Life of Giuseppe Verdi
by Collin Mitchell

Fermi's Gifts
A Novel Based on the Life of Enrico Fermi
by Kate Fuglei

First Among Equals
A Novel Based on the Life of Cosimo de' Medici
by Francesco Massaccesi

The Flesh and the Spirit
A Novel Based on the Life of St. Augustine of Hippo
by Sharon Reiser and Ali A. Smith

God's Messenger
A Novel Based on the Life of Mother Frances X. Cabrini
by Nicole Gregory

Grace Notes
A Novel Based on the Life of Henry Mancini
by Stacia Raymond

Guido's Guiding Hand
A Novel Based on the Life of Guido d'Arezzo
by Kingsley Day

Harvesting the American Dream
A Novel Based on the Life of Ernest Gallo
by Karen Richardson

Humble Servant of Truth
A Novel Based on the Life of Thomas Aquinas
by Margaret O'Reilly

The Judicious Use of Intangibles
A Novel Based on the Life of Pietro Belluschi
by W.A.W. Parker

Leonardo's Secret
A Novel Based on the Life of Leonardo da Vinci
by Peter David Myers

Little by Little We Won
A Novel Based on the Life of Angela Bambace
by Peg A. Lamphier, PhD

The Making of a Prince
A Novel Based on the Life of Niccolò Machiavelli
by Maurizio Marmorstein

A Man of Action Saving Liberty
A Novel Based on the Life of Giuseppe Garibaldi
by Rosanne Welch, PhD

Marconi and His Muses
A Novel Based on the Life of Guglielmo Marconi
by Pamela Winfrey

No Person Above the Law
A Novel Based on the Life of Judge John J. Sirica
by Cynthia Cooper

The Pirate Prince of Genoa
A Novel Based on the Life of Admiral Andrea Doria
by Maurizio Marmorstein

Relentless Visionary: Alessandro Volta
by Michael Berick

Retire and Refire
Financial Strategies for People of All Ages to
Navigate Their Golden Years with Ease
by Robert Barbera

Ride Into the Sun
A Novel Based on the Life of Scipio Africanus
by Patric Verrone

Rita Levi-Montalcini
Pioneer & Ambassador of Science
by Francesca Valente

Saving the Republic
A Novel Based on the Life of Marcus Cicero
by Eric D. Martin

The Seven Senses of Italy
La Luna di Miele
by Nicole Gregory

Sinner, Servant, Saint
A Novel Based on the Life of St. Francis of Assisi
by Margaret O'Reilly

Soldier, Diplomat, Archaeologist
A Novel Based on the Bold Life of Louis Palma di Cesnola
by Peg A. Lamphier, PhD

The Soul of a Child
A Novel Based on the Life of Maria Montessori
by Kate Fuglei

What a Woman Can Do
A Novel Based on the Life of Artemisia Gentileschi
by Peg A. Lamphier, PhD

For more information on these titles and
the Mentoris Project, please visit
www.mentorisproject.org